IN A DEEP DARK WOOD

TINA PRITCHARD

INKUBATOR
BOOKS

PROLOGUE

She liked the fact that most of the inmates feared her. When she first arrived, some of the women tried to give her a hard time. She found it weird that even those who had committed the most horrific of crimes took the moral high ground when it came to kids. The first time they came for her, she was taking a shower. The big butch-looking one grabbed her by the hair and smashed her face into the tiles, while her skinny friend with the squint laughed shrilly, clapping her hands in excitement. Even though her nose was broken, she refused to tell the guards who was responsible. She learned two important lessons that day: never turn your back on anyone, and get your hair cut as short as possible.

There was something about her that made people uneasy. Even though keeping on good terms with everyone was encouraged, she didn't want friends. Using people was her forte. She was a master manipulator with an extensive repertoire of behaviours. These she employed to get exactly what she wanted. A cat playing with a mouse, she picked up and discarded at whim, and this made her dangerous and unpredictable. She exuded power like an odourless chemical, and all except the half-witted and pugnacious, their brains addled with drugs, picked up on it and kept her at arm's length.

Mostly she was alone. It made it easier that she had her own cell, a tiny space, more like a cubicle, with a bunk, a desk and chair, a toilet and a compact wash-basin. A small bookshelf held a line of toiletries and a few books borrowed from the prison library. It was her choice not to have anything personal out on display.

Her reflection in the mirror above the sink often caught her unawares as she glimpsed her pallid features and new, short hairstyle. Having her hair cut in the prison hairdressing salon had given her the idea. A plan to work towards. It was something that gave her a feeling of assurance. The seed took root, and she nurtured it, even when it became sickly and struggled to grow. It was her secret. Her responsibility. She loved the sense of it, nestling in the deepest, darkest recesses of her being. When she lay in her cell waiting for the lights to go off, the thought of it gave her comfort. Relief from the vortex swirling around her. The shouting, the screams, the shrieks of laughter, the slamming of doors, the discordant music: The noise was incessant. The background psychodrama of the mad, the sad and the bad.

The sweet eighteen-year-old inside for repeated attempts at shoplifting, and who worked in the textile workshop, was easy to bribe. The squares of fabric were smuggled out and handed over during break time. Signing up for the hairdressing course gave her access to scissors, supposedly under supervision, but it was easy enough to slip them into her waistband when she went to the washroom. Here, she cut each piece of cloth into three strips, which she guessed measured around a foot in length when laid end to end.

It took a month until she had what she needed. Her only concern was that her little stash would be found if there was a suspicion that illicit drugs had been brought in, and there was a cell search.

The barred window was small and positioned above head height. If the weather was good, it lifted her spirits to see a patch of blue sky. At night, it never got completely dark in her cell; lights were dimmed but never turned off completely, and this made her task easier. It took over an hour to tie the knots. The rope, fashioned from an incongruous selection of strips of brightly coloured material, looked almost cheerful, like party bunting.

Tying an end around one of the window bars, she pulled hard to check its tensile strength, feeling a level of satisfaction when it held fast. Fashioning the ligature into a noose with a running knot, she placed the chair on her bunk and the noose around her neck. In her hand, she held a crumpled photo of two sweet-faced boys dressed in identical outfits. Her boys.

Kicking the chair away, she knew there would be a few seconds when instinct would cause her to claw at the rope, and she held the photo up in front of her for as long as she could. She did this until the ringing in her head ceased and the darkness closed in. Until everything faded into oblivion.

1

The house is quiet. Too quiet. The hallway still smells of paint. Was it really only two days ago that we folded away the dust sheets, washed the rollers and brushes, and closed the lid on the tin of paint? The colour, a heritage green, looks bilious in the pale afternoon light. Not long ago it might have offended me enough to think about repainting it in a warmer colour. Now the idea seems ludicrous. When I push open the lounge door, it squeaks on its hinges. Even though I'm expecting it, I still jump in response, heart rate accelerating. I am jittery as hell, and I try to calm down by breathing deeply, using the techniques learned at my yoga class. All I can manage are shallow gulps. My throat feels as dry as sandpaper. Despite this, I can't control the tears running down my cheeks or stop the snot pouring from my nose. Sniffing inelegantly, I wipe my nose on the sleeve of my jumper, past caring about propriety.

The lounge is untidy. Books and papers litter the coffee table, and the cushions remain unplumped. Dust motes dance in shafts of light struggling feebly through the slats of the window blinds. The atmosphere is stuffy, and paint fumes mingle with the aroma of stale food and sour coffee. I want to pull aside the blinds and throw open the windows. Let in cool, clear air to banish the musty odours.

I want to, but I can't. I'm afraid. I feel unsafe in my own house.

My phone is displaying numerous voice and text messages. I ignore all except the last one. It's from Laurie. I hit redial, and he answers immediately.

'Fran, it's me. Are you okay?' His voice is placating. He's trying to keep calm.

'Yes. I feel shaken up, but I'm all right. What time will you be home?'

'I'm just picking the car up now. If there are no hold-ups, I should be with you before seven.'

'Are you hungry? I think there's stuff in the freezer,' I say.

'Something reheated will be fine. Did you get Buddy?'

Oh shit, Buddy. On my instruction, the police had taken him to Jenny's house. I need to pick him up from there. The pair of them will be climbing the walls by now.

'I'm just on my way to get him.'

It had slipped my memory, but I don't tell him that. The last thing I want to do is talk to anyone, and I steel myself for what is to come. Jenny will ask questions, and I really don't feel like telling her about what happened. Not yet.

'Laurie?'

'Yes, I'm still here.' His voice is fading in and out. I'm worried he is losing the signal. I want the continued reassurance of his voice. Even if it's on the end of a line.

'He was dying, Laurie. He was dying, and I couldn't help him.'

'I know,' he says softly.

Picking up my keys, I let myself out, pulling the handle with force to ensure the door is properly closed. The air is fresh and tinged with cold, and I draw my coat around me. The street lights are already on, casting pools of white light in the autumn gloom. With the change in the weather, the leaves have started to fall, spiralling to the ground in a languid pirouette. The Council recently replaced the yellow sodium lamps with LEDs. At the time it irritated me. I preferred the older-style lamps with their softer, sodium glow to the glare of the replacements. Now the extra illumination is welcome.

With my senses heightened, I'm scanning the road for anything unusual or out of place, including any strange cars. My legs feel heavy, and it takes twice as long to cover the short distance to Jenny's house. The dense mass of woodland surrounding our small horseshoe-shaped close of houses stands in silhouette against the darkening sky. The familiar image looks oppressive and threatening. A place once so full of happy memories has become tainted. A combination of anger and sadness overwhelms me. Poor Buddy, he loves his walks in the woods. There's going to be a lot of pavement pounding in broad daylight for the foreseeable future.

Jenny eventually answers the door to my knock. As usual, she is smartly dressed and well groomed. In comparison, I'm dishevelled, and my face is blotchy from crying. To her credit, if she has noticed, she doesn't comment.

'He's been as good as gold,' she says, ushering me in. 'But I didn't have anything to feed him, so he's had some bread and butter and a rich tea biscuit I hope that's all right? Oh, and I've taken him out into the garden a couple of times for a wee. I kept him on the lead. I didn't want him disappearing at a time like this.'

Buddy is subdued. He peers at me through fuzzy eyebrows, head resting on his paws. He wags his tail, but doesn't come to me. It could be he knows where his best interests lie, though it's more likely he doesn't like the change in his routine. Reaching down to stroke his head, I speak to him in what I hope is a reassuring voice.

'Come on, Bud, we're going home. Dad will be back soon.'

I slip on his lead, and he gets to his feet, albeit reluctantly.

'Thanks so much for having him,' I say. 'It was a weight off my shoulders knowing he was with you.'

'It was no problem. I was glad to help. I'm going to make a cup of tea. Do you want one?' She is already filling the kettle. If I stay any longer, I will get drawn into a detailed explanation, and I can't face that. Not yet.

'No, thank you. I must get back. Laurie is on his way, and I need to make us something to eat. It's been a long day.'

'I do understand. It must have been awful for you?'

'It really was dreadful. I feel so weary. I hope you don't mind, but I won't stay. I promise I'll call and see you in a day or two. We can have a chat then.'

'Of course,' she says. 'It's been a terrible shock. Do let me know if there's anything I can do to help. You have my number, and Buddy is always welcome.'

She accompanies me to the door, Buddy trailing behind.

'You do know it's not the first time there's been a suicide in the woods?' Her voice is low and conspiratorial.

My heart lurches, then beats faster. The bright flash of recollection a physical pain.

'Yes, I was aware.' I sigh heavily and look down at Buddy to hide my tears. 'But it wasn't a suicide this time, Jenny. It was cold-blooded murder.'

2

With Buddy at my side, I'm less anxious, but I still jump in response to a sudden noise. People are starting to come home from work. The thud of car doors slamming and raised voices echo around the close. Our house is now in complete darkness. As I approach the porch, the motion sensor on the security light flickers, but doesn't fully illuminate. I keep meaning to buy a new bulb and curse my stupidity for not switching on an inside light before leaving the house.

Buddy slinks in as I open the door, tail between his legs. He seems to sense everything is not as it should be. I follow, lighting the table lamps and closing the blinds in the lounge. He noses the door to the kitchen, and I flick the switch, bathing the space in light. The array of spots located in the ceiling and under the kitchen cupboards throw out bright, white heat, and I lower the light levels with the dimmer switch.

Everything is as it was before I took Buddy for his morning walk. Breadcrumbs litter the granite work-tops, and my breakfast dishes are still in the sink. A cursory tidying will do for now. Decorating has made everything dusty anyway, and a deep clean is well overdue. We can blitz the house on Saturday morning. Laurie doesn't mind housework, and if we pull together, we can have it all spick and span by lunchtime.

Once Buddy is fed, I get some leftover takeaway from the fridge. My phone does a little dance across the worktop before the message alert pings. It's from Laurie. *Traffic slow, so stopped for a coffee. Back 7:30ish.*

A bubble of irritation rises in my throat. He's aware of what I've been through, yet he thinks it's all right to stop for a coffee? It's uncharitable of me, but I feel justified at being annoyed. It has been a shit day. I could do with him being here to support me. Pouring a glass of wine, I sit waiting, unable to concentrate either on reading or the TV.

The sweep of headlights and crunch of gravel alerts me to his car pulling onto the drive. Buddy woofs excitedly and runs for the door. I hear the click as Laurie puts his key in the lock. There's a solid clunk as the door encounters the safety chain.

'What the fuck?' Laurie curses loudly, and I jump up to go and release the chain, Buddy running excitedly between my legs as I do so.

'Sorry, love. I'm a bundle of nerves,' I say.

'I wasn't expecting it, that's all. I don't think we have ever used that chain since we moved in, have we?'

He wheels his case into the kitchen and leaves it by the washing machine. Buddy is demanding his attention in his usual way. I can't help but smile as he jumps as high as his short legs will allow before rolling onto his back for a tummy rub. Not for the first time, I observe it's the dog getting all the attention. I can't really begrudge the bond they have formed. After all, it was I, with additional persuasion from the kids, who pushed for a dog in the first place.

Once Buddy has been rewarded with a treat, it's my turn. 'Come here. You look absolutely shattered.' Laurie hugs me and plants a kiss on top of my head. 'Do you want to talk about it now, or shall we eat, and you can tell me the full story over a glass of wine?'

His tone suggests his preference for the latter.

'It's only reheated Chinese takeaway,' I say. 'I'm afraid preparing food has been the last thing on my mind.'

We sit side by side on the sofa. The combination of noodles with chicken and rice is greasy and unpalatable, but Laurie polishes off his portion and takes a long swig of wine.

'The police officer who rang me said you made an excellent witness. It was a detailed account, and you gave a very precise description of the men. The police are fortunate to have you as a witness. You've always had a good eye for detail.'

'Oh, God, Laurie, it was awful. To make matters worse, I felt like a criminal when they took me away in a police car. I'm sure there was a lot of curtain-twitching in the close. The detective interviewing me was great, though. Her name is DI Jo Holmes, which did make me giggle a bit. I almost asked where Watson was.'

'Do you feel up to going through it all again now, or is it too upsetting?'

'No, it will be good to go over it with you as long as you're not too tired,' I say. 'It might even jog my memory for something I might have missed.'

The dirty plates, mine displaying a heap of congealed noodles, are making me queasy. I scrape the residue into the bin and run the plates under the tap. After stacking the dishwasher, I return with the wine bottle and top up our glasses. The heating has gone off, and it's getting chilly. With Buddy snuggled between us, I pull a throw from the back of the sofa and drape it over our knees.

'So, let me get this clear?' Laurie says. 'You and Buddy went through the gate into the woods at your usual time?'

'Yes, thereabouts. Flynn rang around eight, and we left soon after that. He was going to come for the weekend, if you remember, but he's been invited to a party. Oh, bloody hell Laurie, I've just thought. The kids will have to know. It'll be all over the media by tomorrow.'

'Don't worry. They would have rung by now if they'd heard anything. We can get up early and call them in the morning. You took the path into the woods, you say. Then what?'

'Everything seemed so normal,' I say. 'I didn't see anyone, not even a walker or a cyclist. I let Buddy off the lead. He was running backwards and forwards through the leaves, as he usually does, and then he took off at speed. You know, like when he's following the trail of a rabbit or a fox. I searched for ages and kept calling his name. There was no sign of him, and I began to feel panicky. I stopped on the path to listen in case he was close by, and it was then I heard a weird noise. I couldn't quite make out what it was, so I walked in the direction it was coming from.'

The words are tumbling out, and I pause to take a gulp of wine before continuing.

'You know that huge old yew tree with overhanging branches where the older kids hang out?'

'Mm, I do. It's a great place for a den, but a bit unsavoury,' he says. 'It's completely enclosed, if I remember correctly. We used to warn our kids about going in there. The youths used to get lairy and smash beer bottles. Didn't someone get a needle-stick injury once after picking up a discarded needle?'

'Yes, yes.' I'm impatient to continue. 'As you know, it's set back quite a way from the path. That's why the kids liked it. You could get up to all sorts without being seen.' My hands are trembling, and I tuck my palms between my knees. 'There was no sign of Buddy, and I thought he might have got himself stuck somewhere. I followed the direction of the noise on the off chance it was something to do with him.'

'What sort of noise was it?' Laurie is leaning forward in anticipation.

'It's difficult to explain. It was like a dull, repetitive thumping. There were muffled voices too, although it was hard to make out what they were saying. As I got closer, I realised it was coming from the space inside the tree. At first, I thought it must be some lads smoking a bit of weed and messing about. I was going to ask them if they had seen Buddy. I pulled aside the branches, and it wasn't kids, it was two men. They were standing with their backs to me.'

A wave of heat rises through my body. I feel light-headed and shaky.

Laurie notices. He pulls Buddy onto his lap and moves in closer, placing his arm around my heaving shoulders.

'Go on,' he says.

'They must have realised that I was there, because they both turned around to face me. It was then I noticed the boy.'

My whole body starts to shake uncontrollably. Laurie moves Buddy onto the sofa and goes to the kitchen. He brings back a glass of water and a roll of kitchen paper. I desperately want to cry, but there is a lump in my chest, like a log damming a river.

He pulls me close. 'Hush,' he murmurs, stroking my hair. 'Do you want some time out? I can make us some tea.'

'No, not yet. It's agonising, but it's helpful, too. I'm just glad I didn't go to pieces like this at the station when they were taking my statement. I was concentrating so hard on getting the facts right and in order, I didn't have time to get emotional. Somehow it feels different telling you like this. I know I must sound flaky, but remembering the small, inconsequential things like the poor boy's trainers is the most upsetting part. Does that sound pathetic?'

'No, it's completely understandable. There's less focus on getting things right, and you're in your own environment. It's why more personal memories are being triggered. Don't give yourself such a hard time. You did incredibly well at the police station, considering you were in shock. That detective said so when she rang me.'

The glass is cool in my hands, and I hold it against my burning cheeks. What I have to tell him next is seared into my memory. I try to swallow, but my mouth feels as though it's full of cotton wool. I force down a sip of water.

'This bit isn't pretty, Laurie. Are you sure you want to hear it?'

'If it helps you, then yes. It's your call, Fran.'

'Okay. I suppose I've got this far.' I wipe a droplet of sweat from my forehead before continuing. 'The boy – I say boy because he didn't look very old. Seventeen or eighteen? He was standing on a crate, and his hands were tied behind his back. His mouth was taped with that sticky silver stuff.'

'Duct tape, you mean?' Laurie says.

'Yes, like packing tape. He was petrified, Laurie. He

was struggling and trying to cry out. I'll never forget the sound. It was horrible. He saw me, and he was pleading with his eyes. It was then I noticed the rope around his neck. It was thick and heavy like the one on the narrow boat when we had that canal holiday. Do you remember?'

He nods in agreement.

'The men saw me, but they just turned away and went back to booting the crate. That was the noise I could hear.' I draw a shaky breath. 'And then, the absolute bastards, even though they knew I was there, they kicked the crate from under him. It was so callous. I ran towards him, thinking I could do something, perhaps even grab his legs to support him. The men seemed to find this funny. One of them got hold of my arms and pinned them behind my back.' I pause, shuddering at the memory. 'That poor boy. He died in front of me, in the most horrible way, and they were laughing. I tried, I really did, but there was nothing I could do to help him. That's the worst of it.'

'Fucking hell, Fran. Did they hurt you at all?'

'No, not really. Everything suddenly went quiet, and the one holding my arms let go. My brain was racing. I wanted to get to the boy even though I knew he was dead. At the same time I was trying to decide which direction I should run to get away. The other one came over and blocked my exit in a jokey sort of way. He was dancing from side to side as though teasing me. Then his expression changed. He drew a finger across his throat and shook his head. That's when I dodged past him and took off at speed.'

For the umpteenth time today, I try to put the horrific tableau out of my head. The boy, swinging slowly in a pirouette of death, beautiful dark eyes bulging, a thin trickle of blood running down from one of his nostrils.

I slump back on the sofa and, at last, the tears flow unchecked.

Nothing is ever going to be the same again.

I will never be the same again.

3

While Laurie goes to make a cup of tea, I sit back with my eyes closed, the events of earlier playing out in a loop like a bad film. Running frantically from that terrible scene had sent me crashing headlong through the undergrowth, tripping over bramble suckers and tree roots and dodging overhanging branches. Convinced they're going to catch up with me, I run until my heart feels as if it is going to burst through my rib cage. My breath is escaping in short, ragged gasps, but I plough on, adrenaline coursing through my veins. By the time I reach the main path, my legs feel like jelly. I can't run anymore, and I slow to a walk, waiting for my breathing to slow. I'm hoping to intercept a dog walker or cyclist, even a driver coming into the car park, but there's no sign of anyone.

Usually the woods are a haven for dog walkers, and most days around this time, there are two or three parked cars. Now, the only vehicle I can see is a small grey van tucked into a gap between two trees. I make my way towards it, then stop short. What if it belongs to the two men? Patting my pockets, I locate my phone and Buddy's lead.

Oh God, Buddy. Where the hell is he?

Just then, a Range Rover drives in and reverses into a space. I wave my arms like a lunatic at the woman driver. I recognise her as a fellow terrier owner. We often stop and chat on walks, sharing anecdotes about the disadvantages of owning such a wilful breed. Her dog is yapping in the boot, and to my great relief, sitting on a towel on the front seat, looking totally unperturbed, is Buddy.

She looks at me sternly. 'He was trotting down the road. He must have been on his way back home.'

Her tone is sharp and accusatory. I can't blame her. She probably thinks I'm a negligent owner. It occurs to me that Buddy has been blessed with more intelligence than I give him credit for. If he had tried to make his way home by following our usual path, he wouldn't have been able to get back into the garden. Reaching the gate, he would have been perplexed to find it locked, and it's far too high for him to climb over.

'I'm so sorry, but I need your help,' I say to the woman. 'Can you drive me down the road a little way? Something awful has happened, and I really don't feel very safe. I need to ring the police.'

Without a word, she opened the passenger door and gestured for me to get in. With Buddy sitting on my knee, the woman listened to my garbled account. I was grateful when she volunteered to drive me home, and relieved when she waited with me for police to arrive.

LAURIE IS TIRED. He was up at five this morning, and I can see he is flagging. I'm exhausted too, but I doubt I will get a good night's sleep.

'Why don't you let Buddy out in the garden and then have a shower and go to bed? I'll potter for a while and then come up,' I say.

With the dishwasher loaded and swishing its way through a cycle, I unzip Laurie's case and empty it. I jam his dirty clothes into the washing machine, but not before burying my nose in his shirts. I feel guilty at being so suspicious. The trouble is that old habits die hard; it's not that long since he was unfaithful.

I check the downstairs windows and engage the safety chain on the front door. It's not normally part of my night-time routine, but from now on I cannot trust anyone else with the task. Both Laurie and I are slap-dash when it comes to home safety. There have been mornings when I have come down to let Buddy out into the garden and the bifold doors have been left unlocked overnight.

Laurie tends to laugh it off. 'We have excellent security and live in one of the safest neighbourhoods. You worry too much, Fran.'

You worry too much. It's his stock phrase when he wants to make light of my fears. Now, I don't think I will ever stop being anxious or feel safe again.

Buddy follows me upstairs and curls up on his bed on the floor. Laurie is lying on his back, snoring, a book open across his chest. He doesn't move as I retrieve the book and his glasses and place them on his bedside cabinet. When I slide in beside him, he turns onto his side away from me, and I curve my body against his. 'Heat thieving' he calls it. Sleep eludes me, and after tossing and turning for what seems like hours, I switch on the radio, notching down the volume to avoid disturbing Laurie. He stirs, and Buddy does too. Awakened from sleep, he does a complete turn, ending up back in exactly the same position he started from. I smile despite myself.

The World Service is full of depressing news, and I'm about to switch off the radio when a report on biodiversity grabs my attention. We as humans definitely have to stop plundering our planet if it is to have any chance at survival. The reporter mentions the importance of trees and their role in the ecosystem. I have always loved being outside in nature. It's calming, and I feel centred when I'm walking in woodland. Now I feel sad, thinking how my perspective has shifted in just a few short hours.

I will never forget walking into 'our woods' for the first time. It was the day after we moved into the house, and the chaos of unpacking was still ongoing. The kids were squabbling, a sure sign they were bored and had too much energy.

'It's a lovely day. Let's go for a walk,' I'd said. 'I'm getting stir-crazy too, and the exercise will do us all good.'

Laurie had been reluctant. There were so many jobs left to tackle, and he only had a few days booked off before he would be returning to work.

'Come on,' I'd wheedled. 'Let's explore. We can check out the cycle tracks. Once we get settled in, we can go for lots of bike rides.'

Flynn, having just reached his eleventh birthday, was still capable of public displays of excitement and whooped his agreement. Alice, two years older and ineffably cool, raised her eyebrows in disdain, then fixed me with a sly look.

'And we can get a dog, can't we, Mum? You did promise.'

Laurie had sighed loudly and thrown an exasperated look in my direction. He'd gone over all the disadvantages of dog ownership on numerous occasions, invariably concluding with, 'And me and your mum will be left with the responsibility of looking after a dog long after you two leave home.'

He was right, of course.

While the kids ran ahead along sun-dappled pathways, Laurie and I followed.

'Worth it?' he'd asked, squeezing my hand.

'Definitely,' I'd said.

It would be another two years before we finally wore him down, and he caved in to the pressure. One Saturday, having viewed a series of canine mugshots online, we all trooped off to a local rescue centre. Here we were introduced to the oddest-looking scrap of a puppy, the last from a litter of indeterminate paternity. He was pint-sized and terrier-like in appearance. There and then, Buddy – as Alice and Flynn named him – inveigled his way into our hearts and, despite Laurie's reservations, became a part of our family.

It was a good decision, although Laurie would never admit to it.

I startle awake to see the clock on the radio showing 3:30 a.m. I have slept briefly. I drift off again, and from an anxiety-laced dream, I am roused by the voice of the presenter reading the shipping forecast. It is now 5:20 a.m. In a couple of hours, Flynn will be getting up for work. I want to ring him before he leaves to catch his train. Alice, on the other hand, only has a short walk to work. She's not great in the mornings and will no doubt be listening to music rather than having the radio or TV on. I decide I will ring Flynn, and Laurie can do the honours with Alice. She's always a bit spiky with me on the phone and is definitely not a morning person. At the age of twenty-four, she can still behave like a stroppy teenager, and I don't need any further angst.

'Flynn, it's Mum.'

I can hear the sounds of crockery rattling in the background and the background murmur of voices from the TV.

'Hi, Mum. What's up? It's a bit early for you. Is everything all right?'

I feel a sense of relief. He obviously hasn't heard anything yet.

'I'm good, thanks. Listen, I don't want you to be concerned. It's just that something happened yesterday. I wanted to tell you about it first, before you hear it from somewhere or someone else. It's all a bit traumatic.'

'That sounds ominous. Are you sure you're okay? Where's Dad?'

'Dad's still asleep. We are both all right. The last thing I want is for you and Alice to be spooked, but once this hits the media, all sorts of lurid speculation could circulate.'

I proceed to give him a shortened version of events, conscious he needs to get ready for work.

He lets out a low whistle. 'Phewee, that sounds horrendous. Look, Mum, I have to go, but I will ring tonight. It must have been a terrifying experience for you. I'm just glad you and Dad are safe.'

'We are. Don't worry about us. Oh, and Flynn?'

'Yes?'

'There is a possibility the press might track you down at some point. I don't think they will, but if they do, don't speak to them.'

'I won't, I promise. Talk to you later.'

Laurie is moving about upstairs, and Buddy is waiting to be let out into the garden. Suddenly, he lets out a low growl and starts barking wildly.

'What is it, boy?'

Through the glass doors, I can see a man wandering around on the patio. He's holding a phone to his ear. He continues with his conversation despite the fact that I am banging hard on the glass.

I shout to Laurie to come down. The man, unconcerned, reaches into his pocket.

He walks up to the glass and holds a business card against it. I'm shaking this time, not in fear but in anger.

'Mrs Hughes, Francesca, Fran? Hi, my name is Tom Harrison. I'm a reporter from the *Derbyshire News*. Can I have a word?'

Laurie is by now at my side. He is rubbing sleep from his eyes and struggling to tie the belt of his dressing gown. He is seething at the intrusion, his face red with anger. I *would* like to know how this stranger got my details so quickly. Do the police give out witness details? If they do, it's wrong. Then again, it's easy enough to find people via the internet nowadays.

'No, you can't have a bloody word. Piss off before I set the dog on you,' Laurie yells. 'And I'm warning you now, he bloody well bites.'

Buddy snarls and shows his teeth as if to order.

'You're trespassing, mate. You had better make yourself scarce before I call the police.'

If it weren't so serious, I would laugh at the sheer absurdity of it all.

Raising his hands, the man backs off and walks away. Laurie waits for him to get onto the path at the side of the house before sliding the patio door to allow Buddy to escape.

'He should just about make it.' He laughs.

Buddy is barking furiously and throwing himself at the side gate in a frenzy. We can only assume Tom has made his escape.

'This is just the start, isn't it?' I say, feeling weary. Laurie nods in agreement.

We hear the snap of the letterbox.

A pound to a penny, it's Tenacious Tom's calling card.

4

L aurie is talking to Alice. He is using his reassuring voice, trying to pacify her. He hands me the phone, and I mouth, 'Gee, thanks,' at him. She sounds uncharacteristically agitated on the other end.

'Mum, I'm worried. Is it possible those men could come looking for you? You are the only witness, after all.'

Great. Thanks for reminding me. It's not like I haven't thought about that possibility.

I hold my tongue and make reassuring noises. Alice switches tack and goes into bossy mode.

'Listen, Mum, Dad is not to let you out of his sight, do you hear me? And it's important that you ask the police for protection.'

She has obviously been watching too many crime thrillers. She does have a point, though. I make a mental note to ask DI Holmes what the procedure is when I next speak to her.

Over the course of the morning, the doorbell rings repeatedly, and a collection of notes and business cards accumulate in the Buddy-resistant wire cage attached to the letterbox. We don't answer the door and throw the stuff into the recycle bin. Anyone who knows us will phone, and we aren't expecting any deliveries. We do need groceries, though, and Laurie wants to get sturdier locks for the garden gates.

He calls me to his side as he stands, looking at the fencing through the window. 'What do you think about putting some of those spikes along the top of the fence? They might act as a deterrent, if nothing else.'

I'm not keen on the idea, but don't dismiss it out of hand, especially as I will be on my own when he is working.

'Let's see, shall we?' I say. 'Isn't that bloke at number five some sort of security consultant? We could always have a word with him. See what he suggests. I think he's called Phil.'

We make soup and sandwiches for lunch and switch on the TV. It's a relief to see there is nothing about the murder on the BBC.

A small segment on the local news, however, catches me off guard. The boy's face fills the screen, and I choke on my bread. The picture was obviously taken a little while ago. Although he looks younger, it is unmistakably him. I don't think I will ever forget his eyes, full of fear and begging me to help him. Bile rises in my throat. As I'm running to the downstairs loo to throw up, I catch a snippet of what the newsreader is saying.

Derbyshire police are treating the death of seventeen-year-old Tyler Ingram, found in local woodland yesterday, as suspicious...'

'WE NEED A PLAN,' Laurie says, 'and not just for the next few days. Right now, we have no idea how long this is going to go on for. It's important we try to get back to some sense of normality and not let it impact on our lives for any longer than necessary.'

I feel a glimmer of annoyance. He is being his usual pragmatic, problem-solving self. In contrast, I'm a wrung-out bundle of conflicting emotions. I should say I agree with him. That we can't let it affect us. That it's a temporary blip in the smooth running of our shared life. I want to, but I can't, because I don't believe it, not for a second. Laurie and I are such different characters and approach problems in very different ways. I'm not good at shaking things off and pretending nothing has happened. It didn't work during the last crisis in our lives, and I'm damned sure it won't this time, either. I want to tell him that I'm not in the frame of mind for having a rational discussion, and I certainly don't want to start planning anything. That the short-term is about all I can cope with, but I'm conscious we might end up arguing. I opt instead to keep my thoughts under wraps. It's a strategy I don't like, and one that generates in me a ripple of dissonance, but I can't bear the thought of a row. Not today. Feeling like a sap for being so feeble, I opt to keep schtum, for now at least.

When we first met, I was not one to acquiesce. Growing up with a single mum and an absent father honed in me a mix of defensiveness and belligerence, and I was quick to anger if challenged or I disagreed with something. This either fascinated or repelled prospective boyfriends. University provided fertile ground for those of us who had decided we were exotic or different in some way.

Seamlessly, I felt myself gravitating towards others, mostly female, who were considered 'characters' in my

Social Science degree course. We called each other 'sisters' and organised sit-ins or marched in support of unpopular causes. Our uniform of choice – paint-splattered dungarees, bandana-style headbands and Doc Martens boots – tended to scare off all but the most robust of the opposite sex.

We heard from one male considered worthy of our patronage that our group was referred to as the Fanatical Feminists. If this was meant to offend, it fell flat. We just borrowed a badge-making machine from someone's kid sister and made button badges. We took satisfaction in getting the uninitiated to guess what FF stood for.

Gatecrashing a party hosted by students from the Mechanical Engineering Department led me to Laurie. For fun, a few of us had decided we would wave the feminist flag at the blokiest men we could find. A house full of engineers seemed fair game. To be honest, they didn't give us that much of a hard time. Just a few snide comments and references to *'Germaine'*, which we took as a compliment rather than an insult. After a handful of Cheez Balls and a couple of pints of weak home brew, I was past caring anyway. Curled up in a chair in a corner of the room, I watched the unedifying spectacle of drunken young men slam dancing to 'Sweet Child o' Mine' by Guns N' Roses.

Obeying the code that says you never leave a sister behind, my friend Ali stayed as, one by one, the rest of our group slunk away in search of a livelier gathering.

Looking through a collection of music tapes, I noticed someone standing in the doorway watching us. I thought I detected a sardonic smile playing around his lips.

'C'mon, Laurie. Have a drink. Studying can wait.'

A guy I knew as Arch pulled the reluctant figure into the room. Laurie was lanky, with dark hair flopping into his eyes. Two thoughts entered my head when we were introduced: one, *where has this extremely good-looking specimen been hiding for nearly three years?* and two, *how on earth am I going to get his attention?*

I decided to go for the direct approach.

'Hi. Would you like some?' I said, handing him a bowl of dry roasted peanuts.

Unlike most men I'd encountered, he didn't eye me up and down pityingly before making a caustic comment. He seemed interested, but not overly so. Later, he walked me and Ali back to halls, holding his coat over us to protect us from the drizzle. It was an old-fashioned gesture, but endearing. I let it pass without making one of my usual sly comments. We arranged to meet the next day for coffee. As the months passed, we found ourselves spending more time together until we were rarely apart. By the time my exams were over, we were in love and looking for a flat together.

'Do you want coffee?' Laurie interrupts my reverie.

'I was just thinking about when we first met,' I say. 'You took me for a coffee the next day. I wasn't too impressed when you suggested the uni café, though. I didn't know you were completely broke and had to borrow a quid from Arch.'

In spite of myself, I find myself laughing at the memory.

Laurie smiles wryly. 'And then you ended up working to support both of us until I finished my degree. You didn't know you were going to be my meal ticket for the next year, did you?'

'I bloody well did not!' I snort. 'If I had known, I would never have given you my bowl of nuts at that party.'

Laurie coaxes me out for a walk with Buddy, who is disgruntled to find we are not going into his beloved woods. Before turning the corner leading onto the main road, we bump into Jenny.

'Hello there. How are we all?' She bends to stroke Buddy, who raises his head in expectation of a treat. I suspect he had more than one rich tea biscuit when he was in her care.

'Just to let you know – and I hope you don't mind – I sent a couple of news reporters packing. They were fishing for information. I told them that people in this neighbourhood are not ones to gossip, and I will phone their editors to make a complaint if I see them lurking in the vicinity again.'

Jenny, with an MBE for services to the community under her belt, is a formidable woman. She also has some pretty useful contacts in high places, and I don't doubt she is capable of exerting influence if necessary.

With Buddy walked, Laurie is keen to go and stock up on some shopping.

'We can place an online order at the weekend. I'll just pick up a few meals at M&S to tide us over for a few days, and then call into that big hardware place. I can get the bolts for the gates and have a chat with them about additional security. I'll only be about an hour. Ring me if you are worried, and I'll come straight back.'

I remember the porch light.

'While you're there, can you pick up a bulb for the security light? I've been meaning to get one all summer.'

As I sit nursing a mug of tea, the letterbox rattles. Startled, I get up too quickly, spilling hot liquid down the front of my shirt. Buddy barks in response and follows me to the door.

I see a folded piece of paper lying at the bottom of the letter cage. I assume it's from another persistent journalist. Retrieving it, I hold it aloft, keeping it away from Buddy's jaws.

The paper is cheap and the edges ragged, as though torn from a jotter. Placing it on the coffee table, I open it out and smooth the folds. Scrawled in a childish script in bright red felt-tip pen, the words seem to leap from the page and dance before my eyes. I feel my skin prickle in fear.

Keep Your Mouth Shut.

aurie's car pulls in, and I hear him unloading bags into the porch. Anticipating the safety chain, he doesn't use his key, but knocks and waits for me to come and open the door. After helping him carry the bags to the kitchen, I spread the note in front of him on the worktop.

'When did this come?' Frowning, he picks it up, examining it from all sides.

'Not long after you went out. What do you think we should do?' The whole thing looks so amateurish, I do wonder if it might be someone's idea of a joke.

Laurie is obviously of the same mindset. 'Perhaps it's kids playing a practical joke,' he says, loading wine bottles into the fridge. 'The handwriting is very child-like. You could give DI Holmes a ring and mention it, or we could just ignore it. It depends on how you feel.'

'I'm spooked. There's no getting away from it,' I tell him. 'But I'm not sure the police will be able to do anything. Let's just leave it for the moment. If anything else worrying happens, I will contact them.'

My attempt at bravado *almost* has me convinced.

We are getting into the habit of eating our meals from trays while sitting on the sofa. Later, Laurie goes to the study to catch up on some work. I try reading a book, then a magazine, but end up distracting myself with a silly comedy program on TV. Hearing the murmur of his voice from upstairs as he makes a phone call causes a pang of painful recognition. There were many secret calls and unexpected nights spent away during the affair. Over the months my suspicions grew, but with no firm evidence, it was difficult to confront him. Looking back, there was obviously a part of me that just didn't want to believe it. There was so much going on in my life, and I was miserable and in a state of denial, clinging onto the thin veneer of normality. Eventually, almost as though he subconsciously wanted me to find out, Laurie got careless and left his phone on the coffee table while he went to the kitchen.

Able to dismiss the faint smell of perfume on his clothing, the unexpected nights away, the furtive late-night calls, I couldn't disregard the brief text that scrolled across the top of his phone. His latest mobile required fingerprint recognition for access, but an incoming message flashed up briefly on the screen.

Ring me. I'm missing you. Nat xx

'Who's Nat?' I had kept my voice as calm and controlled as I could manage.

He had looked cornered, but tried to bluff it out. 'Just someone from work. What's the big deal?' He was blustering, and I knew he was lying.

'Why would someone from work be missing you and want you to ring them?' I had remained composed, sensing his discomfort, which had been almost palpable.

His face had crumpled; he'd looked as if he was about to cry.

'Christ, Fran. I'm so sorry...'

'Please don't say you didn't mean for it to happen, or I will fucking lose it.'

He had sat with his head in his hands, and I stood over him, waiting expectantly for a response. Head down, he made a steeple with his fingers, as he always does when he's anxious.

'I need to know, Laurie, all of it.' My tone had turned glacial. 'And then we have to decide what we are going to do.'

'I'M GETTING a glass of wine. Want one?' Laurie has come in, startling me and interrupting my train of thought.

'That would be nice,' I say, trying to shake off the punch to the gut I always feel when I'm reminded of that time.

With things better between us and everything almost back to normal, I experience a pang of guilt at having resurrected such a painful memory. *There is so much going on, what possible good can come from rehashing the past?*

While Laurie watches a wildlife documentary, I flick aimlessly through the book Jenny has lent me. It's a historical romance set in eighteenth-century Derbyshire. She has told me to look out for the reference to our village, but I've lost interest in the story. I know it's mean on my part, but studying the blurb before I next see her should give me enough of the storyline to convince her I've read it.

Opening my laptop, there are a few junk emails and some notifications on social media, none of which are important enough to attend to. It strikes me that the dead boy might have a Facebook page. I search for his name, but draw a blank. There are a number of individuals called Tyler Ingram. None are a good fit. They are either too old or live in different countries.

The list does include a Melanie Ingram from Derby. I click on the name. It's possible she might be a relative. The page opens to reveal a cover photo of two large dogs. They look like Dobermanns. The profile picture is of a woman. She is, I would guess, in her late thirties. Blonde and pretty with a too-dark fake tan, she is wearing far too much make-up for my liking. The latest post shows a picture of a teenager with dark eyes and hair. It's unmistakably Tyler. He is standing next to a motorcycle, smiling and giving a thumbs-up into the camera. Superimposed across the top of the picture is a black banner with white writing. It says *Tyler Ingram RIP. Gone but never forgotten.*

The majority of those clicking the like button have selected the crying face emoji. There are hundreds of comments:

We will never forget you, Ty.
Love you and miss you always.
Sleep tight, bro, you woz the best.
RIP Ty, why did it have to happen?
Night-night, cuz. The angels have you now.

The list of tributes goes on, and I'm pretty sure the majority are from his friends, given the sentiments. I begin to feel uncomfortable, as though I'm prying into something personal. It feels intrusive, peering into the life of someone I don't know, like eavesdropping on a private conversation. I close the lid of my laptop. It's apparent the page belongs to Tyler's mother. I find it difficult to imagine the pain she must be feeling having lost a child. I hope she has a support network and is comforted by the expressions of sympathy. Although she doesn't know me, she will be aware that there is someone out there who witnessed those last, awful moments of her son's life. What horrors are occupying her waking thoughts and invading her dreams? It's been a bad enough experience for me; how much worse must it be for her under these circumstances?

I vow from now on to count my blessings. Instead of looking back on the difficult times, it now feels more important than ever to move forward and appreciate all that I have. Those schmaltzy platitudes found in greeting cards used to make me want to throw up. Now I see that messages of positivity and hope can keep you moored when it feels as though your world is spinning out of control. I'm not religious and have no prayers for Melanie Ingram or her dead son. The best I can do is offer up a heartfelt wish that her questions are answered and that she ends up finding some peace in her life.

A wave of emotion washes over me, and I look across at Laurie. He's still boyish after all these years. He's been lucky. Unlike many men his age, he has remained trim and still has a good head of hair, even if it is sprinkled with grey. It seems as though now is as good a time as any to get close again. I pour us both more wine and reach for his hand. The emotional distance between us has meant making love has become less of a priority over the last few months. My disinterest in anything apart from a hug or a cuddle on the sofa has put distance between us. I realise that. It's up to me to make the effort and get things back on track. While Laurie takes Buddy into the garden, I go through my nightly ritual of checking windows and doors. When they are back in the house, we double-check the lock on the patio doors together before leaving Buddy on his favourite blanket in the kitchen.

We are tipsy from too much wine, and the anxiety of the last few days is dulled by the alcohol. I reach up to kiss him, and giggling like schoolkids, we stumble upstairs, our bedroom a bastion of security against a world that has become full of threat and uncertainty.

6

I wake not exactly refreshed, but not drained and exhausted either. A glance in the bathroom mirror, however, reveals a sorry sight. My hair, desperately in need of colour, is hanging limply to my shoulders. My face is drawn and sallow, and there are dark shadows resembling bruises under my eyes. A visit to the hairdresser for a trim and to get my roots retouched will help. I switch off the light above the mirror, which is doing a good job of highlighting my imperfections, and make a mental note to call Tash to book an appointment.

Laurie makes croissants and coffee for breakfast, and we watch as Buddy hares across the lawn after squirrels and digs furiously into the odd molehill. The trees in the distance are starting to change colour, the leaves gradually becoming muted and dull. In a week or so, they will explode into a profusion of reds, yellows, browns and gold. Autumn is such a beautiful season, and we are fortunate to be able to witness the full spectacle at such close proximity.

In previous years, we looked forward to the cooler,

shorter days. Then we would wrap up and go for long, brisk walks, returning to light the wood burner as the sky darkened. The idea that those carefree days will ever return seems remote. It's childish, but tears are close to the surface; I push down a rising resentment at the injustice of it all. *Why me?* I want to shout. *Why do I feel like I'm being punished when I've done nothing wrong?*

The thought of what my mother would say is enough to encourage me to snap out of my self-absorption. She hated self-pity and brought me up to confront challenges, not to get browbeaten by them. It was true we didn't always get on. Sometimes we clashed horribly, especially once I became a teenager – just as Alice and I do on occasion – but I loved and respected her. Now she is no longer around to keep us all in check. Years of smoking dope during her younger years and cigarettes throughout the rest of her life took a toll on her health, and she died from cancer at the age of seventy-five. I miss her. In fact, we all do. She was not only a force to be reckoned with, but was also a fierce defender of her family, adoring Laurie and her grandchildren unconditionally.

I now know our battles resulted from the high expectations she had of me. She was especially intolerant of my 'teenage melodramas', as she called them, but I always knew she loved me. Her life hadn't been easy, and she was a proponent of the *'curtains approach'* when faced with any emotional crisis. *Just pull yourself together and get on with it.* I can hear her familiar voice in my head and decide that is a good piece of advice – for now, at least.

'Why don't you come for a walk? You'll feel better for it,' Laurie says.

'I was just coming around to that idea myself,' I tell him, slapping on my brave face. 'I don't think I'm up to taking our path into the woods yet. We could go the long way round, though, and take the path from the car park. The one that doesn't go past that bloody yew tree.'

'Are you sure?' Laurie looks hesitant, but I can tell he's pleased. 'If you can manage it, Buddy and I will be delighted. Won't we, boy?' He tickles Buddy's floppy ear.

I don't feel quite so confident when we reach the car park, which today is full of vehicles. My former faux bravery is beginning to waver, and my heart is starting to hammer in my chest. We wouldn't have been able to take the path that leads past the yew tree even if we had wanted to. The access is sealed off with crime scene tape, and a police officer stands guard, preventing anyone from entering.

In the far corner, away from the parked cars, a crowd of people have gathered. They are all sobbing quietly and leaning against each other for support.

As we hurry past, I see cards and flowers have been placed in front of a laminated photo of Tyler. His smiling face is flanked on either side by tall glass jars containing strings of lights. On the ground, a large heart shape has been fashioned out of tea lights.

One of the figures from the group turns and reaches out to hug a young woman who has just arrived and looks distraught. The older woman has blonde hair tied back in a ponytail and is wearing a long, dark coat. Although I only catch sight of her for a fleeting moment, I recognise the woman from her Facebook page. It's Tyler's mother.

I am beginning to suspect I've made a mistake in coming today. I don't want to turn back and risk drawing attention to myself, so with Buddy still on the lead, we take a path less used by walkers. It is more of a rutted, muddy track and is frequented mainly by cyclists and occasionally motorbikers, despite the fact that motorised vehicles are banned from every part of the forest. A couple of cyclists whiz past, and we have to jump to the side to avoid being splattered with mud, but mostly we have the path to ourselves.

The circular walk eventually brings us to the other side of the car park. We are close to where the van was parked that aroused my suspicions. I am relieved to see that there are now very few vehicles remaining. There's no sign of Tyler's friends and family either.

Many of the tea lights on the ground have gone out, but those in the jars sparkle incongruously. It's such a melancholy scene, and I struggle to hold back the tears.

Twinkling lights have always been a reminder of happy times in our family. Over the years, I hosted barbecues for friends and prepared parties for Alice and Flynn on so many special occasions. Together, we would string fairy lights along the fence and drape them in the trees and bushes until the garden looked like a magical grotto. Normally a symbol of joy and celebration, today they represent sorrow and loss. I notice Laurie is subdued, and I sense he is also affected by the scene. I take his arm, and we walk back home, neither of us in the mood to talk about what we have just observed.

I AM CLEANING the kitchen floor when a thought pops into my head. Laurie is hoovering the lounge, and when I hit the off switch with my foot, he looks up from his task in surprise.

'What do you call those pictures that people stick in their car windows?' I ask him.

'What's this, a quiz?' he jokes, then sees I'm serious.

'Do you mean car stickers? Decals, I think they're called.'

'That's the word, decals,' I say. 'When we were in the car park today, something must have jogged my memory. When the police asked me about the van, I couldn't tell them much, just that it was a Volkswagen, because I remembered the VW symbol, and the fact that it was grey. But I do remember there was something in the back window. Let me try to draw it for you.'

Grabbing a piece of paper and a pencil, I sketch out what I remember of the image. Two spheres, one above the other, wrapped around with a blue ribbon. Laurie initially looks confused, but then takes the pencil from me and adds to the drawing, filling in some more of the details.

'Like this?' he asks, turning it towards me. The top circle is now a world globe, and the bottom one is a football.

'Yes, exactly like that,' I tell him. 'What does it mean?'

'It's a Birmingham City Football Club badge. The men were probably not from around here, or it would more likely have been a Derby County or Nottingham Forest sticker.'

'It's probably not that important, but I'll give the police a ring on Monday and mention it,' I say.

I feel the faintest flicker of relief. If the men are not local, then maybe they have left the area. And if that's the case, the note through the door was probably a prank after all.

7

'You're not sleeping well, are you?' Laurie asks me over breakfast. 'Might be worth going to the doctor's to get something to help you relax. You don't want to make yourself ill again.'

I know he doesn't mean it, but that *make yourself* comment jars. It's not as if it is a choice I have made. Lack of sleep is becoming a problem, though. When I do eventually drift off, I wake with a jolt, drenched in sweat, fragments of nightmares hovering at the edge of my consciousness. Although we have always laughed at Laurie's ability to sleep soundly, I must be disturbing him if he is aware of my restlessness. The fact that I'm wide awake for long periods during the night, combined with my wrung-out dishrag look, can't be very appealing first thing in the morning.

'I will,' I say, not very convincingly.

He knows I dislike taking medication unless it's absolutely necessary, but his concern is justified. The previous year had exhausted all my physical and emotional resources. There had been the trauma associated with the investigation at work into the death of a baby, mum's death, and then the emotional aftermath of Laurie's affair. It was overwhelming, and I found for the first time in my life that I was unable to cope with even basic day-to-day tasks. The doctor I saw at the time was young and newly qualified, but sympathetic when I dissolved into a whimpering heap in front of her.

'Everyone needs a bit of help at some point, Mrs Hughes. It isn't a sign of failure to admit you are struggling,' she'd said as I blubbed into the paper towel she had handed to me.

'I'm going to prescribe a short course of tablets, which should help, and I'd like you to come back in two weeks. Don't hesitate to ring in the meantime if you have any concerns.'

Leading me out of her room, she had placed a hand on my shoulder, a gesture I found oddly reassuring, given I'm old enough to be her mother.

Leaving the surgery, I had experienced a mixture of emotions: pathetic gratitude at being listened to and embarrassment at confiding in someone not that much older than my own daughter.

I did try to take the tablets, but they left me feeling woozy and forgetful. After persevering for over a week, I went back to tell the doctor I didn't want to continue taking them.

She had gently rebuked me for not giving the medication longer to kick in, and sent me off with a pile of leaflets on sleep management and mindfulness training. These I placed in the recycle bin when I got back home. I decided I would instead make myself walk at least once a day in the fresh air with Buddy. It seemed to work wonders, and gradually, over the weeks, I began to feel better in myself. Mum would be proud of me, I thought at the time. Little did I know how naive I was, expecting to shake off anxiety and grief like a summer cold. Recovery was never going to be straightforward, despite what I thought. In times of crisis, what is submerged and concealed by layers of self-deception will always bob back to the surface, like a genie in a stop-motion animation film, escaping from a bottle.

LAURIE BANGS on the kitchen window, startling me. He wants me to come out into the garden to survey his handiwork, and I follow him outside. He has added stronger bolts to the gates and strengthened the hinges. The bolts, made from galvanised steel, are large and ugly, but it does look like it would be virtually impossible to kick in either of the gates if you wanted to access the garden.

'The weather forecast is good for today,' he says. 'Why don't we have a run out to the Peak District this afternoon? I've got some work to do this morning. It won't take long, and we can drive to Youlgreave later and walk by the river. We can stop for an early evening meal at a pub on the way home.'

'That sounds great,' I tell him. 'We could all do with a change of scenery.'

I make a flask of coffee, and with Buddy safely secured in the boot of the car, we head for the A515. We pass mile after mile of uniform green fields until the road begins to rise and the landscape starts to alter. The flat fields give way to rolling hills, unfolding like crumpled paper and stretching into the distance, reaching far away to the horizon. Approaching the town of Ashbourne, the Gateway to the Peak District, we catch a glimpse of the elevation that is Thorpe Cloud. With its distinctive flat top, it's a spectacular sight. Once an ancient coral fossil, it emerged from the ocean floor as a reef knoll. Now, it's a popular beauty spot, attracting tourists from far and wide.

We can just make out a few moving dots on its incline. These are walkers making their way up the steep, rugged path to the summit.

When it was still possible to encourage Alice and Flynn to come with us on family walks, we would cross the river Dove using the stepping stones, then join the snake of climbers following the path up from the limestone ravine at the base of the hill. It was well worth the climb for the view. Below us, spread out like a 3D patchwork quilt, sprawled steep-sided wooded valleys and emerald green fields enclosed by flint-coloured, drystone wall boundaries.

Now, as we drive through the town, we pass the gated development where mum's flat is located. I feel a pang of sadness thinking of how much she had loved her warm, cosy home. Having lived for so many years in a rambling old cottage where it was necessary to have a car, Ashbourne had everything she needed on the doorstep, including decent supermarkets. Over the years, the town has become increasingly choked with traffic and crowded with tourists and walkers, but it retains its old-fashioned charm, with its cobbled marketplace, quaint tea rooms and high-end shops.

The draughty money pit of a cottage I grew up in was bought by mum when it became apparent that my father was not in it for the long haul. She saved for a deposit on her teacher's salary and took out a small mortgage to ensure we had a roof over our heads. There was never enough money to keep abreast of the repairs, and everything was make-do and mend, but it was home, and I felt a sentimental attachment to it despite its many flaws. It came as a surprise when she decided to sell, but it turned out to be a canny decision on her part. Rising prices in the area guaranteed a quick sale of the cottage. This allowed her to buy her new flat, fit it out in a quirky mix of modern and antique furniture, and have some cash left over. Of course, the expectation was that she would have many more years. Sadly, it was not to be. Following her death, apart from the small sums of money she left to Alice and Flynn, the bulk of her estate, including the flat, came to me.

Youlgreave is basking in warm sunshine when we arrive. There aren't many visitors at this time of year, and the village is quiet. We manage to park in front of a row of mellow stone cottages. Buddy is raring to go and launches himself out of the car, eager to explore after being confined for the best part of an hour. We take the lane that winds down to the river, admiring the cottage gardens we pass along the way, still a riot of colour despite summer being almost at an end. When we reach the bottom of the hill, Buddy runs ahead and pads into the shallow water beneath the footbridge. He returns to shake vigorously, showering us with a cascade of water droplets.

It's relaxing walking in the sunshine, and for the first time in days, my anxiety levels drop. Resting on a wooden bench, we enjoy a cup of coffee from the flask. With Buddy safely tied up at our feet, we watch a heron poised like a statue. It's standing on the edge of one of the weirs that drop into pools where trout breed in the crystal-clear depths of the river.

'We should do this more often,' I say, tilting my head to catch some rays. 'I feel as though I can breathe easier being away from the house.'

'We will, once I eventually retire,' Laurie says. 'It's all right for you. You are a woman of means. Not everyone has the luxury of retiring at fifty.'

He's teasing, I know, but I do feel guilty. Since quali-

fying in social work, and with only short breaks for
maternity leave, my career spanned almost three
decades. Towards the end, the stress of the job, alongside everything else I was having to cope with, left me
emotionally and physically drained. No longer enjoying
the work and heading for burnout, I made the decision
to take early retirement in exchange for what I hoped
would be peace of mind. Mum's money, although it
wouldn't have been the way I would have chosen to
acquire it, came at just the right time.

Once her property was cleared, I chose to rent it out
rather than sell. The first couple who came to view it
seemed ideal tenants, and I felt confident the flat would
be in safe hands. It also gave me a guaranteed income,
and if I did decide to sell it later, I would acquire a not
insubstantial lump sum. I was lucky, I knew that, but
more importantly I felt sure Mum, who got so much
enjoyment out of her own retirement, would have
approved.

'It will be great once you do retire,' I say to Laurie.
'We can go on all those cruises with the other rich baby
boomers the kids are always complaining about. You
know, the ones who have bankrupted their children's
futures.'

'Well, our two haven't done too badly. We subsidised
them through university, and they are fortunate not to
have any debts apart from their student loans. And
don't forget, we have helped them with deposits and
furniture in their respective flats. We never had any help
when we were starting out. I seem to remember we did
without. If there was anything we wanted or needed,
we saved up for it. They have it too easy now.'

He's frowning, and I want to make him smile. 'Cur-
mudgeon,' I say, grabbing his arm and tucking it inside
mine.

On the way back, we call at a country pub we've visited on many occasions. The couple who manage it greet us like old friends. They bring Buddy a dog biscuit from behind the bar, and he wags his tail and offers a paw like the consummate performer he is. We sit in an alcove close to the open fire piled high with logs that spit and hiss in the grate. Buddy, tired from the walk, curls up under the table and promptly falls asleep.

Laurie orders our food and comes back with two halves of cask ale, pale amber in colour and topped with a creamy head of froth. As we wait for our meals, he reaches across the table for my hand. 'It's been a lovely day, and you look better for being away from the house, but I do have to go to work, Fran. Next week I have those presentations for the new contracts, and much as I hate the thought, I will have to spend a couple of nights away most weeks, right up until Christmas.'

If he notices the micro expression of pain that crosses my face, he doesn't acknowledge it. I let him continue without interruption, not really listening and pushing down the feelings of unease that surface whenever he tells me he will be spending nights away from home. I want those feelings to subside, and I want to trust him again. *It can only be a matter of time, can't it?*

Laurie *has* noticed. 'I could try to pass the work on to someone else if you want me to be at home. It's just that it would be a nightmare having to prep them at such short notice. That's the problem with consultancy; it's so difficult to delegate.'

He's looking for reassurance, but I turn away to watch the flames reflected in the horse brasses lining the beam above the fireplace.

'I was thinking.' He waits for me to turn back to face him. 'What if I ask Mum to come for a few days? She'd love a break from Dad. Once I get next week out of the way, I can look at booking the odd day off here and there. What do you think?'

I *think* my worries about him being away are complex, and not just to do with any fears I might have of being alone in the house. On the other hand, much as I love his mum, Verena, she is probably not whom I want with me at this point. I *think* that although not depressed, my anxiety levels are off the scale, and I am as fragile as an egg. Despite this, I don't want anyone, including Verena, seeing my vulnerability; it's the last thing I need right now. This is what *I think*, but I say nothing to that effect.

Instead, I give him a brittle smile. 'Let's just see, shall we? It's short notice for your mum, and I've got plenty to do next week. Oh, and I forgot to say, Alice texted. She and Flynn are coming to stay next weekend. It will be something to look forward to.'

I've got plenty to do next week. We both know that's not true, but he doesn't challenge me. If nothing else, the kids will be a much-needed distraction. It's just what I need to fill the empty chasm opening up in front of me.

8

'Hello. I'd like to speak to DI Holmes if it's convenient.'

There's a click on the line as they put me through to her extension.

'This is DI Holmes speaking.'

The voice on the other end of the phone is light and reassuring. I imagine her sitting at her desk, compact bob, neat earrings, striped linen shirt and tailored black trousers, for all the world looking more like a travel consultant than a senior police officer.

'It's Fran Hughes. Is it possible to have a word? I can ring back if you're busy.'

'Hi, Fran. I was actually going to call you this morning to have a bit of a chat. The team is meeting at ten. Can I ring you later? Actually, I've just had a thought. Are you in this afternoon? I'm going to be in the area. I could come and see you about two if that suits.'

'That will be fine,' I say. 'I'll have the kettle on.'

Laurie has gone to work, with the promise he will be back early this evening. I walk Buddy and return to tackle my to-do list, which is pinned to the fridge. When I'm stressed, my memory becomes unreliable. There's not much point in adding things to the checklist facility on my phone, either, as I have a habit of deleting that by mistake. No, I'm a big fan of lists; as old-fashioned as it is, pen and paper suits me just fine.

I ring Tash to make an appointment for a cut and colour. She's had a cancellation and fits me in at 4 p.m. this coming Thursday. Laurie will be away overnight on Tuesday and again on Thursday, which means I can relax with a baked potato in front of the telly instead of cooking after I get back.

I also want to order some flowers for Jenny, as she was such a help looking after Buddy. The choices online are not great, but I find a small florist in Derby who does a seasonal, hand-tied bouquet, which I think she'll like. I phone and arrange delivery, adding a thank-you note. Buddy and I will call to see her on Wednesday afternoon, to check if the flowers have arrived.

The food order for the weekend can wait for a couple of days, but I will have to remember to include lots of snack foods to keep Alice and Flynn happy. Marshmallows will be good. We can toast them on sticks in the fire. It will be just like the old days.

The doorbell rings, and I look through the front window to check before putting Buddy into the kitchen out of the way. DI Holmes is accompanied by a younger male, whom she introduces as DS Mark Georgiou. Tall, with black curly hair and brown, soulful eyes, he looks as though he is no stranger to the gym. It occurs to me that he could be quite popular down at the station with males and females alike.

They both decide on coffee, and I make a cafetière, which I place on a tray with the cups and a plate of biscuits.

'Ooh, lovely. Fresh coffee,' DI Holmes says. 'We're usually lucky to get a cup of weak tea. This is quite a treat.'

My early guess as to her attire is not that far off the mark. She is wearing a white shirt and a navy pencil skirt, which finishes at the knee. She notices a photo of us all on the mantelpiece and enquires about the kids.

'Yes, that's Alice and Flynn,' I say. 'It was taken a while ago when we were on holiday in Wales. They have both left home now. We don't see much of them, but they are coming this weekend.'

I try not to sound like the pathetic empty-nester she must view me as.

'Do you have any children?' It's forward of me to ask, but I've noticed she is wearing a wedding ring, so it's not beyond the realm of possibility.

'Yes, we do. Twelve-year-old twins, a boy and a girl.'

I can hear the pride in her voice.

'I'm really lucky,' she says. 'My wife works part-time, which means she can be there when I am working antisocial hours.'

She gives me a cool look, as though she is expecting a challenge. I wonder how much explaining she has to do about her family situation. Whether she attracts any judgemental comments, even in these seemingly enlightened times.

'It must be lovely having two at the same age,' I say. 'At least you get them through the teenage years together.'

She smiles. 'They are quite a handful already. I dread to think what they will be like in a year or two.'

She puts her cup down on the table and turns to face me. 'I realise this might be difficult for you, Fran, but I was wondering if you would be willing to come with us to the crime scene? You did a great job, but it's just to see if you can remember anything else of significance.'

She has reverted to brisk and efficient, seamlessly steering the conversation away from the personal, a tactic I recognise from my own work with clients.

She takes a biscuit and bites off a corner. 'Sometimes going back to where it happened can trigger memories. It doesn't have to be now. We can arrange to take you when it's more convenient.'

If I am going to do this, I don't want to spend too much time thinking about it and lose my nerve. I agree to go with them there and then.

Pulling into the car park, we attract the attention of a group of Lycra-clad members of the local running club limbering up in preparation for a circuit of the woods. As we wait in the car for them to leave, I realise I have forgotten to mention the sticker in the rear window of the van that was parked up on the day Tyler was killed. I tell them, trying to remember as much detail as I can. With my description, a look passes between the two of them that I can't quite decipher.

'It didn't mean anything to me,' I say. 'Laurie recognised it, though. He said it's the Birmingham City Football Club logo.'

Before joining the path from the car park, we pass the pile of floral tributes. It has rained, and the bouquets from last week are brown and shrivelled in their cellophane. Fresher bunches have been added more recently. I resist the temptation to bend down and read the accompanying cards. The plastic is starting to lift from Tyler's photo, and the colours from the print are beginning to run, but the lights in the glass jars, powered by batteries, continue to shine as brightly as ever.

'How are you feeling, Fran?' DI Holmes gives me a

sympathetic look, as though aware of what an ordeal this is going to be for me.

'Okay so far,' I tell her.

We have reached the edge of the path and are about to turn in towards where the yew tree is located. A stray piece of plastic crime scene tape is fluttering loosely in the wind, and I jump at the sound. My head starts to pound, and I feel queasy. I pause and take deep breaths to steady myself. I don't know how I am going to react once the curtain of branches is pulled aside. One thing I can't rule out is an embarrassing meltdown. Taking another breath, I steel myself. What will face me can't be worse than what I have already seen played out in this haven of tranquillity. Of this I am sure.

The overhanging canopy of yew tree branches reaches almost to the ground, shading the splinters of light coming in from above. The area looks as though it has been swept clean. Forensics have obviously done a thorough job of collecting evidence, because there is no sign of the crate Tyler was standing on. Peering closer at the branch from which he was suspended, I can see that the reddish-brown bark has been rubbed away by the rope, exposing the lighter tissue beneath. I shiver as I gaze in mute fascination. Where the pale afternoon sun has penetrated the dense foliage, by a strange trick of the light, the bare wood appears to be suffused with blood.

DS Georgiou has taken out a notebook and pen from the pocket of his jacket and is waiting patiently. DI Holmes has placed her hand under my elbow for support. I'm glad of her presence, as without it, I'm sure I would have bolted from the scene by now.

'What I'd like you to do is to try to think back to the unfolding events that led to Tyler's death. Don't worry about the order. You can start at the end and work backwards if you want to. Just go through it all at your own pace. DS Georgiou will make a record of what you say. Do you feel up to giving it a go?'

I nod, and she steers me into the centre of the space. It's so still I can't even hear birdsong. Shafts of light cut through the branches, and in that suspended moment it feels as if we are in a church.

'It might help if you can remember how you were feeling up to and during the incident,' DI Holmes is saying. 'Taking yourself back to that morning and focusing on what was going on around you will help with recall. But please, let us know if you need a breather. We can stop at any point if it gets too much.'

I'm familiar with the cognitive interviewing techniques she is using; I've utilised them myself in my own job. Closing my eyes helps. Under pressure, my memory works more effectively if my thinking is linear. In my head, I run through the timeline from when Buddy and I first entered the woods. It's going well until I try to give a description of the two men. It must be fear impacting on my ability to recall. I was able to give a good description during the original interview. Why then has the mental picture I had of the men become occluded? Details of their height and build, one tall and of slim build, the other shorter and stockier, one with crooked teeth. These details aren't problematic. I also know they were wearing dark clothes, and both had shaved heads. Beyond that, their faces have become insubstantial in memory, as flimsy as gossamer.

I know it's possible that I have suppressed the memory because it was too traumatic, but if that's the case, why then has everything else associated with what happened remained imprinted on my mind with such heightened clarity?

I stop trying to force myself to think. It's giving me a

headache anyway. I turn in preparation to leave when a fragment of memory flashes into my consciousness. Closing my eyes again, I wait for the image to take form. I hadn't recalled it in the first interview, yet here it is, taking shape and becoming recognisable. In my eagerness, I shout triumphantly, the words running into each other as I do so.

'A clock face! The shorter guy, not the one who grabbed my arms, but the other one, who made the cutthroat sign. When he turned away, I noticed something on the back of his neck. It was a tattoo in the shape of a clock face.'

I ask for some paper, and DS Georgiou tears a sheet from his notebook. He hands it to me along with his pen, looking over my shoulder as I sketch out the shape.

DS Georgiou squints at the paper. 'You haven't drawn any hands. Is that correct?' he asks.

'That's correct. No hands,' I say. 'What can that mean?'

Again they exchange a look, although both remain non-committal. Perhaps they think I'm getting carried away. I start to feel my initial exuberance ebb. DI Holmes, seeing my expression, seems keen to try to bolster my confidence.

'You did really well, Fran. You have given us some very useful additional information. It looks like you have had enough for today, so I suggest we take you home now. But we will arrange for you to come in to work with an officer and prepare an e-fit of the men based on your description. Meanwhile, you can always contact us if you think of anything else.'

It is only after they drop me back at the house that I realise I haven't mentioned the threatening note posted through the letterbox.

9

In my dream, I am following a cloaked and hooded form. We pass through a labyrinth of dark streets lit by fog-encircled lamps. It feels important that I don't lose sight of the figure, and I hurry to try to keep up, but each time I get within touching distance, they turn down yet another increasingly narrow alleyway. The walls on either side are becoming so close I can feel the water coursing down the brickwork and splashing onto my arms. My nostrils twitch at the smell of damp and decay. Reaching a dead end, I follow the figure up a set of stone steps and in through a door. A spotlight clicks on, illuminating a large empty space. I offer an outstretched hand towards the figure, and it turns slowly until it is facing me. The hood is a void of darkness in which a head is suspended like a pale moon. It is featureless apart from the eyes, which burn with a fierce intensity, desperately begging me for help.

Clawing my way back from the heavy sluggishness of sleep, I see the room is unnaturally bright. It takes a few minutes before my head clears and I can start to make sense of what is happening. Despite all my checks before bed, I've forgotten to close the bedroom door or drop the blind on the landing window. An animal must have triggered the security light in the back garden, which goes on and off a number of times. My limbs still feel heavy, and with no Laurie to cuddle into, the chill of the night air on my sweat-stained face causes me to shiver. I'm reluctant to get up, so I curl into a ball, pulling the quilt over my head. Buddy has crept up onto the bed beside me, and I settle for stealing some of his warmth. Eventually, I fall back into a fitful sleep.

After breakfast, I walk Buddy to the park, where there are always a few mums with excitable children playing on the swings and slide. We are on our way back home when I see Jenny reversing out of her drive in her car. She pulls up alongside us.

'Thank you for the flowers. They arrived this morning. All my favourites, and beautifully presented, too. You didn't have to, you know? I'm always more than happy to help.'

'I know you are, Jenny. It's just a small token of our thanks, isn't it, Buddy?'

Buddy has been wagging his tail the whole time at the sight of Jenny, and also manages a cute side turn of his head in response to his name.

'We were thinking of popping to see you this afternoon, but you appear to be off on an outing,' I say.

'Oh, I'll be back by lunchtime. I'm just doing a bit of shopping. It will be nice to see both of you. I've tried out a new recipe this morning. You can give me your verdict on my banana bread, and I'm sure we can find a treat for this little man.'

She closes her window and gives Buddy a smile and a wave before driving off. I would swear, if I didn't know better, that he grinned in return.

Back home, I retrieve a message on my phone from Verena. As it's late morning, she will be in her kitchen, having fed the animals earlier. She and Laurie's dad, Bryn, have retired to rural Wales. They now own a smallholding with a motley collection of rescued animals. Grabbing a coffee, I dial her number, and she picks up immediately.

'Fran? It's good to hear your voice. Laurie phoned to let me know what happened. It's terrible. Poor you, and how awful for that boy and his family.'

She prompts me for the full story and sounds genuinely shocked when I tell her about returning to the scene with the police.

'Really?' she says. 'I can't imagine anything worse.'

It's on the tip of my tongue to challenge this statement. I don't want to be provocative, so I resist. Years ago, I wouldn't have been able to help myself, and I would have made a snarky comment about the life of refugees or something similar. The art of diplomacy came into my life rather late.

I can hear Radio 4 in the background and the rattle of crockery. Bryn is probably making a pot of tea, and the thought of their warm, cosy, chaotic cottage, with discarded wellies by the door and washing drying over the Aga, fills me with nostalgia for all the happy times we spent there as a family.

'Fran?'

My daydreaming means I have missed some of what Verena has been saying.

'Yes, I'm here. I thought I heard the door. Sorry,' I say by way of an excuse.

'I was saying that I could come to stay while Laurie is away. He rang to suggest it, and I think it's a good idea. It will only take me a couple of hours to drive to you. I just need a bit of notice beforehand. Bryn will manage without me for a few days, but I still need to organise him and the animals before I go.'

'That's so kind,' I say in my most upbeat voice. I weigh my words carefully, not wanting to hurt her feelings. 'It's just that I've got a few things coming up. If you come, I really don't think it's fair to leave you by yourself if I'm flitting here there and everywhere. It would be a waste of your time. I'm fine, really. I promise I will let you know if I need you.'

It's all bullshit, of course. I have nothing planned that can't be changed.

Verena and I are on good terms now, but this was not always the case. Early on, it had been a tense relationship. We first met soon after Laurie and I started going out. She was grey-haired even then, with a penchant for dangly earrings and hippy clothes. At that time, they were living in the suburbs of a nondescript town near to London. It was an easy commute for Bryn, who worked as a buyer for an independent wine merchant in the City. Despite their urban location, Verena made her own bread and grew vegetables long before it was trendy to do so. She even kept a couple of chickens and a feisty cockerel, much to the exasperation of her neighbours. When I came on the scene, I knew immediately she didn't think I was good enough for her precious son.

Looking back, I can hardly blame her. A bolshy, opinionated, pint-swilling leftie would not be what most women would view as an ideal prospective daughter-in-law. Over the years, we settled into an uneasy relationship based around a genial competition for Laurie's affections. The arrival of the children unified us. Eventually, I grew to admire, respect and then love the quirky free-spirited woman who had given birth to the man I loved.

Having told Verena I'm busy, I feel the need to at

least attempt to keep up the pretence of something resembling a social life. Perhaps I can rustle up a meeting with some of my old work colleagues?

After leaving my job, I was disinclined to join in with the regular social meet-ups. Feeling so wretched at the time, it was difficult to feign sociability. We had been a close-knit team, but were subjected to an uncomfortable level of scrutiny following the death of a child. The Serious Case Review into the circumstance surrounding Baby C's death affected us all. Even though we were eventually exonerated, the death of a baby under such tragic circumstances left us all devastated. Perhaps I was being hypersensitive, but I got the impression that some of the team thought I had chosen the easy way out by leaving when I did. The upshot was, with nothing to contribute to the work-based gossip pool, the invitations eventually dried up. A few have kept in touch via social media, but I'm not really included in their nights out anymore. One thing is certain, me being a witness to a particularly gruesome murder is more than likely to generate a flurry of interest around the water cooler. It may even trump discussion centring on the plot line of the latest Scandi noir. I decide against making contact. I can't face any of them. Not yet, anyway.

Catching up on my emails, I see there is a message from my yoga teacher. She wants to know if I will be coming back, as she has a waiting list of people wanting to join the class. I message her with my apologies for not attending for a while, and confirm that I will be there for the next session. I find yoga relaxing and look forward to the class. My reputation for being so relaxed that I fall asleep during the closing minutes always generates a great deal of amusement amongst my fellow practition-ers. I'm hoping the effect continues despite my distinctly wobbly state of mind.

JENNY SEEMS pleased to see us. She has prepared a tray with her best china tea set and generous slices of home-made banana bread. Buddy has not been forgotten. She produces a treat ball filled with chunks of doggy sausage. He sits for a while looking perplexed, as though expecting it to automatically dispense the elusive bits of meat. Jenny laughs indulgently when he discovers he can roll the ball with his nose until pieces of sausage drop onto the rug.

Returning the book she lent to me, I offer Jenny a reasonable enough account of the plot for her to believe I have actually read it. We sit in her conservatory, looking out over immaculately kept gardens. Since her husband Peter's death, Jenny has employed a gardener, but most of the plants and bushes were planted during their almost fifty years of marriage. I enjoy hearing her stories about moving into the house as a newly-wed.

'So much has changed since we came here in 1969, but the one constant is that beautiful expanse of wood-land,' she says. 'It's such a pity that this has happened, Fran. I'm guessing it will take time for you to recover and begin to feel safe again?'

If ever, I think to myself, nodding in agreement.

I update her on my return to the scene with the two CID officers.

'How dreadful. It's like something out of a television drama. It's such a quiet village,' she says. 'I really hate the thought of always having to be on alert from now on. I suppose it's a necessary evil and a sign of the times. Let's just hope they catch those awful men soon.'

The autumn sun is a watery shade of lemon as it sets behind the trees. With a drop in air temperature, we watch as a grey mist rolls in, obscuring the top of the tree canopy. It's an eerie sight. I collect my coat and Buddy's lead, along with a piece of cake for Laurie. There is a definite nip in the air. I take Buddy for a quick walk to the top of the road and then turn back, eager to get home and light the wood burner before cooking our evening meal.

The drive is shrouded in gloom, and I'm fumbling for my keys in my coat pocket. Stepping into the unlit porch, I don't notice the figure crouching in the shadows until they push past me, tripping over Buddy's lead in the process. Taken by surprise, neither Buddy nor I have time to react. A flailing arm catches me a glancing blow on the cheek, and then they are gone, melting silently like a wraith into the encroaching dusk.

10

'It's weird, Laurie, but it didn't feel like it was an adult who pushed past me in the porch. I'm pretty sure it was a kid. I really don't think there's much point in phoning the police.' I'm visibly shaken, but rational enough to realise that calling the police won't achieve much. 'You know what teenagers are like, if that's who it was. They don't think about the consequences of their actions. It was probably a dare between friends, and he or she drew the short straw.'

On the other end of the phone, Laurie is furious and worried on my behalf. He is also annoyed with himself for not sorting out the porch light. 'I knew there was something else we needed,' he says. 'That bloody light is unpredictable. It may need more than a new bulb.'

'Don't blame yourself,' I say. 'I forgot, too. I'll phone up an electrician tomorrow. By the time you get home on Friday, it will be like Colditz when you pull onto the drive.'

'Are you sure you're not too shaken up? I could drive home tonight and go back early in the morning if you are worried.'

'No,' I say with as much conviction as I can muster. 'You are not doing anything of the sort. Buddy and I will be fine. I'm not having you run yourself off the road after falling asleep at the wheel. We would rather have you back safe and sound, if you don't mind.'

Finding an electrician who can come and do the job at short notice proves more difficult than I imagined, but eventually I manage to locate one. He has time between jobs and is only in the next village. He arrives just as I am finishing a sandwich, and accepts my offer of a cup of tea. As we stand chatting in the kitchen, he gestures towards the woods.

'It's a lovely location. Awful what happened, though. The murder, I mean.'

I nod, but don't volunteer any information.

'There's nowhere safe now. I've had quite a few more calls from around here since last week. Security always becomes a big issue when something major happens, but a dog is as good a deterrent as you can get, I always say.'

He looks at Buddy curled up on his blanket in his usual pose, nose tucked into his backside.

'Terriers are good guard dogs. I've got two borders of my own, and people think they look cute, but they are pretty fierce when it comes to defending their territory.'

I let him out through the front door. Five minutes later, there's a tap on the window.

'It's not the bulb,' he says. 'The whole unit needs replacing. I've got some spares in the van, or you can get your own, and I'll come back and fit it for you.'

I decide on the former, and he brings a selection of boxed lights for me to have a look at.

I decide on a cast-iron effect lantern.

'This will give you light in your porch, but not in the

whole of your garden. Do you want me to put up a PIR spotlight to cover your drive and garden, too?'

In for a penny, I think to myself, taking his bank details to pay his bill online.

IT'S DRIZZLING when I set off for the hairdresser's. Even though it's only a ten-minute walk away, I arrive soaked to the skin. The little shop is sandwiched between the Co-op and the post office, and the window display is end-of-summer beach-themed. Hair products are artfully lined up on pieces of driftwood. A light scattering of sand contains a selection of realistic-looking starfish and brightly coloured seashells. I push open the door, and the bell tinkles to announce my arrival.

Tash is in the back and comes out armed with a sweeping brush. Her own hair has undergone a number of incarnations in terms of colour and style over the years. The spiky cut in an eye-watering shade of fuchsia pink she is sporting, does not disappoint; I compliment her on the colour. She takes my coat and hangs it up on a wooden peg. While I perch on her tiny, uncomfortable chaise longue, she sweeps away the hair from underneath the salon chairs.

'Window looks great,' I say, moving across to take a seat in front of one of the large mirrors. 'I can't wait to see what you do with it for Halloween.'

Tash gives me a mischievous smile. In previous years, she has come to the attention of the local Parish Council, who were not best pleased with her wacky interpretation of the celebration. Someone had complained about the coffins and blood-soaked figures with glowing eyeballs, all displaying the latest trends in hairstyling. Tash being Tash, she left the display up, but endeared herself to local mums by providing a bran tub with a lucky dip for passing children, and no more was said about her display.

'Okay. Now we have coffee and Polish cake. Yes?' She has already disappeared into the back without waiting for a reply.

Tash is from Poland and has been in this country for over ten years. She still has an accent, but I love the way she has incorporated Derbyshire idioms into her speech. She made me laugh out loud once when she referred to her husband as 'mardy' when he was ill, and a 'big whinge bucket' when he had been bad-tempered.

She is tall and well-built, with a somewhat unconventional dress sense. Today she is wearing a short tartan pleated skirt with chunky boots and tights. Her cold-shoulder top only partially obscures her tattoo sleeve, which begins just below her shoulder and ends above her wrist. The intricate pattern of blood-red roses, encircled by leathery green leaves and topped with dewdrops, trails down her arm. It's a sight I find both beautiful and unsettling every time I see it.

She brings me a slice of her cake and a mug of strong brewed coffee and places them on the shelf in front of me.

'Right, ducky. What are we doing with this?' She takes a handful of my lanky locks from either side of my head and extends them outwards. 'Definitely need a trim as well as some colour. Shall we do some highlights to brighten it up? Looks like it needs it.'

Tash's brusqueness conceals a heart of gold. She is as good with the old ladies who come in for a perm as she is with the little ones having their first haircut. I also know she donates to a lot of the less high-profile charities in the area, shying away from any recognition for her contributions.

'How is szarlotka? It's family recipe.'

'It's delicious, Tash. Cinnamon goes so well with apples. Can you message me the recipe? I'd like to have a go, but I doubt it will be as good as this.'

She huffs in response, but I can tell she is flattered. 'Of course. Now let's get going on this hair. I'm glad no one else coming in, or I could be here until midnight.'

Tash attacks my hair with vigour, cutting and shaping it into a choppy bob and applying half a head of blonde highlights. We chat like the old friends we are, Tash keen to know all about Alice and Flynn. They were both impressed enough to trust Tash to give them trendy haircuts during their teenage years. I'm eager to hear all about the renovations on the house she and her husband, Alex, moved into three years ago.

Over the years we have become confidantes, sharing intimate details of our lives from that odd position of trust occupied by someone outside of your family who doesn't fit in neatly with your circle of friends. It was Tash I turned to for advice when I was considering leaving work. By this time, the Baby C story was all over the media, and it was possible to discuss the case without leaking any important facts.

'I don't think I can continue with the job, Tash,' I'd said. 'It feels like the final straw. There was nothing to alert us that anything was wrong, yet I still want to beat myself up about it.'

Tash knew the background to the case from what she read in the papers, and was less than sympathetic towards the parents of the child. Given her own circumstances, I could hardly blame her.

'You should get out, Fran. People like that are take the piss. Have lots of help and still mess things up. They don't deserve to have baby.'

'She was just so young,' I told her. 'It's true she had

been using heroin, but she was stable on her methadone. She was doing really well with support from her mum. Her little flat was immaculate; the baby seemed well cared for. We had no real concerns when we visited. True, she kept quiet about the boyfriend coming to stay. The baby was fractious. Poor little mite was still withdrawing, and they would give him tiny amounts of methadone to settle him to sleep.'

Tash had clicked her tongue in annoyance. 'How stupid to give baby that muck. People should stay away from drugs in first place. Don't deserve baby if take drugs. You getting too old for this, what you say, Fran, *malarkey?'*

I had to agree with her; I was tired and jaded from it all. I longed to leave behind the chaos that people generated in their lives, increasingly as a result of drug-taking. It was social workers who were left to pick up the pieces, and we got little thanks for the work we did. Damned if we intervened and took a child away from its parents, and damned if we didn't, as had happened in this case. Tash was harsh to blame the parents in this case. More accountable are those who bring the stuff into the country and distribute it. They are the real villains.

Over the years, Tash has been party to all the major crises that occurred in my life, ranging from my moans about teenage tantrums, the affair, the death of my mum and my subsequent spell in the doldrums after leaving work. I was therefore more than happy to offer some support in return when she suffered a series of miscarriages. I shared in her joy when she became pregnant again. This time, she carried the little boy she and Alex had named Iwo, after her father, for twenty-eight weeks. Then she went into early labour. The baby was stillborn.

Incapacitated by their sorrow and unfamiliar with

British norms, she and Alex had no idea if it was possible to have a funeral for Iwo. I was able to assure them they could, and helped with the arrangements.

Early on a cold January morning, I joined them for a short ceremony at the crematorium, where I read an extract from a poem in front of the tiny white coffin. In the background the Polish lullaby 'Rest Young Child' played as the curtains closed.

Verena has always enjoyed painting in her spare time, and I had asked her if she would paint a watercolour of a lily of the valley. When it was finished, she posted it to me. On the back, I wrote out the verse I read at the funeral, and packaged the painting up to send to Tash and Alex. Tash tells me that Iwo is always in their hearts, but the little painting, she keeps in her bag. When she feels down, she finds it comforting to take it out and read the words of the poem.

A lily of a day
Is fairer far in May,
Although it fall and die that night –
It was the plant and flower of Light.
In small proportions we just beauties see;
And in short measures life may perfect be.

It is close to six o'clock before Tash finishes my hair. She holds up a hand mirror to show me the sides and back of my head. She'sworked wonders, but the face looking back at me in the main mirror is pinched and drained.

'You look tired, Fran. Not sleeping?'

'No, not well,' I say. 'It's all the stuff surrounding the murder. You heard about it, I assume?' 'Yes, it's a terrible thing,' she says. 'It would give me nightmares too.'

I wonder if she is aware that it was I who witnessed the murder. Surely the village grapevine has been active since it happened?

'You know I saw the whole thing, don't you?'

I hold off mentioning the threatening letter or the intruder.

I can tell by her reaction that she had no idea. '*Gówno.*' She draws out the Polish expletive, then places her hands on my shoulders. 'No, I didn't. People have been talking about it in salon, but I had no idea…' Her words tail off, and she sits down heavily in the chair next to mine. 'You saw the boy Tyler being murdered?'

I nod, the familiar knot of tension in my stomach twisting in response.

'He lived in Willington, you know, not far from me, with his mum and brother,' she says.

'A brother. How old is he?'

'Teenager too, but younger than Tyler. Fifteen maybe? His name is Gabe.'

'I don't know why, I'm surprised he had a brother,' I say. 'I have been thinking a lot about his mother, but it never occurred to me that she might have other children. Stupid really, not to realise. It must have been devastating for them both.'

Tash does not respond immediately, and I look across at her.

'Pah,' she says. 'Bad lot. She likes money too much.' She makes a face and flicks imaginary banknotes through her fingers to illustrate her point. 'No one know how she make a living,' she adds.

It sounds as though Tash is not a fan of Melanie Ingram, but I decide against challenging her on the subject.

It's still raining, and she offers to drop me off in her car after locking up the salon. She deftly reverses into our drive to avoid having to make a turn in the road, and triggers the security lights.

'Look like Blackpool Illuminations,' she says, making a face and pointing at the front of the house. I laugh at her expression; I can see she's not impressed. She tells me she will ring if she finds out anything further about Melanie and Gabe, then gives me a hug and a wave before driving off.

Laurie will be pleased. The thought of his face when he sees what I've done makes me giggle. When he returns home tomorrow, as soon as his car noses onto the drive, the motion sensor will trigger the security light, and its powerful beam will bathe the whole area in incandescent white light.

I just hope the neighbours appreciate our attempts to make our property resemble a gaudy seaside resort.

11

Laurie Skypes as I'm sitting having my baked potato. I'm not that hungry, but I've started losing weight with all the stress, and I need to eat.

'Hey there, is everything okay? Nothing else untoward happened?' He leans sideways, then peers close-up into the screen. 'The hair looks good from here. How was Tash?'

I assure him all is well, then tell him about my conversation with Tash and what she said about Melanie Ingram and her surviving son. He listens attentively but doesn't offer much in the way of comment.

We chat about more mundane matters. He tells me about his day and uses his computer to give me a tour of the hotel room. It is slightly more luxurious than his usual accommodation.

'I'm going to try to get ahead of the traffic tomorrow. All being well, I'll be home by five. I'll text when I'm setting off,' he says. 'By the way, did you place the food order? You know the kids will be starving. They always are.'

'I'll do it now,' I tell him and sign off, but not before I turn the screen to show him a sleeping Buddy stretched out on the sofa next to me.

'Night night, both of you. Love you. And you too, Fran,' he says, his words a standing joke between us.

Pouring a glass of wine, I sit back down with my laptop and place the grocery order, ensuring there are lots of extra goodies for Alice and Flynn. Scrolling through my emails with the TV on in the background, I glance up at the screen. A close-up of the laminated photo of Tyler appears, and my arm jerks involuntarily, knocking half the wine out of my full glass.

'Bloody hell!'

Grabbing a handful of tissues, I mop up the spill, with one eye on the screen. The camera pans out to reveal the shrine in the car park, then turns towards the female reporter, who speaks directly to the camera.

Residents of a quiet village in Derbyshire have been left shocked by the events that occurred at a local beauty spot last week. The death of seventeen-year-old Tyler Ingram, found in this local woodland, is being treated as murder. A post-mortem report has revealed that the teenager died as a result of hanging. Police officers have spoken to a witness to the attack and have started house-to-house enquiries in the area. Two white men wearing dark clothing, both with shaved heads, are being sought in connection with the crime. One is described as tall and of slim build, the other shorter and stockier with a distinctive tattoo on the back of his neck. A grey Volkswagen van seen in this car park close to the time of Tyler's death has been found burned out in a suburb of Birmingham. Members of the public who may have information crucial to the investigation, no matter how small, are asked to ring the Major Crime Investigation Team at Derbyshire Police on 101 or contact Crimestoppers anonymously online or by phone.

The reporter references again there being a witness. Thankfully, I'm not mentioned by name, which I'm pleased about. It's probably only a matter of time before they do get around to it though. The media obviously have my details. I've thought hard about whether I should speak to them and made the decision not to. DS Georgiou did say it can be helpful during a murder investigation to talk to the media. I told him I would think about it. After discussing it with Laurie, I'm pretty sure it's not something I can see myself doing anytime soon. I decide against contacting Victim Support, which was also suggested, even though they work with witnesses. It's silly, I know, but the idea of being labelled a victim doesn't sit easy with me. Something also stops me from telling the police about the note through the door and the figure in the porch, despite Laurie's insistent reminders that I should do so.

THE FOLLOWING EVENING, Laurie makes good time and arrives as I'm packing away the food delivery. Buddy heralds his arrival by running around in circles, his level of excitement almost off the scale. The security lights are obviously working. Going to the window, I can see that as Laurie is getting out of his car, he's shielding his eyes against the glare. 'You weren't joking, Fran. I was almost blinded as I pulled in. The bloody place looks like a prison compound. .'

He takes his bags out of the boot and tries to avoid stepping on Buddy, who is weaving ecstatically through his legs. He hugs me, then turns his attention to Buddy, who is behaving as though his master has been away for months.

'I'll take him for a quick walk and settle him down for the evening,' he says, grabbing the harness and lead.

When they return twenty minutes later, Laurie is carrying a rectangular box. 'Did you order something? This was in the porch.' He unclips Buddy and places the package on the kitchen worktop.

'No,' I say. 'Who is it addressed to?'

'There's no name or address. I don't think it's come by post.' He turns it over, searching for a clue to the sender.

'Don't open it,' I say, feeling suddenly uneasy. 'It might be something nasty.'

'But it could be innocent,' he says. 'We have two choices. We can just chuck it in the bin, or we can satisfy our curiosity and open it. At least if we see what it is, we will know and not keep wondering.'

I shrug my shoulders nervously. He gets a sharp knife from the kitchen drawer and slices through the packing tape, pulling aside the cardboard leaves of the box. Inside, nestling amongst the tissue paper, is a soft toy dog. Its face is terrier-like, and with its short legs, it looks very much like Buddy. It's even wearing a collar similar to his. The toy looks up at us with glassy eyes.

It takes a moment before we notice the tiny replica knife embedded in the fur of its chest. Crafted to scale with an embossed rosewood handle, the knife is surrounded by a patch of red viscous-looking liquid the colour and consistency of blood. I wedge my hand into my mouth to stifle the scream rising through my throat. My legs start to shake, and I lean against Laurie for support. Grabbing my elbows, he holds me at arm's length.

'No arguments, Fran,' he says. 'This time we have to tell the police.'

12

It's almost midday on Saturday before a female officer arrives to take a statement. Her name is DC Kira Bennett. Although she appears young, she has the self-confident air that comes with experience. She records our statements in a notebook, then asks us to verify and sign them. She looks concerned, but doesn't discount the suggestion that it could be either bored local kids messing about, or perhaps someone with a sick sense of humour trying to spook us.

'Although if it is kids, they have gone to a lot of trouble and expense acquiring the knife. Those little replicas are not cheap,' she says.

'Would have to be a kid with a lot of pocket money, then?' I'm trying to sound flippant, but I'm not convincing anyone, least of all myself.

'That's true. I can't imagine a young person spending so much just for a practical joke,' she says, peering into the box lying on the coffee table.

'Do you think we need to be worried?' Laurie says. 'Those men are cold-blooded killers, and when I'm away overnight, Fran is in the house alone. If it is somebody trying to intimidate her, is there anything else we can do to improve security?'

'I don't think we can rule anything out at this stage,' DC Bennett says. 'It's a sad fact, but unfortunately, pranksters and those with mental health problems do come out of the woodwork when they see things on the news or on social media. What I do want to emphasise is that this will not be treated lightly. We take any threat of intimidation, however small, very seriously. I'm going to recommend you have a panic button with a direct link to the station. Someone will be in touch about setting it up. I am also going to arrange for an unmarked car to make a regular drive past. If you have any concerns, ring us immediately.'

DC Bennett also leaves us with contact numbers for the local PCSOs, saying she will ask them to keep a look out for any new faces or unusual activity in the village. Retrieving a pair of gloves and plastic evidence bags from her car, she places the note, the soft toy, and its box into separate bags before labelling and sealing them shut.

After she's gone, there's no time to talk about the interview, as Alice and Flynn are due to arrive on the two o'clock train. Laurie and I hurriedly prepare a salad to go with the quiche I've made. I'm going to heat it up once they arrive.

'I don't think we should say anything about this to the kids, Laurie. Let's try to have a nice weekend. They don't come that often, and telling them will just make it miserable for everyone.'

'I agree, but a panic button…?' He shakes his head in disbelief before picking up his car keys.

'I know. It does seem a bit extreme. I guess it would give me some peace of mind when I'm on my own, though.'

Alice and Flynn arrive in high spirits and seem pleased to be back home. It's not long before they revert to their usual tetchy squabbling as we have lunch. Buddy, happy that all his family are back together, lies under the table, snoring contentedly at Flynn's feet.

I'm keen to hear their news. The last week has been so full of negativity that the ebb and flow of their conversation, spiked with inappropriate jokes and raunchy anecdotes, makes everything seem almost normal. My children have always been as different as chalk and cheese both in looks and temperament, but they never fail to induce a sense of pride and accomplishment within me.

Flynn, fair-haired and green-eyed, grew tall and lithe during his teenage years, while Alice, with her darker hair and eyes and her square features, has remained shorter and sturdier than her younger sibling. Today, she is sporting a pixie cut dyed a shade of coppery brown.

'It suits you,' I say. 'The colour is great, too. I'll have to talk to Tash and ask her if that colour would work on my hair.'

Alice rolls her eyes. 'Oh, Mum. It's bad enough that you dye your hair at your age, but choosing the same colour as your daughter would be ridiculous. You should just let it go grey. It's very fashionable now, you know.'

I feel a familiar sense of annoyance at yet another of Alice's casual, throwaway remarks aimed in my direction. I look across at Laurie, who raises his eyebrows. We both elect not to comment. Instead, I ruffle Flynn's hair. 'What about you, Flynnie? Have you been applying product to your locks?'

He reddens, and I realise I've spoken out of turn. I notice the clothes he is wearing are slightly more expensive than his usual casual T-shirt and cargo pants. He has also been working out at the gym, if I'm not mistaken. *There's a love interest*, I think to myself. I don't want to tease him in front of Alice, though. It's obvious he needs a bit of time before he feels able to talk to us about whom he is seeing.

Alice is looking through the patio doors at the trees, their dappled leaves shimmering in the afternoon sun. 'We should go for a walk in the woods like we used to.' She jumps up and claps her hands. 'Come on, everyone, let's do it. It will be fun.'

Flynn throws a fierce look in her direction.

'What have I said, Flynn? There's no need to scowl at me. It's a simple request.'

'Alice, come on now. Think of your mum. It might be better if we walk somewhere else.' Laurie is using his appeasing voice. I can feel his discomfort, but I know he will be wary of Alice's short fuse.

She sighs in exasperation, but doesn't pursue the issue. Catching my eye, she gives me a weak smile and mouths, '*Sorry.*' I feel heartened, even though I know she has preserved her dignity by not letting her dad or Flynn see the gesture.

It's a beautiful day, and it does feel a shame not to make the most of it. Autumn can be a short season. Soon the nights will lengthen and the grey, rainy November days will be here. I suspect it will be winter, maybe even Christmas, before they come to visit again.

'We should go,' I say decisively. 'Let's clear the table and load the dishwasher. Buddy will be stoked to be back in the woods. And guess what? I have marshmallows for when we get back. And for tea…' I do a drum roll on the table. 'We have, ta-da – pizza!'

'Yay,' they shout in unison, reverting to a teenage show of exuberance at the prospect.

It's definitely turning colder, and I'm doing what they insist on calling 'mum fussing', trying to ensure everyone is wrapped up warm enough for the walk. Flynn and Alice, along with Buddy, head for the gate at the bottom of the garden. Laurie and I will take the longer route and meet them at the car park. We grab our coats and boots and leave by the front door.

Our road is tree-lined, with mostly detached houses of varying sizes and ending in a cul-de-sac. Beyond, and curving around the back of the properties on both sides, are acres of woodland; beyond that it is rolling country-side. The woodland is one of the reasons we chose to purchase in this location. Perfect for Alice and Flynn and the dog we planned to get when the time was right. The proximity to the woods also means the houses have always been sought after and have a premium price attached to them.

How lucky we felt to live in such a beautiful area. The presence of a good school within walking distance only added to our smugness at securing the house at a bargain just before house price inflation sent the prices soaring.

Although not strictly allowed, we and the other occupants whose houses back onto the woods have taken out a fence panel at the bottom of the garden and replaced it with a gate. Having direct access means we don't have to skirt around the perimeter via the main road to join the path leading from the car park. Over the years, those of us with children and dogs have flattened the undergrowth to create our own paths. Ours takes us through a small patch of dense conifer plantation. From here, it is possible to join one of the many walks criss-crossing the miles of deciduous and conifer trees that make up the forest. A mile or so in, the path leads into a clearing. Here, a dozen or so ancient oaks, their gnarled branches spreading wide, provided the perfect play-ground for the few children living in the neighbourhood when Alice and Flynn were youngsters.

Now, the population in the close is ageing, and those children, including my own, have grown up and moved on to start lives of their own. There are only two houses with younger children, and as both sets of parents are working, leisure activities tend to be accessed by car.

Flynn and Alice always enjoyed their after-school sports, but were at their happiest dragging tree trunks and branches into the clearing to make dens. With their friends in tow, sun-kissed and breathless, they would make regular forays back to the house to raid the fridge for drinks and food to take back for a picnic. How inno-cent those times seem now, when viewed through the prism of current events.

Our neighbour Phil across the road is putting the finishing touches to a patch of fake grass he is laying. Laurie waves, and Phil comes down the drive to talk to us.

'Saves getting the mower out,' he says. 'Personally, I would have been happy having it all slabbed, but Gina wants a patch of green to break it up.'

He leans on his expensive, bespoke, farm-style gate as though resting after completing an arduous task.

'I heard about what happened, Fran. It must have been really scary. It's put the wind up Gina, I can tell you. Not that she ever really walks anywhere, but it feels too close for comfort, being as it's on the doorstep.'

I only ever see Gina to wave to when she is getting into her car. She works in the city centre, doing some-thing in the field of beauty therapy, and always looks immaculately turned out.

'I see you've got some hardcore security lighting on the front now,' Phil is saying. 'Just give me a shout if you want any advice. There are always weak spots that can benefit from being tuned up. Hang on. I'll get you my card.'

He rummages in the glove compartment of his top-of-the-range Audi A6. I smile and thank him. I can't help but think that being in the security business is a pretty lucrative job.

Flynn and Alice are waiting for us in the car park. They are close to Tyler's shrine, and both look pale. I suspect they have been reading the condolence cards and the messages attached to the flowers. Alice is on the verge of tears, and I go to embrace her. She snuggles into my shoulder just as she did when she was a little girl. Flynn shuffles his feet, then moves towards us, as does Laurie.

'Family hug,' Flynn says, and we all stand together, arms entwined until Alice breaks free. She sniffs a couple of times, then bends down to pick up Buddy, who allows her to bury her head in his wiry fur.

'It just brings it all home, being here. It must have been the most horrible thing to see, Mum. He looks so young in that photo.' Her voice is muffled, and Buddy starts to whine, unsure of what is going on.

'He was.' I sigh.

Seeing everyone's dejection, I try to inject some jollity into my voice. 'Come on, I think we've all had enough. Let's go home and get the fire going. We need to get warm and heat up those marshmallows.'

13

W ithout the heating on, the house feels cool. Laurie lights the wood burner, and Flynn brings in a basketful of logs from outside.

'You did make sure the gate to the woods was locked when you came back, didn't you, Flynn?' I say as he hands Laurie some smaller logs to get the fire burning.

'I did, but we had a bit of a job getting it open on our way out. That whopping great bolt is stiff, and there's all sorts of debris starting to pile up on both sides of the gate. You're not using it, are you, Mum?'

'No,' I say, threading marshmallows onto kebab skewers. 'It's too soon.'

I don't elaborate, but their faces tell me they know I'm upset. Perhaps I'm being overprotective in not revealing the full extent of my disquiet. I don't want them to know about my lack of sleep, the nightmares, or how I'm in a constant state of anxiety. For my own self-preservation, I want to project an aura of balance and rationality. They don't need to know that I'm continuously looking over my shoulder or that I'm fearful of coming back into the house on my own. They have previously seen me at a low ebb, and it unnerved them. It's important that I at least maintain a pretence of holding it all together. Being pitied by my own children is the last thing I want.

I visualise myself as the person I was when they were growing up, hoping my self-perception isn't too far off the mark. There were, of course, moments of self-doubt, particularly when I was a new mum. But generally, I thought of myself as strong, consistent, dependable and a good role model, although Alice might have a view on that one. I wasn't a perfect mum. I made mistakes, but between us, Laurie and I have not done too bad a job of bringing them up.

'How's work, Alice?'

She looks up from toasting a fluffy pink mound of marshmallow, and eyes me warily.

'It's fine. Why?'

'Can't I ask my children about their jobs without being viewed with suspicion?'

I try to keep my voice light and jokey, but there's never a good way to broach certain issues with Alice, no matter how hard I try. Her present job is one of particular sensitivity. After graduation, she went to work in a large department store in Birmingham and got a flat-share a short walk away with Jess, a friend from university. Two years on, she is still there. Her defensiveness stems from being unable to secure a graduate job, despite her Social Policy degree. For Alice, salt was further rubbed into the wound when Flynn walked straight into his dream job as a video game developer for a small company in Worcester.

'Actually, I'm thinking of applying to the graduate program. I've already been given lots of responsibility anyway. I might as well be getting paid big bucks for the privilege.'

Her face is pinched and defiant. Despite her bravado, I know she really does care about what Laurie and I think.

I look across at Laurie. He's about to speak, but I jump in first, fearing he might say something to upset her.

'Your dad and I will support you in whatever you do, because we love you and trust you to make the right decision,' I say, choosing my words with caution. 'You know we will be here for help and advice, but you are an adult, Alice, and you must make your own choices.'

Her face relaxes, and she jabs a skewer into another marshmallow before holding it over a flame.

'Oh, and Alice.'

'What?' she says, through a mouthful of puffy goo.

'You have pink marshmallow all around your mouth.'

Flynn barks like a seal, then, dodging a well-aimed cushion launched by his sister, follows me into the kitchen. I light the oven while he strips the packaging from the pizzas.

'What about your job? Still enjoying it?' I say, putting the pizzas into the oven.

Flynn, always the diplomat, is careful about what he says in front of Alice, but he is keen to tell me about how much he is enjoying his work.

'It's great, Mum. Not like a job, really. Being paid to do what you love is ace, and it's a tight team. Someone new started last week, and she's really cool. She's called Eloise.'

Ah, Eloise. That explains the new look.

The next morning they both have a lie-in. When they

eventually emerge, it's after eleven. After getting dressed, they disappear into the woods to walk Buddy. When they return, Laurie cooks a huge brunch for us all.

'Don't leave it so long before you come again,' I say as we sit drinking coffee in the kitchen. 'And bring a friend if you want to. It's a breath of fresh air having young ones in the house again.'

Flynn looks at me. There's concern on his face. It's apparent he thinks I'm about to mention Eloise.

I turn instead to Alice. 'It would be nice if you brought Jess. We haven't seen her in ages.' Flynn visibly relaxes and pops a sausage into his mouth.

They leave mid-afternoon in a noisy whirl, jamming their hastily packed belongings into the boot of the car. With their departure, the house seems to sigh and fold in on itself. Laurie gets back from dropping them off to find me dozing on the sofa, a cup of tea going cold on the table in front of me.

'I'd almost forgotten how loud and untidy they are,' he says, stretching out next to me.

'I know, but it's so lovely to see them, even though it was only a short visit. I thought Alice behaved quite well for once,' I say.

'Did you think Flynn was a bit quiet?'

'He was, but that's because he has got something else on his mind.'

'Oh yes. What might that be?'

'I think a certain girl from work called Eloise may have something to do with it. It's quite possible your son might be in love, Laurie.'

The short time they've been here has provided me with – superficially at least – a semblance of normality. I can, if I try, convince myself I *feel* almost normal. Maybe the worst is behind me, and with time, everything will slot back into its rightful place. Well-oiled cogs will turn well-oiled wheels, and the machinery will propel me forwards to a place where there is hope and light, not death and darkness.

Just maybe.

14

I can't speak for Buddy, but I'm getting bored with the pavement walks. On impulse, I put him in the car and drive to Willington, a pretty village if you can ignore the giant concrete cooling towers dominating the skyline. It's located on the Trent and Mersey Canal. Although the village is quiet at this time of year, an influx of boaters during the summer months swells the population considerably. It's a popular spot, as you can moor your boat alongside the towpath adjacent to the local pub and have a meal. Or you can walk a short distance to the Co-op and restock supplies for your onward journey.

The village also boasts a pretty church, a small train station, a post office, a florist's, and a couple of gift shops. When Alice and Flynn were youngsters, we hired a narrowboat for a week during the summer holidays and spent a night moored here on the last leg of our return journey. Tired after a long day spent operating the locks, the kids were famished by the time we had tied up and refilled our water tank. That night we ate our pub meal outside, sitting on one of the wooden picnic benches. We were all in bed by 9p.m. and fast asleep soon after that, rocked by the motion of the boat as it pulled gently against its mooring ropes.

There are no free spaces in the car park, even at this time of the morning. It tends to be used by commuters taking the train to Birmingham and is often full. I turn my car around and drive over a little humpbacked bridge and park in a layby close to Tash and Alex's terraced house. I notice they have replaced the front door and put in new wooden windows. Outside, there are signs of ongoing building work. Bits of old carpet and planks of laminate flooring are stacked neatly in a corner of the tiny front garden. From a basket hanging on a hook next to the door, a profusion of bright orange and yellow nasturtiums spill over the edge, trailing their fleshy stems almost to the floor.

Tash and Alex will both be at work, so I walk Buddy down the road and through the car park to join the towpath.

A slight mist hovers over the water, and the few boats still moored up look ghostly in the pale grey light. They vary in their degrees of neatness. Some are freshly painted with bright canal ware and tubs of colourful flowers on their roofs; others are tatty and neglected, with logs piled onto every available space and fly-specked curtains at the windows. As a general rule of thumb, the newer, better-maintained boats are owned by Alice's favourite target, the well-off retired. The older, scruffier ones tend to be 'liveaboards' with a motley assortment of owners – not always, but almost invariably, single males of a certain age.

The canal gives the area an illusion of space, and the trees look as though they have recently had their branches lopped. They are a sufficient distance away for me not to feel too hemmed in as I make my way along the towpath towards the nearest lock. Buddy is in his element, chasing the odd mallard or moorhen off the path and back into the water. He stops short at entering the canal himself, happy to just dip the tip of his nose and his paws into the shallows, where tufts of reeds protrude and rushes grow in abundance.

We pass the newly built marina, the gleaming boats arranged in serried ranks, looking to all intents and purposes like a caravan park on water.

A man is fishing in the canal. He is sitting on a low canvas chair surrounded by rods and buckets of bait. He nods a greeting at me and gives my inquisitive dog a scratch around the ears.

'Lost my dog a couple of months ago. Died of old age. He were a terrier, too.'

The man's voice is gruff. It doesn't sound as though he is used to doing much talking.

'I'm really sorry to hear that,' I say, grabbing Buddy before he gets stuck into a plastic box full of wriggling maggots.

We reach the lock just as a narrowboat is coming up. The boat is as neat as a new pin with her blue and cream livery and tubs of pink and red geraniums on the fore-deck. The name *Minerva* is emblazoned across her gleaming side. A man jumps off, and I help him close the heavy gates after the boat exits the lock. It is being steered effortlessly by his female companion.

She 'hovers' the boat alongside the towpath just long enough to allow the man to jump back on board, then aims the prow for the middle of the canal. The familiar putt-putt of the engine can still be heard long after they have disappeared from sight.

I was planning on having a coffee at the lock-side café, but I see it's closed, so I round up Buddy for the walk back. The sun breaks through the cloud cover, burning off the haze over the water, and the sound of birdsong fills the air. I'm thinking how peaceful it is when there is a low rumbling sound, then a whoosh of air, which flattens the tops of the trees that still have foliage. This is followed by a strident blast of a horn as a train passes at speed within feet of where we are walking. Despite being aware of the proximity to the track, I'm still startled by the noise.

The normally bombproof Buddy looks shocked and stands stock-still with his tail tucked between his legs until he is sure the threat has passed. 'It's all right, boy,' I tell him, bending down to stroke his head. Reassured, he resumes his exploration of the hedgerows and dense thicket of brambles edging the towpath.

The couple from the lock have found themselves a sheltered spot not far from the pub and are tying off *Minerva*. I give them a wave and head for the path exiting from the towpath. This will take me back to the main road. We are about to turn onto it when I hear a woman's voice, loud and urgent.

'Kai, Dexter, get here – now!'

Then all hell breaks loose as two dark shapes hurtle in my direction. Before I have time to react, they are jumping up at me, snarling and barking in a fevered combination of excitement and aggression. The cropped tails and upright ears suggest the dogs are Dobermanns. Turning their attention to Buddy, they pin him to the ground. They are twice his size, muscular with powerful jaws. Although my instinct is to try to get a hold of the dogs, I know they could easily overwhelm me. I've read somewhere that grabbing a dog by the tail can interrupt a fight, but the docked tails make that impossible. In desperation, I look around for a stick but can't locate anything suitable.

To my great relief, the man from the boat appears,

brandishing a broom. The woman, whom I take to be his wife, follows, carrying a bucket overflowing with water. Buddy is now squealing in pain, which seems to incite the dogs into a greater frenzy. One has him by the scruff of the neck and is shaking him like a rag doll. I can see a thin trail of blood on the ground. The man, though a little unsteady on his feet, gets in a couple of blows with the brush handle as the woman douses the dogs with water from the bucket. I'm relieved to see that the dog mauling Buddy has slackened its jaws, releasing Buddy's motionless form from its grip. The cold water seems to have dissipated their aggression, and they shake vigorously before withdrawing almost sheepishly to the side of the path.

Crouching on the ground next to Buddy, I can hear the man berating the owner of the dogs, who has arrived, breathless from running. All I can see are a pair of leopard-print wellingtons and the bottom of a pink cashmere coat as she clips leads on the dogs' collars. She ignores the angry tirade of abuse coming from the man and leans over to talk to me instead.

'Shit, is your dog hurt?'

Stupid question, I want to say, stroking the blood-matted fur around his muzzle. Buddy doesn't stir for a few minutes, and I feel sure he is badly injured or even dead. I cry out in relief as he stirs, whimpers, then reaches out to lick my hand. A superficial check reveals no significant damage that I can see, apart from a couple of fairly deep bite wounds around his mouth and a chunk out of his ear. He is, however, wobbly when he tries to stand, so I scoop him up and cradle him in my arms.

'I'm so sorry,' the woman says. 'They are usually fine with other dogs. They just don't like terriers for some reason.' She sighs in exasperation. 'It's my own fault.

They've been cooped up for a couple of days. I shouldn't have let them run off the lead. I hope he's alright.'

I have a good ear for accents, and I detect a slight rising inflection that is not local.

Although obviously modulated over the years, her accent is still discernible, the distinctive vowel sound for *i* a dead giveaway. It's only in Birmingham that *alright* becomes *olright*.

I've been so worried about Buddy, I haven't really looked properly at the woman. She is still leaning over and talking to me, but the curtain of blonde hair falling across her face is concealing her features. The shock of the attack has left me struggling to process what she is saying, and, still clutching Buddy, I stagger to my feet. By now, I am boiling with anger and ready to give her a piece of my mind, but I stop short as I realise just who is standing in front of me.

15

Melanie Ingram has slender fingers topped by pink gel nails glittering with diamanté. I watch in admiration as she expertly taps a number into her phone.

'Hello, yes, it's Mel Ingram. Kai and Dexter have attacked a dog on the towpath. I'm coming in with the owner.' There is a pause as the person on the other end speaks. 'No, I haven't a clue.' Her tone is firm but impatient. 'It's a small dog, some sort of terrier cross, I would guess. I want you to check it over and see if it needs any treatment. We'll be with you in twenty minutes.'

She is used to giving orders, that much is clear.

The man and woman from the boat look on in concern.

'Poor little lad,' the man says, fixing Mel with a fierce look. 'Best get him checked out. And make her pay for any treatment. It's the least she can do after what her dogs have done.'

She ignores him and turns to talk to me. The man might as well be invisible.

'Are you alright carrying him a little way? I say him. I'm guessing it's a male?'

'Yes. He's called Buddy,' I croak, dry mouthed.

'My house is not far. I just need to take the dogs back, and then I'll drive you to the vet's. I'll pay, obviously. Come with me. It's this way.'

She doesn't wait for a reply and walks off. I thank the couple and, still holding Buddy, I follow her retreating back as she heads off towards the main road.

The house is post-war red brick and compact, with a well-tended front garden. A relatively new silver Range Rover sits on the drive, and Mel opens the boot.

'Put Buddy in there. It won't take me long to sort the dogs out, and the vet's is only a five-minute drive away.'

Buddy has perked up and seems unperturbed by being placed in a stranger's vehicle. Mel clips a seatbelt onto his harness, and he does his usual circular turn, albeit a little stiffly, then curls up on the rug lining the boot.

His back right leg does seem to be sticking out at an angle. Apart from that, he seems to have forgotten the trauma on the towpath.

Mel beckons me inside, and I slip off my walking shoes, placing them on the shoe rack in the hallway. She leads the way into a spacious lounge tastefully decorated in shades of grey and cream. The seating consists of two deep leather sofas and a low-slung Barcelona chair. A couple of white shag-pile rugs have been strategically placed on the expanse of blond wooden flooring, and a huge glass coffee table occupies the centre of the room. The overall look is too clinical for me, but it's obvious she has expensive tastes.

There is not much evidence of any personal effects or clutter, certainly no books or ornaments, but on the wall above the fireplace hangs a large black-and-white framed photo. It's a studio shot, professionally posed, and the smiling blondee woman is obviously Mel. She is younger in the picture, and her hair is a shade darker, but it's unmistakably her.

The boys, I would guess, are aged around six and eight. They stand at her side, dressed in identical plaid shirts, hair brushed up and back into spiky quiffs. It's obvious they are brothers, and the older one is definitely Tyler. His gaze is open, clear and untroubled; a faint grin plays around his lips as he looks directly into the camera. The younger boy must be Gabe. In contrast, he appears bored and sulky, his body language defensive. It looks as though he has been chastised and made to stand in front of the camera against his will.

A large bunch of white lilies sit in the fireplace, and I start to feel headachy and faintly nauseous; the cloying scent of lilies has always been for me a pungent symbolisation of decay and death. The flowers, surrounded by sympathy cards, serve as a reminder that in this house, a boy on the verge of becoming a man lived, laughed, argued, cried. Perhaps he had dreams and had started to plan for his future. A future denied to him in just a few, short brutal minutes. The thought fills me with an overwhelming sense of melancholy, and I want to weep at the unfairness of it all.

Mel appears at my side and gestures towards the photograph. Turning my head, I sniff and blink away the tears that are forming. I hope she hasn't noticed.

'The older one is my Tyler, the family protector, even then. The cheeky-looking one, playing up as usual, is our kid Gabe. He's the youngest,' she says.

I don't tell her I have already worked that out. Something does strike me as odd, though. She has made no reference to Tyler's death. Surely, as a bereaved mother, you would want to mention something so important?

I have never met her in person, and she doesn't know me either, but suddenly I feel uncomfortable, as though caught out in a lie.

There hasn't been time for me to mention the fact that it was I who found Tyler. I want to bring it up, but for some reason, I am conflicted and uneasy in her presence. I notice she is scrutinising me with a cool detachment, and her gaze is making me feel even more ill at ease.

I swallow hard. 'They are lovely boys, a real credit to you. There is something I need to tell you though. It's about your oldest son.' I am stammering in my haste to get the words out. 'The thing is, you don't know me...' Now I'm gabbling, the words tripping over each other. 'You don't know me...' I say again, trying for more conviction in my voice.

She puts a hand on my arm, silencing me. I see a shadow cross her face. It's fleeting, and she quickly regains her composure.

My uneasiness persists. I want to say something meaningful and consoling.

'I'm so sorry for your loss. It was I who saw what happened. It was I who witnessed Tyler's murder.' It's all I can manage to blurt out.

Mel's face remains impassive. 'The police said someone was there and tried to help him. I want to thank you for that. It must have been terrifying, getting caught up in what was going on.'

Getting caught up in what was going on. Mel's choice of words is odd. Before I have time to think about it further, she has picked up her keys and is ushering me out of the front door. A quick glance through the rear window of her car and it looks as though Buddy is still in the same position. I tap lightly on the glass, and he lifts his head wearily before dropping it down onto his paws and going back to sleep.

The veterinary surgery is, as Mel has said, only a short drive away. I carry Buddy inside while Mel speaks to the receptionist at the desk. While we wait, I try placing him down on the floor, but he winces in pain and holds up his back leg. I pick him back up and cuddle him until the vet calls for us.

'Right, little Buddy. What have you done to yourself?' Clodagh, the vet, is soft-spoken, with an Irish lilt that reassures both of us. She examines Buddy gently and skilfully. 'He was attacked by dogs, is that right?'

'Yes,' I say. 'The woman who brought us in, Melanie Ingram, it was her Dobermanns that went for him.'

Clodagh raises her eyebrows. 'Ah, yes. Those two are pretty powerful dogs. They must have given him an awful fright, but I don't think there's a huge amount of damage done to the little fella. He needs a couple of stitches over that eye and some antibiotics, that's all. I think his leg is just bruised. If it's alright with you, I'd like to keep him in overnight for observation. We'll give you a ring in the morning to let you know what time you can pick him up.'

Knowing Buddy is in safe hands, I start to feel less tense. During the drive back to pick up my car, Mel juggles calls from two phones, one of which is in her coat pocket. From the other, located in her bag at my feet, we are treated to a succession of message alerts. The pings are irritating, but she doesn't seem to notice.

'Sounds like someone is trying to get hold of you?' I say by way of conversation. I'm hoping for some information to give me a clue to her life, but she remains enigmatic, eyes fixed on the road ahead.

We reach the layby where my car is parked, and she

pulls in behind my little powder blue Fiat 500. The alerts are now coming through thick and fast on the phone buried in her bag.

'It's just work,' she offers by way of explanation.

It's on the tip of my tongue to ask her about her job, but she seems eager to get away. She takes the phone from her coat and waves it in my direction.

'Add my number and ring me when you are coming to pick up Buddy. I'll go with you to settle the bill.'

I do as she says, and feeling as though I have been dismissed, I get into my car. It's just after 1 p.m., but seems much later. It's certainly been an eventful day. Driving home, I rehearse in my head what I'm going to say to Laurie when he gets back. I'm reluctant to phone him while he's at work. If he's busy, he won't pick up; and if he's tired, he can be tetchy. Even though he is usually easy-going and we don't argue so much now, I suspect he will be concerned about me and angry about what happened to Buddy.

Whatever I tell him, I will need to choose my words carefully.

16

Clodagh rings the next morning. She tells me Buddy has had a good night and is ready for collection. When I try Mel's number, it keeps going to answerphone. It occurs to me that she might be avoiding my call. It's even possible she's had second thoughts about footing the vet's bill. I leave her a message, and just as I'm getting into my car, she calls me back. She sounds flustered.

'Sorry, the engine warning light has come on, and I've had to take my car to the garage. They've just dropped me off at home. Do you mind picking me up from here?'

My ring on the doorbell is answered not by Mel, but Gabe. At least, I assume it's him. He is wearing a beanie hat under the hood of his sweatshirt, and the drawstring is fastened tightly under his chin, concealing the lower part of his face. If he does recognise me, nothing in his sullen gaze betrays that fact, but I still feel a sense of disquiet in his presence. Standing behind him is another youth dressed in almost identical clothing. He is slight, with reddish, cropped hair and freckles. He looks about fourteen. Neither of them speaks or moves aside to let me in.

The uncomfortable silence is broken by Mel, who appears in the hallway.

'For God's sake, Gabe, where are your manners? Don't leave Fran standing on the doorstep.'

As Gabe and his friend move to the side to let me pass, I notice they are both wearing backpacks.

'Not at school?' I ask as I step into the hallway.

'Inset day,' Gabe murmurs. His friend sniggers and rubs an inflamed spot on the side of his cheek.

Today Mel is casually dressed in a tracksuit and trainers, her hair pulled back into a loose ponytail. I follow her into the lounge, which is considerably untidier than it was yesterday. There are discarded Xbox controllers on the sofa and energy drink cans and empty crisp packets scattered across the coffee table.

'I've got to go out,' she says, getting her purse from her bag. She takes a handful of banknotes and hands them to Gabe. 'What time is your train?'

Gabe takes the money and jams it into a zipped pocket in his rucksack. ' 'Bout 11:30,' he mumbles.

'Better get going, then, but when you get back, I want you to walk the dogs and get this place cleaned up. It's a bloody tip. I've got a lot to do today. I don't have time to chase around after you and your mates.'

'They're off on a day trip to Birmingham,' Mel says to me, by way of explanation. 'Keeps them out of trouble. They only get bored and into all sorts of mischief if they hang about in the village.'

She picks up her bag and jacket, and I lead the way to my car.

It's the end of surgery, and Clodagh is waiting for us. She goes to collect Buddy while Mel chats to the receptionist, who is preparing the bill. I hear the woman say,

'That will be £250,' as she hands over an itemised print-out. It's an awful lot of money, but Mel appears unconcerned and hands over the payment in cash.

Buddy is ecstatic to see me and yips in relief at not having been abandoned. We leave with a repeat prescription and a set of instructions relating to his care.

Mel asks if I will drop her at the garage. Her vehicle needs some work, but they have a courtesy car that she can use until hers is repaired.

'It's a bloody Fiesta,' she says scornfully. 'I haven't driven anything as small as that since I was a teenager.'

I look at my little car and then at her, debating whether I should say something amusing or even sarcastic. She seems oblivious to the irony and squeezes herself into the front seat without comment. She ignores the constant barrage of messages coming through on her phone and gazes out of the car window instead.

'Work again?' I say.

Her look is diffident. There is an awkward pause before she replies.

'Yes,' she says. 'I sell make-up. Today is one of my delivery days.' She turns back to the window, ending the conversation abruptly.

After leaving Mel at the garage, I am at a loose end. She had exited the car with a wave, leaving only the faint lingering scent of her perfume, a heady floral fragrance I recognise but can't recall the name of.

'What should we do now, Buddy?' I say to the snoring figure on the back seat.

I decide to go back to the canal to see if the couple on the narrowboat are still moored up near the pub. They were concerned about Buddy, and I'm sure they will be pleased to see how well he has recovered. This time, I manage to get a space in the car park, and sure enough, *Minerva* is still moored in the same place.

Standing on top of the boat, the man is cleaning the
roof with the mop and bucket. Through one of the side
windows, I can see his wife. She is chopping vegetables
in the tiny galley kitchen. Seeing me, she smiles and
gives me a nod and a thumbs-up when she sees Buddy
trotting happily alongside me.

The man steps down to the small brass toe-step at
the side of the boat, then lowers himself onto the
gunwale before hopping off to land on the towpath in
front of me. He bends down to give Buddy a stroke.

'Well, he looks much improved on yesterday. I
thought he was a goner when those two set about him.
Vicious buggers. I hope she sorted out the vet fees. It's
the least she could do under the circumstances.'

'She did. I've just picked him up from the vet's.
They've given him some antibiotics and painkillers. His
ear is a little wonky, and his back leg is stiff, but he'll be
as right as rain in a few days.'

The woman joins us on the path, and Buddy is
treated to an additional bout of fussing.

'Lovely to see him in such fine fettle. You two off for
a walk?' she says.

'Just a short one. I think he's actually quite worn out
after all the excitement. I'm glad I caught you,' I say. 'I
just wanted to thank you again for all your help
yesterday.'

'We are just relieved he's alright. He's a sweet little
thing,' the woman says, 'And by the way, I'm Sal, and
this old codger is Alan, although everyone calls him Al.'

Al smiles and winks. 'Just like the song,' he says.
'Call me Al.'

'I'm Francesca, but everyone calls me Fran,' I say.
'And, I think you already know Buddy.'

A man passes us walking two Staffordshire bull terriers, and I instinctively pull Buddy close to me by his

lead. Sal sees my apprehension and looks at Al, who nods his head as though in agreement.

'Why don't you go for your walk, and then come back and have some lunch with us? It's just home-made soup and bread, but you would be very welcome.'

'That would be lovely,' I say, eager to see inside. The layouts of narrowboats are fascinating, given the space available, and it will be interesting to see what they have done with the interior. This time, I walk in the opposite direction and away from the man with his dogs. We don't get very far. Buddy's initial enthusiasm for a walk has waned. His pace has slowed, and his tail is down. Turning around, we take a leisurely stroll back to the boat.

I knock on the roof to announce our presence and take off my boots. I remember to duck down to avoid banging my head as Buddy and I enter the cabin where Sal and Al are waiting.

To my surprise, the interior is completely different from what I expected. Instead of dark planking and twee furnishings, it's light and airy with grey linen curtains, lime-wash paintwork and Laura Ashley–style furniture. Matching checked Sherlock chairs sit either side of a small wood burner. Loaded with crackling logs, the fire is throwing out heat, and Buddy stretches out on the rug, soaking up the warmth. Like all narrowboats, space is at a premium, but it doesn't feel cluttered or cramped. A pull-out dinette table has been set for lunch, and my stomach gurgles in response to the delicious aroma of vegetable soup and freshly made bread.

I take my place on the banquette, a selection of tasteful cushions at my back.

'This is so kind of you, and your boat is absolutely beautiful. I love a traditional style of narrowboat, but this feels so spacious in comparison. And there's not a horse brass in sight. How have you managed it?'

'It's all down to Sal, really,' Al says, looking at his wife in admiration. 'I'm good with my hands, but Sal is the one with an eye for design.'

Sal clicks her tongue as though in annoyance and shoos him away. But not before I see the colour rise in her cheeks. *They are still in love*, I think to myself, with a pang of envy.

Soon I'm savouring their home-cooked food and starting to feel relaxed. Al pours me a small glass of elderberry wine, which he tells me he has made from fruit picked from the hedgerows last autumn. They don't live on board all year round, he says. They own a house, which they return to for the winter. The boat was purchased and designed to their own specifications when Al retired. With no dependents to worry about, and being free agents, they feel they have the best of both worlds: the joys of the canal in the summer, and a nice warm house to return to in the winter. A look I can't interpret passes between them. Sal seems pained, but the moment passes, and I wonder if I imagined it.

It's difficult not to admire the lifestyle they have chosen. Life is full of compromises, and I know I have so much to be grateful for. It's ungracious to want more or to wish that things could be different. It's true I've had a difficult time recently, but unlike Mel Ingram and poor Tash, I am fortunate not to be mourning the death of a child. Still, deep down, there is a niggling worm of dissatisfaction. A part of me that yearns for a simpler life with fewer complications.

While Al prepares the boat for departure, I help Sal wash the dishes. A low thrumming and a vibration through the floorboards means he has started up the engine. The wine must have loosened my tongue because I tell Sal all about Tyler's death, the threats, and my interactions with Mel Ingram.

Sal looks shocked. They had overheard people talking about it in the pub, she tells me, but hadn't realised the connection to Willington and to my village.

'It's incomprehensible that such terrible things can happen in rural areas. It's such a quiet part of Derbyshire. I really don't know what the world is coming to. That poor young boy, and poor you. It must have been a terrible experience. That mother of his sounds like a piece of work, though.'

She doesn't express any sympathy for Mel, having already formed her own opinion of her. I do wonder if I painted too harsh a picture of my encounters with Mel. After all, grief can affect people in different ways, and it might be that this is how she is coping with her loss.

There's no time to elaborate, because Al taps on the kitchen window. It's time to leave. Sal and I exchange telephone numbers, and I rouse a reluctant Buddy to get him on to the lead.

'By the way, Sal, why the name Minerva?'

'We get asked that a lot,' she says. 'Young 'uns think she's named after Professor McGonagall in Harry Potter, but our Minerva is the Roman goddess of wisdom.'

Sal gives me a farewell hug, and I pull on my boots and jump down onto the towpath.

Reaching the car park entrance, I turn to see Sal is on the back deck, hand ready on the tiller. Once the ropes are untied, Al nudges the front of the boat with his foot, and *Minerva* glides away from the bank. He then hops up alongside Sal, who expertly steers towards the centre of the canal. I wave as they pass me, sending out a silent message to Minerva to grant me the gift of wisdom.

I'm going to need it, if the last week has been anything to go by.

17

Buddy is eager to get out of the car and back to familiar surroundings. He rushes inside when I open the front door. I hesitate, one foot on the threshold, palms sweaty. This is starting to become a habitual behaviour; I can't seem to break the pattern. I am reminded of a cat we had when I was a child. She was poised to go through a door left slightly ajar when my mother had pushed it open from the other side and whacked the cat hard on her head. For the rest of her life, the cat always paused on the verge of doorways, tail and whiskers twitching, only moving forward when she was sure she was safe.

This is me. I am that cat. Senses alert to possible danger, feeling as though I am in constant peril, always waiting for something awful to happen.

A ping on my phone breaks the spell. It's a reminder about my yoga class tonight. I've completely forgotten about it. I'm a bit peeved at giving up my evening. I was hoping to talk to Laurie about today's events. It will be close to nine when I get back, and by then, he will be too tired. After getting stuck in traffic last night, his main concern was Buddy. He wasn't in the mood to listen to anything but the bare facts about Mel Ingram, even though I was buzzing to tell him about what had happened.

Can it really be the case that the dog's welfare is of more importance than anything else I have to say?

I give myself a mental dressing-down. I'm being silly and, worse, unfair. Working and travelling is leaving him exhausted. I text him to let him know when I'll be home then get myself ready for the class.

WHAT IS it about some middle-aged women that they have to squeeze themselves into the most inappropriate, tight-fitting, lurid-hued Lycra to participate in an exercise class? My preferred outfit is harem pants and an old baggy T-shirt. The one I'm wearing tonight once belonged to Alice and dates from when she was going through a short-lived heavy metal phase. It bears the legend 'Rock Until You Drop'.

One of the Lycra brigade tears herself away from her similarly clad sisters and bears down on me. She has on a garish-coloured exercise headband and is clutching one of those trendy flask- type water bottles aimed at active urbanites. I think she is called Avis, which suits her, as she is bird-like, with spiky greyish-blonde hair. She looks like a wizened cockatiel.

'Fran, it's so good to see you. How are you?' She doesn't wait for an answer. Instead she grabs my arm and lowers her voice to a whisper. 'It must have been terrible for you. It's shaken us girls to the core, I can tell you. We are all terrified to go out, *terrified*, I say.'

The word *terrified* is communicated in such a theatrical way, I want to laugh out loud. Fortunately, the instructor arrives, followed by a vision dressed in a botanical-print training bra and shorts. On her head, she is wearing a bright green turban from which tufts of bright pink hair are escaping in every direction. The effect is weirdly stylish and zany. I'm impressed by the outfit. She has managed to outdo even Avis in the Lycra stakes.

'Tash, what are you doing here?'

'You tell me to come. Every time I see you, you say come, so I here. Alex is working, and tonight I am free.' She stretches her arms wide to illustrate her point. 'I think it will be good for making a baby,' she says.

I look at her in puzzlement. 'You mean the yoga positions will help?'

She howls with laughter, and those huddling around Avis look at the pair of us in alarm.

'No, no, Fran. Not for the sex, for the relaxation.'

There is an audible gasp from across the room, but Tash appears oblivious. She balances on one leg and cups her hands as if in prayer, in an approximation of the Tree pose.

Recognising some members of the group from the salon, she gives them a loud 'yoo-hoo' and a wave. A few return the greeting with a feeble flutter of the fingers, then gather back around Avis like a flock of well-trained birds.

It has been a while since I attended the class, but soon my stiff joints unwind and start to become supple. We spend the last twenty minutes of the session in meditation, and for the first time in ages, the tension leaves my body, and I start to feel relaxed. On this occasion however, it's not me who falls asleep, but Tash. Lying next to me on her mat, she is snoring gently.

I prod her with my foot. 'Oi, wakey, wakey,' I say.

'Do you want to come back with me and undo all the good work by having a quick drink?'

'What about Laurie? He will be home from work, no?'

'Yes, but he'll either be in his study working or fast asleep on the sofa. I wanted to tell him about visiting Mel Ingram's house, but he was too tired to listen when he got in last night. I suspect tonight isn't going to be any different. He'll probably go spark out when I try to tell him about having lunch with the couple on a narrowboat who helped when Buddy was attacked.'

Tash is jamming her yoga mat and water bottle into a shoulder bag. She stops and turns in my direction.

'Wait. Wind back, Fran. You went to her house? That Mel Ingram?' A shadow crosses her usually cheerful face.

'Yes, twice. Once when her dogs attacked Buddy, and again today, before I picked him up from the vet's.'

'What vet's? What happened?'

Of course, Tash doesn't know about the attack. How could she?

'Let's get going. I'll explain over a glass of wine.'

Tash follows in her car and pulls in behind me on the drive, alongside Laurie's car. We duck inside, trying to avoid being blinded by the security lights, and throw our bags down in the hall. The lamps are low in the lounge, and there is no sign of Laurie.

'Upstairs working, I'll bet,' I say, making my way to the kitchen to grab some wine. Buddy barges past, ignoring me, and launches himself at Tash instead.

Laurie is by the oven, holding a frying pan in his hand. The overhead spotlights have been dimmed, and the table is set with the best cutlery. In the centre of the table is our wedding present from my friend Ali from uni. It's an elongated piece of driftwood with holes cut in the top for tea lights. It casts a soft, flickering glow across the tabletop.

You're not the sort of couple who would appreciate a silver candelabra, Ali had written in her card at the time. *But I hope this alternative graces your table for many years to come.*

'Ah, there you are,' Laurie says, wiping his hands on the tea towel wrapped around his waist. 'I'm making a frittata. Grab a glass of wine. It will only be a few minutes. I'm sorry I was so tired and grumpy yesterday. Let's eat, and then we can talk.'

Just then, Tash pokes her head around the door.

'Oops. I think drink can wait for another time.'

Laurie attempts to persuade her to stay, but she has picked up her bag and is heading towards the front door.

'I should get back. Alex will be home soon,' she says, adding, 'You must come for Polish meal. House is not ready yet, but soon. We have from holiday in Poland, *Soplica Pigwowa*. Is liqueur. Will blow your socks off.'

We hug, and I promise to phone and update her before the next yoga session. Laurie and I stand at the door and wave her off, both wincing as she gives three long beeps on her car horn. The sound echoes around the close, no doubt disturbing those neighbours already in bed who have to get up early for work.

'What on earth was she wearing? She wouldn't be out of place in the Palm House at Kew.'

Laurie says this without malice. He likes Tash, for all her brashness, and he finds her eccentric use of local idioms endearing. Although he has only met Alex on a couple of occasions, he gets on well with him, too. It will be nice to have dinner with them once the house is finished. They are always so hospitable, and I'm looking forward to seeing what they have done to the house.

'Ah yes, the yoga outfit,' I say. 'You should have seen

the old dears' reaction. I think Avis was put out by the competition.'

'Come on,' he says. 'The frittata will be burnt to a crisp if we don't eat soon.'

I follow him to the kitchen, feeling abashed, especially after what I said to Tash. Laurie has a demanding job; it's no wonder he gets tired and irritable and is not up for late-night conversations.

Note to self: Be grateful for having someone as considerate as Laurie in your life, and stop being so bloody selfish and wrapped up in your own issues.

18

Later, as Laurie sleeps beside me, I reflect on our conversation over dinner. I had asked about his day, but despite my best intentions, I was only able to focus on what he was saying for a short span of time. I tried to concentrate; I really did. His work is our bread and butter after all, but I was eager to move onto the topic of Mel and Gabe and my return to the canal.

'So this couple on the narrowboat helped rescue Buddy from the dogs?'

'Yes, they were really lovely. They even gave me lunch when I went back today to thank them. What came across loud and clear is that Sal doesn't have a very high opinion of Mel.'

I tell him about the narrowboat and how impressive the interior was in comparison to most of those we have encountered. We joke about the possibility of buying our own liveaboard and spending the summer cruising the waterways like Sal and Al.

'Think how relaxing it would be. Sailing along with just the sound of birdsong and the lapping of water to disturb the tranquillity.'

Laurie is more prosaic. 'The British weather, nowhere to dry your clothes, having to collect water and empty the toilet. Plus, with the limited space, we would probably end up killing each other. Honestly, Fran, I don't think it's one of your better ideas.'

'Hmm, I suppose you're right. It just seemed so idyllic when I was on board *Minerva*. We could always hire a narrowboat next summer and give it a try. We've never done it without the kids. We could see how we got on.'

'That's a good idea. I'd be up for it as long as we avoid being on the canal when it's busy. You get some real idiots during the holidays. Now, tell me about going back to Mel Ingram's house. She does seem to have got under your skin.'

Although I don't want to admit it, he's right.

'She is a bit of an enigma,' I say. 'Raising two boys alone must have been very difficult, but there seems to be no shortage of money, considering her job is selling make-up. There's no expense spared in the house, and she has a top-of-the-range four-by-four. She was most put out when the garage lent her a Fiesta, although she didn't say anything about slumming it in my little motor when I dropped her off.'

'Was anything said about what happened to Tyler? Did she even know it was you at the scene?' Laurie says.

'I told her it was me, and she thanked me for trying to help him. She's a bit of a cold fish. Very unemotional, almost businesslike. I don't really know what to make of her!'

'What about the brother?' Laurie says. 'He's younger than Tyler, isn't he?'

'Yes, by a couple of years. He was there today with a friend. They were going to Birmingham on the train, which I thought was a bit strange. I would have assumed they'd be at school, but he said it was an inset day.'

Laurie suddenly goes quiet and looks perturbed. He turns his face away from me and starts to clear the table. I can see the tension in his shoulders. The clattering of plates is making my nerves jangle.

'What is it? What's wrong?'

He stops what he's doing and looks over at me, a worried frown furrowing his brow.

'I don't know, Fran, it's just a feeling. I'm not a great believer in intuition, as you know, but I have a sense that there's something going on in that family that's not entirely wholesome. I know you think you have some connection with Mel Ingram because of Tyler, but I'd prefer it if you stayed away from her. For all our sakes.'

Now, lying in the dark, tossing and turning as sleep evades me, I realise Laurie is right to be worried. The truth is, my suspicions were also aroused after my first visit to the house. He has just helped crystallise my thoughts and given substance to the conclusion I had already started to come to: that Mel Ingram and her son Gabe may not be innocent victims. I don't know in what capacity, but something tells me they are connected to Tyler's murder, even if it's indirectly.

If that is accurate, then what is the link? Is Mel in trouble? In debt? You would need a lot of money to maintain her lifestyle. Is it possible that she has got herself caught up in something criminal, and Tyler's killing was some weird act of revenge?

My fevered brain wrestles with a range of permutations, but nothing really seems to fit. Eventually, I sink into a fitful sleep punctuated by lurid anxiety dreams in which I am lost in some foreign city. As darkness falls, each twist and turn I take leads me to a dead end. I have a sense that time is running out, and if I don't escape soon, something terrible is going to happen.

I must have cried out in my sleep, because I wake to find Laurie has switched on the light and is sitting up in bed, looking at me.

'Christ, Fran, you gave me a shock. You were shouting and flailing your arms about. Did you have one of those dreams again?'

I don't answer, but slide upright and lean against the pillows, slowing my breathing until the feeling of panic recedes. Laurie stretches out his arm and places it across my shoulders, offering a space for me to snuggle into. I turn, pulling the duvet up under my chin, and sink into the crook of his arm, my head resting on his chest.

The dreams first started when I was around six or seven. Technicolour nightmares invaded by monsters or ghosts. Recurring visions in which walls of water would sweep the house away with me and Mum inside. Or deep cracks would open up in front of me and I'd plunge, cartwheeling downwards, my screams echoing around the dark cavernous space.

'If you hit the bottom, you will be dead.' This nugget of information was offered by Freya Brown, the class swot. I had chosen to confide in her, as she always seemed the most knowledgeable and sensible of my classmates.

'That's not true. You're a big liar,' I shrieked, pulling her hair, then pushing her so hard she lost her balance. She fell, cracking her head on the corner of a desk. After a telling-off from the head teacher, Mum kept me in for a week as punishment.

This incident and the fact that I had started to wet the bed galvanised Mum into action, and I was taken to our local GP, who prescribed a light sedative. This had the effect of knocking me out to such an extent I couldn't function without falling asleep throughout the day. Mum, not satisfied with the long waiting list to see a child psychologist, managed to pull some strings, and for six months I spent every Thursday afternoon in the company of Dr Poole.

With her frizzy hair, buck teeth and wispy voice, Dr Poole created an oasis of calm in which I played with figures of indeterminate sex, drew pictures with an exciting array of coloured pens, answered questions about my dream diary, and sometimes even spoke into her recording machine. I was sorry when it all ended, not least because I became less interesting to my school friends. They had hung on my every word as I fed them an embellished version of what occurred in the sessions. Even Freya forgave me, taking delight in my confabulations. It was many years later before Mum informed me of Dr Poole's diagnosis.

'You have a very bright and imaginative child, my dear,' she had told her. 'Many of the parents of the children I see would give their eye teeth for what you are defining as 'problems'. The nightmares are likely to reduce in frequency as she gets older. She may even grow out of them, but they could return at times of high emotion. Apart from that, I have seen nothing that concerns me about your daughter.'

Dr Poole was right. The nightmares took a back seat in my life, reappearing infrequently at times of stress. Like now.

I must have fallen back into a deep sleep, because when I eventually wake around nine, Laurie has already left, and Buddy is stretched out in the space he has vacated. There is a note on the pillow in Laurie's neat handwriting:

Morning, Sleeping Beauty. You looked so peaceful it would have been cruel to disturb you! See you around 7 xxx

My phone is ringing somewhere in the house, but I don't rush to answer it. I know it will have clicked onto answerphone before I reach it.

I dress casually in leggings and a jumper and pull my hair back into a loose bun. . Feeling hungry, I make a boiled egg and some toast. It has rained overnight, and a grey mist hovers above the lawn. It's a melancholy sight. Soon the high winds will come, as they always do in autumn, and the deciduous trees in the woods will be stripped bare of their foliage. The skeletal sentinels that remain are not only a stark reminder of the power of nature, but also of the cycle of life and death.

I let Buddy into the garden before locating my phone. Someone has left a voicemail. I dial the number to retrieve it.

There's a long pause before whoever is on the other end starts speaking. It's a woman, and when she does speak, the message is garbled. I'm guessing she is not in the habit of leaving messages on mobile phones.

'Yes, oh… um, hello, Fran, it's me Sal, from the narrowboat.' There's a gap and a series of mumbles before she resumes. 'Could you give me a ring, please? I have something to tell you, and I don't want to do it over the phone. My number is…' Some more shuffling, and then I hear Al's voice in the background. 'Just a minute. What did you say, Al? Was the last bit 776?' Sal asks him. She comes back on the line and recites the full number. She has probably forgotten we exchanged details, and is obviously unaware her number will have been saved to my phone anyway, but I appreciate the effort.

I bring Buddy in from the garden and dry his paws, wet from the lawn, before giving him his breakfast. Then I phone Sal back. It rings out, and I am about to give up and try again later when she answers.

'Hello. Who's that?'

'It's me, Fran. You left me a message.'

'Ah, Fran. Thanks for getting back to me. This might sound a bit strange, but there's something I think you should know. Both Al and I saw something suspicious, but I'd prefer to tell you face to face rather than on the phone.'

'Well, that all sounds very mysterious,' I say. 'I've got a few things to do this morning, but I could get to you this afternoon. Would two o'clock suit?'

She gives me the address, and I set about my tasks, eager for the morning to pass.

I'm intrigued to find out just what has triggered the call.

19

The satnav takes me on a circuitous route around the ring road. Eventually, I end up in a neat suburb west of the city. The road is long and straight, flanked on either side by bungalows, each with their own patch of well-watered lawn or gravel garden. Some of the orderly beds or raised planters still contain tidy clumps of summer annuals, with marigolds, geraniums, dahlias and busy Lizzies, the popular choice of plants. I drive slowly, looking for the number of the house.

The satnav tells me I have arrived, and as there is room for my car, I pull in onto the drive behind a small grey hatchback. Sal opens the door and greets me like an old friend. I can see Al hovering behind her, dressed in what looks like work clothes: dusty jeans and a sweatshirt that's seen better days.

'You will have to excuse me,' he says. 'I've been tackling the back garden.'

Sal ushers me inside, into the kitchen, which is compact, but light and modern. She switches on the kettle. 'Tea or coffee?'

'A cup of tea would be lovely,' I say.

Al is eager to return to his gardening, and Sal says she will bring him coffee after we have had a chat.

'Fran might be interested in what you have been up to. You can show her before she goes.'

I carry the tray of tea and biscuits into the lounge and place it on a coffee table. We sit in comfortable chairs on either side of the patio doors, positioned to take full advantage of the view of the garden. It's a surprisingly large plot, and I can just about make out Al in the distance, beyond the pale yellow sandstone patio and a lawn so flat and green it looks like baize.

'There's always so much to do when we get back from mooring the boat for the winter. We've made the garden as low maintenance as we can, but it can still be a chore.'

Sal looks weary, and I try to work out how old she and Al are. I'm guessing they must be in their seventies. I notice a cluster of photographs on a sideboard and cross the room to take a closer look. A large silver frame holds a black-and-white picture taken on what looks to be their wedding day. They stand awkwardly, peering into the camera, Al in a dark suit and Sal in a white below-the-knee dress stiffened with petticoats. She is clutching a posy of flowers tied with a trailing ribbon. In the photo, Al has substantially more hair than now, and the curls framing Sal's face are dark brown rather than grey, but it's obvious it's them.

'You both look so young,' I say.

'We were. I was eighteen and Al was twenty-one. He had finished his apprenticeship and got a job at Rolls-Royce. We were both keen to leave home, so we decided to get married. We will be celebrating our fifty-fourth anniversary in April.'

'And who is this?' I pick up a smaller frame containing a picture of a young man with the same brown curly hair as Sal's. He is dressed in graduation robes. I assume it's a relative, as no mention has been made of them having children.

Sal takes it from me and looks wistfully at the image. 'It's my son, Nicholas. He died twelve years ago.' She is on the verge of crying , and I feel guilty for stirring up such painful memories.

'Oh, Sal, I'm so sorry. You don't have to talk about it if you don't want to.'

'No, it's fine.' She wipes away a tear and takes a shuddering breath before placing the frame carefully back in its place. She tops up our teacups from a flower-sprigged teapot and takes another deep breath.

'It's not a story with a happy ending, I'm afraid,' she says. 'We had tried for a baby early on, and nothing happened. Nicky came along when I thought I was going through the menopause. We were both thrilled, of course, and Al and Nicky were especially close. They went everywhere together: cycling, fishing, watching the motor racing at Donington. He was a joy as a child, so good-natured. Then, as he got older, he started to get argumentative and defiant. Just adolescent stuff, or so we thought.'

She pauses, fiddling with a heart-shaped stone around her neck before continuing.

'He did scrape through his exams and managed to get a place at university, but he never fulfilled his promise. His tutors predicted a First, but he ended up with a Third. We found out later he had been experimenting with drugs, cannabis and stimulants, mostly.' She sighs, holding the necklace between her fingertips. 'This is all I have left of him.'

I look closely at the pendant to see if it holds a photo of her son, but it's just black glass with a faint sparkling effect.

'It might seem a bit odd, but this stone contains some of Nicky's ashes. It means I get to keep him close to me.'

'It doesn't feel odd at all,' I say. 'It's a beautiful way of remembering him.'

'Thank you. I imagine some people would be repulsed by the idea, but I find it comforting.'

She raises the pendant and brushes her lips over its smooth surface.

'Please don't feel you have to tell me, but how did Nicky die? Was it to do with drugs?' I say.

'I don't mind telling you, and yes, he died of an overdose. We had tried everything we could to help. Bailing him out constantly, paying off his debts, attending groups with other families affected by the problem. We tried to get ourselves as informed as possible. Nothing we did worked. He seemed determined to self-destruct. In the end, he and Al had a blazing row, and Nicky left home.

'We tried contacting him, but we didn't know where he was, and he never answered our calls. The police told us that he had been living in a squat with other users and had started injecting heroin. The wrap he'd bought that killed him came from a batch with high purity levels. Nicky's was just one of a number of deaths during the time that batch was circulating. I know every death is a tragedy, and this is going to sound awful, but we feel cheated. Nicky had so many opportunities and so much potential. We couldn't believe that this could happen to our family.'

Sal blinks away tears, and I lean forward and reach across for her hand.

'Please don't blame yourself, Sal. You will know from the meetings you attended that this problem cuts across all boundaries. You did the best for your son. As parents, that's all any of us can do.'

Sal takes a tissue from a box on the coffee table, dabs at her eyes, and blows her nose.

'I know you're right, but there are so many 'what ifs,' and people we know don't really understand. It's almost shameful to admit what happened. I know Al blames himself. He shut down after Nicky's death. He even cleared the house of everything associated with Nicky apart from a few photos. He deals with his grief by keeping himself busy. That's his way of coping, whereas I'm inclined to ramble on if anyone will listen.' She tries to smile, but it doesn't quite reach her eyes.

'You ramble away if it helps,' I say. 'And if people are judgemental, that's their problem. There but for the grace of… whatever. I'm not religious, but you get my meaning. Nobody should be smug and think their loved ones are immune. It can happen to anyone.'

I think back to another death that occurred as a consequence of the drug trade. Another child loved and cherished, but failed by those who should have protected him. I wasn't deemed culpable, but the guilt is there nevertheless. Baby C died under my watch, and I will never forgive myself for that. I will tell Sal the full story, though not now. This is her time to remember, unsullied by my hurt and remorse. I glance at my watch and see over an hour has passed. I need to get going.

'I will have to set off soon, Sal. Buddy will need a walk, and the traffic will be a nightmare if I leave it too late.'

'Oh my goodness,' Sal says. 'I've been going on, and I haven't even got around to giving you an explanation for why I asked you to come in the first place. Let me put the kettle on, and then I will reveal all.'

When she comes back, she seems composed, lighter somehow, as though talking has released some of the dam of emotion that had built up since Nicky's death.

'Thank you for listening, Fran. I'm sorry for loading it all on you. What must you think of me? Al doesn't want to know. He thinks talking about what happened is just picking at a sore. Like most men, he finds it difficult to show his emotions.'

'You're right,' I say. 'You can't force the issue, but if everyone, especially our men, talked more openly about their feelings, there would be a lot less unhappiness in the world.'

I know that reticence on the part of men is not even a generational thing. So much dissatisfaction and unhappiness stems from bottling up emotions, and this occurs in all age groups. It's not that talking is a panacea for all ills, but never has the maxim *a problem shared is a problem halved* seemed so pertinent when male suicide is at an all-time high.

Sal is standing at the window, looking down the garden to where Al is still working. She raises her hand and waves. He is obviously engrossed in what he is doing and doesn't look up.

'He'll be out there until dark if I don't go and interrupt him.' She laughs, sitting back down in her chair. 'Now, I've got distracted, but the main reason I asked you to come here is simple; I dislike conveying important information by phone. It's a pet hate of mine. Call me old-fashioned, but so much nuance is lost when you can't read people's expressions.'

'Mm, yes, I suppose I agree…' I say.

'Anyway,' Sal says before I can finish, 'I wanted to

tell you directly. The woman from the canal whose dogs attacked Buddy, Mel, I think you said her name was?'

I nod in agreement.

Sal's face hardens, and she purses her lips as though tasting something unpleasant. 'Well, Fran, I'm not going to mince my words, but from what we saw, Al and I are pretty sure that she is a drug dealer.'

20

I agree to another cup of tea, resigned to hitting the rush-hour traffic. While I wait for Sal to come back, I consider the implications of what I have just heard. I'm not naive, and I'm aware Mel's lifestyle has got to be subsidised in some way; it's patently obvious, but drug dealing?

I had already worked out she was involved in something underhand. The nice lifestyle, the expensive car and the large amounts of cash she carries all point to something dodgy. She's living beyond her means, that's apparent, but I was thinking more along the lines of grey-market activities like knock-off computer games or replica shoes and clothing. It didn't occur to me that she could be involved in drug dealing. I consider Laurie's reaction after I had described my visit to Mel's. He had been alarmed and worried about my safety. Had he figured out what was happening? And if so, why hadn't he been more explicit in spelling out what he thought was going on?

Sal tells me the reason she has asked me to come to the house. They had seen Mel when they stopped for a bar meal before taking *Minerva* through the final lock on their journey back to the marina. The pub had been busy, and they had gone for a walk along the towpath while waiting for the pub to quieten down..

'There's a little boatyard and general store on the opposite bank,' Sal says. 'We go there a lot to buy fuel and pick up provisions when we are on the boat. We have got to know the owner quite well. We noticed some activity in the car park and crossed the canal bridge, thinking if Fred was working late, we would go and have a chat with him. It was Al who noticed her first. She had parked in the far corner of the car park. She drives a newish, silver-colour four-by-four, right?'

'So do a lot of women,' I say, trying not to sound too dismissive.

'It was definitely her. Although we were well concealed behind a wall, we could see her very clearly. She was wearing that very distinctive and expensive pink coat when she got out of the car.'

'So far, so innocuous,' I say. 'What on earth makes you think she was drug dealing?'

Sal shakes her head in exasperation and wags her finger at me. 'That's not the end of it. *This* is where it gets suspicious. A car pulled up alongside her, and a man got out. They spoke for a few minutes; then he made a call on his phone.'

'And? It could still all be very innocent,' I say.

'You would think so, but wait until you hear this. Within a few minutes of the man making the call, half a dozen teenagers arrived on bicycles. They were all dressed in tracksuits and had rucksacks on their backs. Mel opened her car boot and passed out packages to the man, who placed them in each of the rucksacks. Once the kids had gone, Mel and the man got into their cars and drove off. It was so quick. It was all over in a matter of minutes.'

'Why didn't you call the police?'

Sal fixes me with a look of not quite disdain, but close to it.

'Because what good would it have done? Al and I know from experience that you need a lot of evidence if the police are going to take any notice. Anyway, by the time the police arrived, they would have gone. We asked about CCTV, but apparently the landlord has to provide any security measures himself, and the pub is struggling to keep afloat, so it's a no-go on that front.'

'And you don't think it could have been stolen stuff, like games or trainers, she was handing over. It just seems so blatant in full view like that if it was drugs.'

Sal gives me a resigned look. 'I suppose you could be right. Perhaps I am letting my imagination run away with me, but I've heard of kids being used by gangs to distribute drugs for them.'

I think of Gabe and his friend in their tracksuits and rucksacks. Is it possible that Mel is a link in a chain of supply? Could she be sending Gabe and his friend to Birmingham to collect consignments of drugs? And where does Tyler's death fit into all of this?

I've read about it happening in other parts of the country. Young people recruited and paid to act as couriers. It's a no-brainer for the drug gangs. The kids are mobile on their bikes and less likely to get caught by the police. If they do end up getting apprehended, their sentences are more lenient because of their age. In my job, many of my more vulnerable clients used both illicit and illegal substances, or had problems with alcohol. I'm aware how endemic drug use is in all communities, but using children – including your own – as a resource in that way would be despicable. Is it possible that Mel is really that calculating?

We walk up the garden, Sal carrying a mug of coffee. Close up, I see the verdant stretch of grass is artificial. Passable from afar, but unyielding and plasticky under-foot. We reach the top part of the garden, and it's very different from the rest. Tinkling wind chimes hang from the branches of a spreading Japanese maple almost devoid now of its russet-coloured leaves. A wooden bench sits in its shade, surrounded by a large patch of waist-high grass scattered through with flowers. Some-thing is etched into the wood on the backrest of the bench, and I bend down to get a closer look. *Nicholas Harris 1982–2007.*

It looks as though Al has been cutting the grass using an old-fashioned scythe. I can smell the sweet scent of meadow grass, even though the summer is long over.

'A wild flower garden, Al? It looks beautiful. It must be a lot of work.'

Al pauses to take a sip from his coffee cup. 'You should have seen it in the summer. The wild flowers have been abundant this year. There were so many bees and butterflies, and of course, the birds love it too. It actually doesn't take much looking after. Just a cut twice a year. I do it in the spring and autumn. We come back from the boat for the odd couple of days to check on the house, and this year, this whole area was a blaze of colour. I don't think I've ever seen it look so splendid.'

'It's something I've thought about doing, but I wouldn't know where to start,' I say. 'It's probably too late for this year, but I'd really appreciate some advice on planting for next year.'

'Actually, autumn is the best time to seed. You can always start getting the area ready at the end of next summer, and then you can sow in the autumn. I'd be more than happy to help. We need more wild areas in our gardens.'

My watch tells me I have been here for nearly three hours. 'Crikey,' I say. 'Time does fly when you are enjoying yourself. I really must go. Buddy will be crossing his legs.'

I wave goodbye to Al, and Sal leads me back to my car. When I move to open the door, she reaches for my arm. Her voice is sombre, with an undertone of anger. 'Al and I despise anything to do with drugs. Scum like that woman are responsible for a lot of broken lives. If there's a way of shutting down that awful network of misery, I'd like to know about it, because the police don't seem to have the resources to tackle it effectively.'

Her vehemence, though not directed at me, takes me off guard. I suppose I shouldn't be surprised. She's still grieving and angry about what happened to her son, and grief can make us irrational and unpredictable. I know that better than anyone. I tell her I agree with her up to a point, but that in Mel's case, we don't have all the facts. It's possible she could be as much a victim as anyone in all of this. After all, she too is mourning the death of her son.

I say all this, and a part of me wants to believe it, but the evidence is stacking up against Melanie Ingram. I'd like to know, one way or another, what the truth is.

'What did you mean when you said the police needed a lot of evidence before they would do anything?' It had been a throwaway remark, but now I wonder about its significance.

Sal looks scornful. 'What a waste of time that was. We went to the squat where Nicky was found. We parked up and watched the comings and goings from the car. We were just so desperate for answers.'

'Did you find out anything?'

'Well, we thought we had acquired a lot of evidence. We would wait sometimes for hours, and then a car, the same one each time, would appear. People from the squat would come down, and the driver would pass something to them through the car window. We weren't close enough to see what exactly, but it looked dodgy as hell.'

'What did the police say when you told them?'

'That was what was so disappointing. We gave them the car registration and some pictures Al had taken on his phone. They said it wasn't enough evidence, and anyway, they told us they were already monitoring the area. They said we should not compromise our own safety or the investigation by being there, and advised us not to get involved. They treated us like a pair of interfering busybodies.'

I find the image of the two of them on a stake-out amusing, like an episode of *Midsomer Murders*, and I struggle to suppress a giggle. I put my head down and get into the front seat of my car, conscious of not wanting to offend Sal after all she's been through. I'd hate for her to think I was laughing at their efforts, but she has given me an idea.

It's a long shot and potentially dangerous, but if it gets me closer to the truth, it will be worth it.

21

The drive home is arduous, with traffic snarled in every direction. Fed up with the bumper-to-bumper crush, I swerve off at the next available junction and take the longer cross-country route. The radio is irritating, fizzing with static and constantly losing the signal. Laurie thinks it's a loose wire and probably a garage job. Being in the car with little distraction does allow me the luxury of thinking time. My defence of Mel Ingram, on the face of it, seems perverse given what I've heard today. But for some reason, I feel the need to at least give her the benefit of the doubt. Mum brought me up with a healthy dislike of injustice and an awareness that appearances can be deceptive.

You should never prejudge without having the full picture. We are all social actors, and what you see might not always be a true reflection of what's going on, she would say. *Like swans, everything may appear serene on the surface, but underneath, any one of us could be paddling furiously.*

As a child, this imagery was so strong that I would look at people, searching for signs of webbed feet. It took a few years for me to work out that this was a simile, and grasp the true meaning of the saying.

Mel, as Laurie identified, 'has got under my skin'. She's abrasive, overconfident, and her values are at odds with mine. She's not really friend material, so what's going on? Why the urge to defend her?

I'm mulling over what Sal said when suddenly I remember something else that was mentioned in the article I read about drug runners. The term 'cuckooing' was used to describe how drug gangs take over a house and use it to stash money and drugs. They may even deal drugs from the property. Some of what was written fits in with Mel's behaviours, but there are discrepancies. The article referred to vulnerable people being exploited, but Mel doesn't come across as vulnerable, not in the sense they were meaning, anyway. But because she doesn't behave like a victim, it doesn't mean she isn't one, though, does it?

Don't worry, Mum. I haven't forgotten the swan analogy. My mind starts to work overtime. Mel may not be especially vulnerable, but she could owe money to someone. It's not difficult these days to build up substantial debt. Worse, what if she stole some of the proceeds and Tyler was killed by gang members in revenge? If it was a considerable amount, she could still be paying off the debt by dealing and allowing the gang access to her house.

I'm getting there, I think. There are chunks of missing information, but this must go some of the way to explaining what's going on.

I feel jubilant and hit the steering wheel so hard I catch the horn. A passing motorist flashes their lights at me in annoyance. I'm eager to get home and read up on the subject with no interruptions, but first I will have to navigate dinner and small talk with Laurie. I feel a bit of a bitch not discussing it with him, but I have the seed of a plan forming, and I'm eager to put it into action without any interference. Do I feel guilty about deceiving Laurie? Undeniably yes. Is that going to get in the way of what I'm about to do? Hell no!

I MADE him promise never to lie to me again, and here I am having to climb down off my high horse. Why? Because I am now lying to my husband. Well, not lying, more omitting parts of the story. Why am I doing this? The honest-to-goodness truth is, I don't really know. It just feels like the right thing to do.

While telling Laurie of my visit to see Al and Sal at their house and what I was told about Nicky, something stops me from mentioning why they asked me to go there in the first place.

'So you had a good day, then?'

'Yes, I did, thanks. They're an interesting couple. I think you'd get on with Al. He's a retired engineer, and Sal is lovely. She can be a bit fractious, but she's a bright cookie. Nothing much gets past her, that's for sure.'

We both pick at the salmon, which I have managed to overcook, and the new potatoes and green beans I have boiled until almost dry.

'It's sad their son died in such tragic circumstances,' Laurie says. 'Can you imagine how awful it would have been for us if Flynn or Alice had gone down that path?'

'Nobody can be smug about substances of any kind. You know it can happen to anyone, however much love and support you pour into them, or whatever their background.' I realise I must sound peevish and preachy when I see Laurie's expression.

'Okay, Fran,' he says. 'No need to snap. It was just an

observation, and I'm certainly not smug about the kids. In fact, I'm damn sure they have both experimented. They certainly enjoy drinking. Either of them could have problems with drugs or alcohol at any point. I was just trying to point out that, like any parent, we would feel deeply upset if it was one of our kids.'

'I'm sorry,' I say. 'It was an enjoyable afternoon, but a sobering one, and it was difficult to hear how awful it was for Sal to lose her son. I came away wondering how much of the problem is personal, how much is societal, and how much is lack of resources. The police do seem to be fighting a losing battle.'

'Probably a combination of all of those things. That's usually the case,' Laurie says. 'I know we dabbled a bit with pills and waccy baccy when we were students, but that seems so innocent now in retrospect.'

'For fuck's sake, Laurie,' I say in mock exasperation. 'Whatever you do, please refrain from saying "waccy baccy". Not in front of me or the kids; in fact, in front of anyone. It makes you sound so old.'

'But I am old.' He laughs. 'And isn't saying embarrassing things in front of your children, especially if they're with friends, par for the course when you are a parent?'

I'm relieved when he says he has to work. Once he has gone up to the study, I sit with my laptop. Searching through a number of sites, I find numerous articles relating to drug problems in rural areas. The term 'County Lines' appears frequently. Further searches and I find I'm being directed to the National Crime Agency website. I feel a flicker of anticipation as I read what's written there.

'County Lines' is a term used when drug gangs from big cities expand their operations to smaller towns, often using violence to drive out local dealers and exploiting children and

*vulnerable people to sell drugs. These dealers will use dedi-
cated mobile phone lines, known as 'deal lines', to take orders
from drug users. Heroin, cocaine and crack cocaine are the
most common drugs being supplied and ordered. In most
instances, the users or customers will live in a different area
to where the dealers and networks are based, so drug runners
are needed to transport the drugs and collect payment. A
common feature in County Lines drug supply is the exploita-
tion of young and vulnerable people. The dealers will
frequently target children and adults – often with mental
health or addiction problems – to act as drug runners or move
cash, so they can stay under the radar of law enforcement. In
some cases, the dealers will take over a local property,
normally belonging to a vulnerable person, and use it to
operate their criminal activity from. This is known as
cuckooing.*

I'm not familiar with the term 'County Lines', but it
fits with the article I read previously, and I do know
rural areas are being targeted by dealers. Not all of what
I have started to uncover makes sense, or even applies
in Mel's case. There are inconsistencies. But bits of the
puzzle are lining up and slotting into place. I just need
to see if I can try to locate the missing pieces without
getting myself into too much trouble.

22

I 'm not going to do anything reckless or stupid. Laurie would say I was being both, and the police, if they knew, would probably lock me up for perverting the course of justice. My motivations are not crystal clear, even to me. What I do know is that I feel the need to resolve my curiosity about Mel's activities. Perhaps then, I might also find an explanation for Tyler's death.

Being angry with myself for not being able to prevent Tyler's death is a recent stick to beat myself with. If I'm honest, the feeling of helplessness began some time ago. It first manifested following the death of Baby C and intensified when I was hollowed out from mourning Mum's death and struggling to hold onto the remnants of my marriage. Seeping like a miasma into the raw, visceral space inhabited by grief, it took me hostage. In moments of introspection, it struck me that having three losses for the price of one could be seen as somewhat unfortunate, to misquote Oscar Wilde.

As the months passed, a change came about within me. The sadness shifted, to be replaced by a sense of unease and dread. This morphed into a generalised and free-floating anxiety. Being fearful of everything rendered me hog-tied and feeble, and I hated the person I was becoming. Refusing to accept that I was ill, I preferred instead to view the process as a functional response to loss. I just needed time to heal, and then everything would get back to normal. That's what I told myself, anyway.

Tyler's death has put me back on shifting sands and is testing my resilience once again. In spite of that, something is driving me on to try to find satisfactory answers for his death. I'm impatient to uncover as much of the truth as I can, although it's become apparent there is another reason spurring me on. If Mel turns out to be culpable, then this changes everything. She cannot be allowed to continue. Making Mel accountable for her actions will, in part, assuage the guilt I feel at missing the signs that might have prevented an innocent life, that of Baby C, being snuffed out. If I find out she is involved, then I have to do everything in my power to stop her. I will just have to figure out how to make that happen.

It's strange, but for the first time in ages, I feel energised, as though I now have a sense of purpose. I know what it must look like from the outside. A silly, bored, middle-aged woman playing amateur detective. I'm a well-meaning, naive version of Miss Marple poking her nose in where it's not wanted. Common sense says *stay away, don't get involved*, but the invisible thread that links me to Tyler and Mel won't allow me to give up on either of them.

So this is my plan. Half-arsed and not very well thought out, but a plan all the same. I am going to attempt to try to befriend Mel Ingram. She has demonstrated she is frosty and difficult to like, but beneath that brittle exterior, I have caught fleeting glimpses of vulnerability. Perhaps I'm wrong, deluded even. Laurie would certainly be worried about my state of mind if he knew what I was thinking of doing. He would be even more concerned if he was to become aware that I stopped taking my medication months ago.

And what about Mel? What if she's suspicious of my motives and doesn't respond to my overtures? The thought is short-lived, and I reject it. I've had a long career working with individuals from all walks of life in and in all sorts of predicaments. I'd like to think there is nothing about people that can surprise me, so I'm putting that to the test. The skills I honed in my job are going to be put to good use in a way that some might consider dubious. I'm going on a charm offensive, and Melanie Ingram is going to be on the receiving end.

IT'S A BEAUTIFUL AUTUMN MORNING, and Buddy is in need of a walk. The temperature dropped overnight, so I wrap up warmly to combat the chill. The leaves are crisp underfoot. Some have blown up onto the pavements, or line up alongside the brick and stone walls. Others settle in clumps on top of drain covers. If it rains, the drains will block, and the pavements will turn slippery underfoot. It will be weeks before the Council sends a worker to clear up the soggy mess. Affected by the cuts to funding, the Local Authority seems to be leaving it later every year before tackling the job. It seems to me like a false economy not to deal with a potential hazard in good time. If someone falls and injures themselves, the cost in compensation will surely outweigh the costs involved in a regular clean-up. I make a mental note to mention it to Jenny and, with her assistance, draft up an email to send to the Council.

The air is clear with just a tinge of woodsmoke carried on the breeze. It's the time of year when people begin clearing their gardens before winter. Although it's not illegal to burn wet wood and leaves, it's antisocial and polluting to send clouds of choking, acrid smoke into the environment. Fortunately, the fire is far enough away for the odour to be just a pleasant reminder of the change in season.

I think of Bonfire Night when I was a child. Holding sparklers in mittened fingers, the sweet crunch of toffee apples, the high-pitched squeal of rockets, and the roar of the fire topped with a straw-stuffed Guy. With Alice and Flynn, it was an altogether more organised affair. Still thrilling, but with the element of danger removed. The event usually consisted of a huge municipal bonfire, cordoned off for safety, and a spectacular firework display. Returning home, we would all have a go at apple bobbing and eat the baked potatoes keeping warm in foil in the oven. The highlight of the evening would be when it came to toasting marshmallows in the wood burner.

Deep in thought, I have walked without being aware of my route. We have ended up close to the shops, and I decide to call and see if Tash is with a customer. If she is, I will have a look at her window display and move on. As I approach, I can see she has placed the bran tub by the door.

Tash does have a customer. I can see her through the window. It's Avis from yoga. Gone is the spiky tuft of hair. Her colour has been softened to a pale gold, and Tash is rolling the brush expertly from root to tip and waving the dryer through each section of hair to form a sleek, close cap.

I wave through the glass in the door, and Tash holds up five fingers.

'Five minutes?' I mouth, and she nods in agreement.

The summer window has been removed and replaced by this year's Halloween display. In front of a dark cloth backdrop are stretched gossamer webs, the largest containing a huge black rubber spider. There is ghostly bunting and an enormous pumpkin, the mouth carved into a rictus of a smile. *So far so ordinary.*

Then in the far corner of the window, set back in a dark recess, I notice a shape propped upright in a rocking chair. Dressed in a mishmash of women's clothing, the addition of boots and a wide-brimmed hat give the figure a happy-go-lucky appearance.

It is only upon closer inspection that it becomes apparent that, from somewhere, Tash has managed to appropriate, not a shop dummy, but a full-sized skeleton.

I walk around the block and arrive back as Avis is coming out of the door. She eyes me up and down, and I flash her a smile.

'It suits you,' I say, pointing to her newly coiffed hair. 'Tash has done a good job.'

'Thank you. She is very talented, and it's nice not to have to drive all the way to the city to have your hair done.'

The window display catches her attention. 'Hmm. Looks as though she has toned it down this year. It's so much better, don't you think?'

I nod furiously, trying my hardest not to laugh. She obviously hasn't seen what's lurking in the background. It occurs to me that it was very likely Avis and her friends who complained about the previous displays.

'And how are you holding up, Fran? Have there been any further developments in the murder case? I

did see in the local paper that the poor boy's body has
been released. The funeral will be a trying time for his
family. I feel for them, I really do.'

She is studying my face, head tilted to one side,
waiting for a reaction. Nosy as always.

'Er, no. I've heard nothing. Um, I must get on. I need
to have a chat with Tash before her next client. See you
at yoga. Bye, Avis!'

News of Tyler's funeral has taken me off guard, but I
don't want to give Avis the satisfaction of seeing how
taken aback I am. I tie Buddy up outside, push the door
and step into the salon. Tash is sweeping the floor and
has her back to me. She turns around when she hears
me come in.

'Fran, you look a bit shocked. Is it the display? The
skeleton is too much? I borrow from retired doctor in
my village. I go to her house to do her hair. She is
named Glenda, the skeleton not the doctor. She is called
Dr Newman. You want a cuppa? Look like you need
one.'

'A cuppa would be nice. And it's not the display.
You've excelled yourself this year. The skeleton is a nice
touch, although once it's been spotted, there are bound
to be complaints. You know that, right? No, I bumped
into Avis on my way in, that's all.' I sigh and smile
weakly.

Tash comes over and puts her hand on my arm.

'What has silly bitch said to upset you?'

'Nothing, really,' I say. 'It just took me by surprise.
She told me about Tyler's body being released for the
funeral.'

Tash clicks her teeth and shakes her head. 'I know. I
hear yesterday in my village shop. Will be a big turnout.
Someone said everyone in his year from school will be
there.'

Tash brings tea and biscuits, and I sip the brew slowly, conscious of the slight tremor in my hands. I have questions for Tash, but knowing how she feels about Mel, I don't want to push it. If she gets angry, she might clam up. I aim for breeziness, which feels forced, but I plough on.

'You know what you said about Mel liking money too much, Tash?' I take another sip from my cup and watch her expression.

Her fingers are circling her mug, and I can just make out the outline of a red petal where her arm protrudes from the edge of her sweater. She nods but doesn't say anything.

'I don't know this for sure,' I say. 'But I'm thinking it's possible that Mel is involved in the drugs trade and that's why Tyler was killed. What I'd like to know is, could she be an unwilling participant? A victim just as much as Tyler was? Willington is a small place. Have you heard anything that might explain exactly what is going on?'

Jesus, I'm beginning to sound like a detective in a cheaply made, trashy American cop show.

Tash stands up and places her cup on the shelf in front of the mirror. Her face, normally animated, is flat and expressionless. When she does speak, her voice is low and husky.

'Why do you want to know these things, Fran? It's not good for you. Best you leave alone, eh?'

She seems prickly, and I wonder why. She knows my mental health has been fragile. Is it that she is trying to protect me? Or does she know more than she is letting on?

'You must take care of yourself, Fran. When baby comes, I need you to be Godmother.'

It takes a couple of seconds for me to realise what

she is saying. 'Tash, you're pregnant. How wonderful, but I've told you before, I can't be a Godparent. I'm not religious.'

'Pah.' She waves her hand dismissively. 'There is always solution. Anyways, is early days.'

I give her a hug and kiss her cheek, sensing her concern. 'It's the best news, Tash. It must have been the yoga.'

We dissolve into giggles like a pair of schoolgirls.

'Alex must be thrilled,' I say.

'Oh yes. Strutting around like big man. He like dog with two dicks.'

This initiates a further bout of laughter, and I grab a handful of tissues to dry my eyes and blow my nose. When we recover, I give Tash a potted version of the attack by Mel's dogs and my meeting with Al and Sal. I skip over a lot of the details, but tell her briefly of their suspicions and what they saw in the boatyard car park.

We are interrupted by the door opening. A well-built woman with a helmet of steel grey hair enters. It's Tash's next client. She is carrying a walking stick that she jabs in the direction of the pavement.

'Is that your dog tied up outside?' she asks brusquely.

'It is,' I say.

'Well, he's been there far too long. I saw him when I went into the Co-op, and it took me at least twenty minutes to get my shopping done and then take it to the car. It's not fair, leaving him tied up for that length of time. Poor little blighter.'

I open my mouth to comment and think better of it. She does have a point. I've been here for at least half an hour.

Tash, waiting at the desk to book in the woman, raises her eyebrows and rolls her eyes.

'I'll ring you,' I say, exiting sharply before I attract any more of the woman's ire.

Buddy, pleased to see me as always, seems unperturbed. He usually likes the attention he gets when I leave him outside to nip in for the odd item from the Co-op store. To compensate for abandoning him, I take him to the park, where he indulges in two of his favourite pastimes: sniffing every square inch of the field and chasing squirrels.

BACK HOME, I sit in the kitchen, picking over the remnants of a cheese sandwich and mulling over what I'm going to say to Mel. That is, if I can pluck up the courage to make the call. My initial bravado is ebbing away, and the more time I have to think about it, the more absurd the idea seems. Mel isn't going to take the bait; I'm now convinced of that. She's too shrewd and knowing. Whereas when I'm flustered or caught out in a lie, I'm transparent and give too much away.

No, I tell myself. *My problem-solving days are over. Rather than looking for a challenge, I should stick to yoga and knitting for the new baby.*

23

'Hi, is that Mel? It's Fran here. From the canal. Buddy's owner.'

I've plucked up the courage to ring her, but I'm having second thoughts already.

'I remember. Is there a problem?' Her voice sounds breathy and distant.

'No, there's no problem. Look, this is going to sound silly, but I was wondering if you would mind me coming to Tyler's funeral. If you only want family and friends there, I completely understand. It's just, I, er, um... It's just, er, you know, me being there when he died...'

I haven't rehearsed in my head what I want to say, and now I could kick myself. I'm making such a hash of it she'll probably hang up on me, and it will serve me right.

It's gone quiet, and I'm about to hang up in embarrassment when I hear what sounds like a sniffle on the other end of the line.

'Mel, are you still there? Are you alright?'

'Yes, I'm fine. It's just that it's been so bloody awful.' Her voice is shaky. I'm almost certain she's crying.

'What's happened?'

'They have released Tyler's body, and I can't face having to see him again lying there in a coffin. They are going to ask if I want to view his body at the funeral place, and I don't know what to say. It's been really bothering me. It was bad enough having to go to the mortuary. I had to identify him, and he was so still and cold. It wasn't my boy anymore. They are going to think I'm a terrible mother if I say I don't want to see him for the last time to say goodbye.'

She sniffs again, and I can hear her blow her nose.

'It's been so horrible. I've been having nightmares thinking about what they did to him during the post-mortem. He's been through so much.'

I feel for her, I really do. You'd have to have a heart of stone not to be moved by her predicament. I'm not sure why she's confiding in me, but I suspect it's not just for sympathy. She's probably had that in spade loads since Tyler's death. It's obvious she has friends. There were plenty of people with her at Tyler's shrine, and hundreds of responses on her Facebook page. Of course, social media contacts are not necessarily close friends, but she must have a family supporting her. What I suspect is that Mel has a network of loose connections, but very few people in her direct orbit whom she trusts. I take a punt on how useful I can make myself to her and go into practical mode.

'I really don't think there's any right or wrong in this sort of situation, Mel. It's up to you to decide. If it doesn't feel right, nobody is going to judge you. The staff handling the funeral are very used to dealing with people who are grieving. They won't think any less of you if you choose not to see him.'

'But everyone keeps telling me I should, and that I'll regret it if I don't,' she wails. I can hear her sobbing steadily. Every now and then she takes a shuddering breath.

'That's everyone else, Mel; it's not you. We all grieve in our own way, and what works for one person is not necessarily right for another. It's a very individual experience. It's good that people care and want to offer advice, but you have to find your own way of coping with it. There's no template to follow.'

'I hadn't thought of it like that.' She sighs, and I can hear the tiredness in her voice. 'Thank you for listening. It's been a big help.'

'It's really no problem. I know it was nothing like you have endured, but I have been through a bereavement myself recently. It's so difficult to think straight and organise everything when you are in emotional turmoil.'

'Yes, it is. It's exhausting. Was it a relative of yours that died?'

'It was my mum,' I say. 'She was a huge part of our lives, and it's been difficult without her around.'

'I'm sorry. I'm not close to my mother, and my dad is dead, but I can imagine that it must be hard.'

She sounds calmer, and I presume she wants to bring the conversation to a close. I'm not in any way prepared for her next question.

'By the way,' she says, almost as an afterthought, 'it's a big favour to ask, I know, but will you come to the funeral director's with me when I go to make the arrangements?'

It's so unexpected that I almost drop the phone in shock. I was looking for a way in to get to know her, but this catches me completely off guard.

'Don't feel obligated,' she is saying. 'It's just that

everyone I know has their own agenda, and they've been bombarding me with ideas for the funeral. I need space to plan it without having all their baggage to deal with as well.'

I'm flattered she's asked me, but cautious, too. I suspect I will be dropped like a hot potato once I have no further use, but this opening is a gift and more than I could have anticipated.

There's a knock at the front door, and Buddy barks wildly. I can hardly hear myself think.

'I've got to go, Mel,' I say. 'There's someone at the door, but I'd be more than happy to go with you. Give me a ring when you make the appointment and let me know the details.'

'I will. Oh, and thanks again.' There's a click as she ends the call.

Lifting a slat, I see through the blind that Jenny is standing in the porch. She is holding a bunch of rust-coloured chrysanthemums and has a newspaper tucked under her arm. Buddy waits expectantly until I slide back the chain, then throws himself through the door at the object of his affection.

'I'm sorry, Jenny. He's such a pain.' I grab him by the collar and signal to Jenny to step inside.

'Come and have a cuppa. I haven't got anything nice to go with it except shop-bought biscuits, I'm afraid.'

'The tea will be fine, thanks.' She perches unsteadily on a bar stool and looks out across the garden. Buddy is at her feet, giving her adoring glances. 'Such a lovely view now you have put in those doors.'

She places the flowers on the countertop. 'I hope you like the chrysanths. I picked them from the garden this morning.'

'They're gorgeous. The colours are so autumnal.'

I put them in a vase and place it on the dining table.

'And I was wondering if you had seen this?' She hands me the local paper, open at the page with the headline about the release of Tyler's body for the funeral.

'I hadn't heard,' I say. 'Not until I met Avis at the hairdresser's. She told me about it. Do you know her?'

'Oh, yes. We are on some of the same committees. Awful woman. Such a busybody.'

Jenny is a dependable confidante and such a stalwart within the community that it's on the tip of my tongue to mention my call to Mel. I stop myself before blurting it out. The fewer who know, the better. I'd hate Laurie to find out before I speak to him myself, and I have no intention of mentioning my recent interaction with Mel to him anytime soon.

Jenny is beginning to look uncomfortable on the stool, so I suggest we take our cups into the lounge. Buddy claims his place on the sofa at her side.

'You do realise we are going to nominate you as his next of kin if anything happens to us, don't you, Jenny?'

Jenny strokes the top of his head, and he snuggles in close to her.

'Have you ever thought of getting a pet? They are good company. Perhaps a little cat? They are easy to manage,' I say.

'We did have a cat many moons ago. She was called Suzy, and Jack loved her. He spoiled her rotten. The little madam had the best of everything, including fresh fish four times a week. Sadly, she disappeared one day. We searched everywhere and put up notices, but not a sign. Not even a body at the roadside. I really couldn't face having another one.'

'That's the worst bit,' I say. 'Not knowing. Laurie and I would be so upset if anything happened to old cheeky chops here. If he disappeared without a trace, it would be even more traumatic. You do hear of pets being abducted and horrible things happening to them.'

Thinking about it, I feel sick at the prospect. Perhaps I should heed the warning from the woman at the hairdressers and not leave Buddy tied up in public places. Living in a quiet village tends to give you a false sense of security. If the stuff I've seen on Facebook is to be believed, dogs can be snatched within seconds and never seen again, and that's in all locations, including rural areas.

'Have you heard anything from the police?' Jenny says. 'Do you know if they are making any progress in the search for the boy's killers?'

'I've heard nothing apart from what's already in the public domain and what's being reported in the media. I don't think they have to keep witnesses updated, only the family.'

'And no other alarming incidents since the parcel?' Jenny had been especially upset by the toy dog episode.

'No, thank goodness,' I say. 'Even though it might be pranksters, the police took our accounts very seriously, which was a relief. They are keeping an eye out in the village for any unusual activity. You may have seen the marked car driving around and the presence of the PCSOs? They've also offered us a panic alarm, which seems a bit over the top.'

'Oh my goodness. Whatever next? It's a sad indictment of our society if you have to resort to such measures to feel safe in your own home. I can only assume the investigation is ongoing, and you will just have to bide your time and let the police do their job.'

'Yes, I will.' Even though the last thing I intend doing is biding my time.

24

The security company rings on Monday morning, and by Wednesday lunchtime, I have in my possession two wireless key fobs. If activated, they connect to a member of staff at a call centre, who will then contact the police directly in an emergency. The fobs are neat and unobtrusive. I place one in a kitchen drawer and the other upstairs on my bedside table.

We now have a secure garden, police-approved locks, a sophisticated burglar alarm and a high-powered outdoor lighting system. Apart from a fireproof letterbox, which the engineer suggested for additional security, we live in a house that is beginning to closely resemble Fort Knox. Despite this, on returning to the house, I still pause momentarily on the doorstep before entering, palms sweaty and heart fluttering. The age-old saying is certainly true in my case. Old habits die hard.

My phone rings, and I rush to pick it up, half expecting it to be Mel.

'Hi, Mum. How are you?'

'Alice, it's nice to hear from you! I'm great, thanks. Is

everything alright?' I'm surprised by the call. She rarely rings me when she's at work.

'Yes, don't worry. I was just wondering if you wanted to come up to town. I'll treat you to lunch for your birthday.'

With all that's been going on, I've completely forgotten about my birthday, which is a week on Friday. It will be just my luck to arrange to meet Alice and then find Mel wants me to go to the funeral director's with her on that day.

'Would you mind if I ring you back to let you know for definite?'

I hear a hiss of irritation on the end of the line.

'But why can't you tell me now? It's not as though you have a packed social calendar. Honestly, Mum, I try to do something nice for you, and look what happens.'

'It's just that I might be doing something next week and…' I start to say.

There's a sharpness to her voice as she interrupts me. 'Well, if you've got a better offer, that's all right with me. There's a really nice bistro opened up just around the corner from work. I thought I'd take you there as a special treat, but if you are doing something else, we can arrange it for another time.'

I'm starting to feel guilty for stalling. Normally, I would have jumped at Alice's offer. She doesn't often initiate a meeting, and it's been a while since we did something together as mother and daughter.

Throwing caution to the wind rather than risk my daughter's displeasure, I agree to meet her. She tells me she will text to confirm the details after the weekend.

I used to worry about the bond, or lack of it, with Alice. She's fiercely independent, and unlike Flynn, who is open and straightforward, she can be sly and secretive about what is going on in her life. She seems to interpret any overtures I make as meddling. She was a daddy's girl from the start; Laurie has never been on the receiving end of her wrath and seems to know what to say and do to avoid conflict.

Looking back, it was a bit pathetic of me, but I committed the classic parenting error. The one where you make comparisons with those who appear to enjoy the perfect relationship. I couldn't help but envy other mums who enjoyed fun-filled shopping trips and pamper days with their daughters. It seemed to me they were more like friends than parent and child. Shopping with Alice for clothes and shoes was always a battle of wills, invariably resulting in one of us getting frazzled and weepy.

Once she reached fourteen and was firmly entrenched in her Goth phase, Laurie and I ended up giving her an allowance, thus avoiding a war of attrition.

I can't say this made her happy, for she remained a morose teenager, but it was one less battle to be fought, and the household was more harmonious as a consequence.

Now the house feels empty, as though the oxygen has been sucked out from within, leaving it stale and lifeless. Looking back, it all happened gradually. Without the volatility that created the sparks of incandescent energy when Alice and Flynn lived at home, the house began to contract, as though drained of its lifeblood.

There was a time when Laurie and I, navigating the emotional peaks and troughs of parenting, craved the tranquillity associated with having an empty house. But, as the saying goes, *careful what you wish for.*

Moving here was the closest I ever got to that most fanciful of notions, the dream home. It seemed inconceivable back then that I would ever consider leaving the place where I felt at my happiest and most secure. Now, with Alice and Flynn gone – and following Tyler's murder – everything has changed. What was once my sanctuary is starting to feel like my prison. I have to ask myself the question: *What exactly am I going to do about it?*

THE GARDEN IS LOOKING LESS than its best. I haven't been out there in weeks, and the leaves that have already drifted down are scattered across the lawn. They litter the paths, accumulate in piles at the corners of the patio, and mount up in front of the garden gates. As the month progresses, the high winds will bring down further flurries, which, if not collected, will turn into a slippery mulch with the arrival of the heavy winter rains. Pulling on an old waxed jacket and a pair of wellies, I step outside.

Buddy is overjoyed to have company in the garden. He hurtles around in ever-widening circles, stopping only to pounce on an eddy of old leaf litter lifted by the breeze, or to sniff at an especially interesting patch of moss. The sun is high and bright in a sky that is a deep chromatic blue. It feels good to be outside on such a beautiful autumn afternoon. Throwing myself into raking and sweeping, I soon have a number of neatly stacked piles ready to transfer into the incinerator bin. Our neighbours on either side are at work during the day. Out of courtesy, one of us will call round at the weekend to check they haven't put washing out or are planning a meetup with friends for drinks in the garden, before we light a bonfire.

It's warm work, and I pause to take off my coat and

survey my handiwork. At this point, Buddy seizes his opportunity. Barking wildly, he runs through the largest of the piles, scattering leaves in all directions. I find an old tennis ball and throw it to distract him while I start to shovel spade loads of dried leaf litter into the bin.

It is close to 4 p.m. when I finish. To amuse Laurie, and as proof of my efforts, I want to take a photo to show him how hard I have worked. It will be dark by the time he gets home, and by the weekend the garden will no doubt look as leaf-strewn as it did before I started.

I've left the phone in the house, and when I locate it, I have had three missed calls and a text message. They are all from Mel Ingram.

"Shit,' I say out loud before retrieving the message.

Hi, Fran. I have made an appointment at the funeral place on Tuesday. It's at 11 a.m. Let me know if you can make it. Mel.

I'm annoyed with myself for not taking my phone into the garden, and I'm also in a bit of a quandary. Should I call her back or just send a return text? I decide on the latter.

That's good for me, Mel. Shall I meet you there or come and pick you up? I will need an address and postcode if I'm going straight there. Fran.

I keep checking the screen, waiting for a response. When there's no reply after twenty minutes, I decide to have a shower. I'm tired and dusty and my muscles ache, stiff from lack of use. Before I do, I nip outside and take a quick photo of the garden for Laurie.

It's still early. Laurie won't be back for at least another couple of hours. Plenty of time to light the fire and prepare food. Not wanting to get back into my old clothes after my shower, I put on pyjamas and a dressing gown and fasten my freshly washed hair into a turban.

Once the fire is blazing, I start preparing vegetables for supper. I'm going to have a go at making a vegetable chilli. Having listened to Alice lecture us on the merits of being vegetarian, despite continuing to eat meat herself, I am going to experiment with having a few meat-free days. It will be good for us to eat less meat, and if it helps the planet, I am all for it. A message alert pings on my phone as I am chopping an onion. Rinsing my hands, I click to read it. It's from Laurie, telling me he is making good progress and will be back before seven.

The meal is ready on the hob when Laurie arrives home. He hugs me and kisses the top of my head. 'Mmm, showered and with freshly washed hair. What *have* you been up to, Mrs Hughes?'

'You will be pleased to hear that I haven't been idle this afternoon,' I say with mock effrontery. 'Buddy and I cleared the leaves, although he was more of a hindrance than a help. Look, here's the proof.' I select the photo of the newly tidied garden and wave the phone in his direction.

'Wow. I'm impressed. That's one thing less for me to do at the weekend. You're a star!' He seems genuinely pleased. As he hands me back the phone, there's another message alert. Even without looking, I know it's from Mel.

'Aha, is it your secret lover? Have I caught you out?' He's teasing me, I know, but the heat rising in my face feels like a kind of betrayal.

'I wish,' I say. 'Who on earth would want a clapped-out overweight woman of my age, when there are so many young, fit women desperately looking for a meal ticket?'

I am trying to be humorous, but now it's his turn to colour. I realise I have pressed a sensitive button, and he probably thinks I'm having a go at him.

'Oh, bollocks,' I say. 'I'm sorry. I didn't mean anything by it…'

'I know you didn't. Come on, let's eat, I'm starving. A glass of red wouldn't go amiss, either.'

I slip the phone into my dressing gown pocket. After supper, there's a film on television that Laurie wants to watch. While he stacks the dishwasher, I light the candles in the front room before we cuddle up together for the evening on the sofa. Buddy has decided to leave us to it and stretches out on the rug in front of the fire, soaking up the warmth.

'Did you find out who was trying to get hold of you?'

I can feel the weight of the phone in my pocket. 'No,' I say. 'It's probably Tash wanting to know if I'm going to yoga.'

The lie slips off my tongue so easily it takes even me by surprise.

25

The message from Mel is short and abrupt. *Meet me there,* followed by the address and postcode. It's Tuesday and at 10:45a.m., I pull into the car park at the back of an unprepossessing red-brick house. It is situated in a not particularly attractive suburb and overlooks a small industrial estate. There is no sign of Mel's car. Rather than go in without her, I turn on the radio and wait for her to arrive. The dark grey jacket I am wearing is lightweight, and with the engine switched off, I can feel the cold begin to creep into my hands and feet. I'm relieved to see her pull in and park at a few minutes to eleven. Stepping out of her car, she is smartly dressed in tailored black trousers and a navy bouclé coat, which she pulls in tight around her to ward off the chill.

The only noticeable sign indicating the purpose of the building is a small, highly polished brass plaque bearing the words *M.T. Innes – Independent Funeral Directors.* Next to it is a bell, which Mel pushes to signal our arrival. A middle-aged woman appears from the back of the building. She is plump and dark-haired, her uniform of white blouse and dark jacket and skirt on the tight side for her frame. She holds the door open to let us in, and a blast of warm, foetid air hits us.

We enter a room carpeted in grey and with subdued lighting. It's sparsely furnished, with a light-coloured wooden reception desk swamped by a floral display. The scent of the flowers mixed with an astringent, anti-septic smell catches in my throat, and I cough. In the far corner of the room, there's a small coffee table flanked by two velvet tub chairs. The overall effect is of a hotel reception area.

The woman shakes both our hands warmly, unsure which of us she should be addressing. Mel introduces herself, then gestures in my direction. 'I've brought someone with me. This is Fran.'

It's an odd position for me to be in. I'm not family, nor am I a friend. I shift from one foot to the other, feeling uncomfortable and out of place.

The woman points to her name badge. 'My name is Natalie,' she says. 'I'm here to help you with the arrangements today. Can I say how sorry I am that we meet under these circumstances, Mrs Ingram? I'm so very sorry for your loss.'

She is welcoming and efficient and obviously used to putting people at their ease. She leads us down a corridor and into a room where we sit on high-backed chairs around a highly polished wooden table. Strategi-cally placed in front of us is a large box of tissues.

'Now I'm just going to go and get the paperwork,' Natalie says. 'Before we begin, can I get you a cup of tea or coffee?'

'Coffee for me. What about you, Fran?'

'Coffee would be lovely. Thanks.'

Natalie returns carrying a black folder and a tray with two cups and a plate of biscuits. She opens the folder and picks up a pen. I notice Mel shifting in her seat, trying to look over Natalie's shoulder at something on the far wall.

'What's that?' she says, pointing at a small stained-glass window. At its centre is a cross. Natalie turns to look, seeming unsure how to respond. 'Erm, well. It's a piece of decorative glass. It was made by a local craftsman. It's a little nicer than a picture, don't you think?'

Mel seems unconvinced. 'It would be better if it didn't have a cross in the middle. Not everyone who comes here is going to be religious, are they?' Her face is pinched and blotchy, and she looks on the verge of tears.

'You're right, of course, Mrs Ingram. People who come here are from all faiths and none. I will make a note of what you have said and pass it on to Mr Innes. You can also mention it on the feedback card we give you after the funeral.'

Mel reaches for a tissue. She blows her nose and takes a sip of coffee. 'Just asking. It's not everyone's cup of tea.' She sniggers at her own joke.

It's an inappropriate response, but I remember how erratic you can be when you are grieving. Natalie appears unconcerned, no doubt used to the full gamut of emotional response. She riffles through the sheaf of papers in front of her and waits for Mel to recover her composure.

'I'm ready. Lesh make a start.' Mel is slurring her words, and I wonder if she has taken something to steady her nerves. Leaning in to check if she is alright, I detect the sour smell of alcohol on her breath.

'Do you need some fresh air before we start?' I say.

Mel swings her hair and lowers her voice to a theatrical whisper. 'Took brandy and tranx on an empty stomach. Need more coffee; then I'll be good to go.' She hiccups and gives me a thumbs-up.

'Let's nip to the ladies' and freshen up,' I say. 'I'm sure Natalie will make you a strong black coffee when we come back.'

I take Mel's arm, and she lets me steer her down the corridor to the washroom. I dampen some paper towels, and she dabs at her face in front of the mirror. From her bag, she takes out a gold compact and matching lipstick case. After patting powder onto her cheeks and under her eyes, she applies a slick of red lipstick.

Despite her initial demeanour, I think I glimpse a look of relief on Natalie's face when we return. I am guessing she is glad it's me and not her who has had to deal with Mel in her tipsy state. With the tray replenished, Mel drains a fresh cup of black coffee. She then sits upright as though chairing a business meeting, placing her hands palms down on the table in front of her.

'Right. Before we start. This funeral is for my boy, and there's something you need to know. It's got to be perfect.' She leans forward and jabs a finger in Natalie's direction. 'And no expense spared. Nothing is too good for my Tyler.'

'Of course, Mrs Ingram. We will do everything in our power to make sure we follow your instructions to the letter.'

I feel sorry for Natalie. She has drawn the short straw being on duty today, but she remains professional and attentive throughout.

'The paperwork is all in order,' Natalie says. 'Perhaps our starting point should be the service itself. Do you want a cremation or burial for Tyler?'

'Cremation. I don't want him rotting in the ground. He's suffered enough.'

Natalie doesn't bat an eyelid and continues filling in the form in front of her.

'On the forms we have, Tyler's religion is given as Church of England. Do you want a Minister of Religion to conduct the ceremony?'

'No, definitely not. You can get a non-religious person to do it now, can't you?'

'Yes, that is not a problem. We can arrange that for you,' Natalie says, scribbling away.

The next hour is spent discussing the flowers, the order of service, cars and coffins. Mel is dismissive of the more traditional faux wooden caskets with brass-coloured plastic handles.

'Tacky,' she says, waving her hand dismissively.

'We can order something more personal. Did you say Tyler liked motorcycles?'

Natalie pulls out a leaflet from her folder. The pictures show a range of eye-catching, brightly coloured coffins, each with an image emblazoned across its shiny surface. Page after page displays coffins to reflect every hobby and interest. Flowers, woodland scenes, boats, cars, bottles of alcohol, bars of chocolate: The choice is overwhelming. Natalie explains that the manufacturers can even customise to requirements using a photograph.

'Then that's what we'll do,' Mel says. 'I'll get Gabe to bring a photo of Tyler's motorbike.'

Natalie leaves the room to check possible dates with the crematorium and to phone the celebrant. We wait for her to return in a room that now feels stuffy and claustrophobic. Mel is starting to look exhausted. Her face has an unhealthy pallor and a sheen of sweat. She looks like I feel when I'm going to throw up. In preparation, I slide the box of tissues towards her. She sits for a while, drumming her fingers on the table, then lifts her bag and retrieves a hip flask from its depths. There is a faint tremor in her hands as she takes a swig of the contents. She offers me the flask, but I decline. One of us has to be sober enough to drive.

'It's an ordeal, trying to get everything sorted out,' I say, trying to show sympathy for her plight. 'You'll feel much better once you get home and you've had something to eat and a rest.'

She takes another tissue and wipes the sweat from her top lip. Since we arrived, her phone has been in front of her on silent. She picks it up and fiddles with it absentmindedly, then sighs.

'You know I said I didn't want to see Tyler?' she says. 'Well, I've changed my mind. I've thought about it a lot, and if I don't say goodbye, it will prey on my mind. Gabe is coming later this afternoon with a couple of Tyler's friends. They've chosen some music for the funeral, and they are bringing in clothes for him to wear. Some of them have said they want to see him. They are only kids, and if they can do it, then so can I.'

She juts out her chin in an attempt, I assume, to look determined. She's faking it, I can tell, although I have to admire her resolve.

When Natalie comes back, Mel is sitting quietly. She has managed to pull herself together and get her erratic behaviour under control.

'There is an afternoon slot on Friday 26th at the crematorium. I've also rung the celebrant, and she is available. Shall we make the booking for then, Mrs Ingram?'

Mel nods in agreement, pushes back her chair and gets to her feet. Steadying herself, she stands for a while as though bracing for some kind of impact. Lifting her bag onto her shoulder, she picks up her phone and collects her coat from the back of her chair.

'Take me to see my boy,' she says.

26

I half expected resistance from Mel when I suggested we leave her car and I drive her home. Surprisingly, she is compliant and follows me without protest. Neither of us speaks on the way back. It's been emotionally draining for her, that's apparent. She came from viewing Tyler looking as though she had been punched in the solar plexus. She managed to sign the paperwork Natalie put in front of her before exiting in haste, without so much as a backward glance. The door closed behind her with such force, the whole building seemed to reverberate. It was left to me to retrieve the folder of paperwork Natalie had prepared and to thank her on Mel's behalf.

I am also tired and drained of energy. The morning has been a reminder of just how much effort was involved in arranging Mum's funeral. She, of course, had left specific instructions as to what she wanted, lodging her wishes with her will at the solicitor's office. This made everything easier. Even so, the experience was still gruelling and overwhelmingly sad. How much harder must it be for Mel, having to deal with the death of her firstborn child, taken from her under the worst circumstances imaginable.

As I drive back to her house, Mel is leaning back against the headrest, her face turned towards the window. She appears lost in thought. I want to say something comforting. To tell her everything will be all right. Time will pass, and she will get to a stage where the pain is not so acute. Say that eventually the good memories will begin to outweigh the bad ones. I'm usually pretty good in these sorts of situations. But not today. I'm all out of platitudes.

A part of me wants to drop her off at home, make my excuses and leave. I weigh up the options. Make my escape, or stay for a while in case I'm needed. Somehow it feels wrong to just abandon her, especially as it becomes apparent when we arrive that there is no one at the house. Even the dogs are absent.. I think back to what was said earlier. Gabe was going to the funeral home later on with Tyler's friends, she had said. I'm hoping his absence means he is at school, where he should be. If I leave now, she will be alone, although it does occur to me that she might prefer her own company.

'Can I make you something before I go, Mel? Maybe a cup of tea and a sandwich.'

She is sitting on the sofa, her legs drawn up under her. I can see she is shivering, and I take a throw from the back of the sofa and place it around her shoulders. There is an electric fire in the hearth with realistic-looking coals. Locating the switch sends a blast of hot, dry air into the room.

'It didn't look like him, you know. He was waxy, like those figures at Madame Tussauds. We took the kids there once when they were little, me and their dad.'

This is the first time I have heard her mention the boys' father, and my ears prick up in interest.

'Tyler thought they were real,' she continues. 'He kept trying to poke them to make them move.'

She has a faraway look, and her voice is distant.

'He was such a lovely baby. All that dark hair and those soulful eyes. People were always looking into his pram and telling me how gorgeous he was. He gets his looks from my side of the family. I know everyone thinks he and Gabe are alike, but Tyler is the spit of my dad. Gabe is an Ingram, but Tyler is a Driscoll.'

I'm still standing after lighting the fire, and she gestures for me to sit in the chair opposite her.

'You might find it hard to believe with this colouring.' She lifts a lock of her hair with her hand, then runs it through her fingers. 'But I'm from an Irish Traveller family.'

I must look surprised, because a ghost of a smile plays around her lips.

'Ya wouldn't think it now, would ye?' she says, putting on a strong Irish accent.

'I wouldn't, no,' I say, thinking of the Traveller families I have encountered in the past. Almost without exception, they viewed social workers with suspicion, convinced we were all potential child snatchers.

They kept themselves separate, outside of society, adhering to their own rules and code of ethics, priding themselves on living on the margins of society. With their cheeky, knowing children, their immaculate homes, the outsides surrounded by rusting scrap metal, their bling-related collections, an overt manifestation of wealth captured in crystal and diamanté, they viewed those not part of their community with suspicion seeing it as fair game to give anyone viewed as part of the establishment the runaround.

You couldn't really blame them for having that
outlook. Building up a level of trust is a time-consuming
business, difficult when you are moving around from
place to place. And Travellers are never a welcome sight
in any community. Overarching everything, mutual
prejudices prevail and are difficult to shift.

I try to place Mel within this community, but it's a
struggle. She is distant and suspicious, and she certainly
has a taste for the good things in life. Taking all of this
into account, I still find it difficult to imagine her living
a life so removed from the one she has now.

She seems to read my thoughts, and her voice rises,
becoming animated. 'It's a bit different to a Gypsy caravan,' she says with a sweep of her arm, taking in the
tasteful, understated opulence of her living room. 'I was
glad to get away, I can tell you.'

'How *did* you get away?' My interest has been
piqued, and I'm keen to find out as much as I can while
she is in the mood for talking.

'I met Joel.'

Joel, it turns out, is the father of Tyler and Gabe. It's
difficult to hear. She makes Joel sound like an
unsavoury character, and there are parts of the story
that set off alarm bells. Mel tells me her dissatisfaction
with her life began at an early age, and she hated the
restrictions her parents imposed on her. At fourteen, she
had started to go off the rails. Moving frequently meant
she had little education and few opportunities. Her
mother and father, fearful of what might become of her,
resorted to the only solution they could come up with.
They decided they would send her to live with relatives
in Ireland.

Once she reached sixteen, arrangements would be
put in place for her to marry one of her second cousins.
Her parents believed an arranged marriage was best for

all concerned. A husband, her own caravan and a baby would settle her down before she got the chance to bring shame on the family.

Her saviour came in the form of Joel, ten years older and, in her words, involved in every dodgy deal going. They ran away together, first to Lincolnshire and then to Scotland, where Joel had connections. When she was eight months pregnant with Tyler, they married in a Register Office in Scotland with only two witnesses present. By the time she was twenty, she had two toddlers, few friends and no family around for support. She begged Joel to take her back to her family, who were by now living on a permanent site in Birmingham. She was heartbroken to discover that her dad had died from a heart attack around the time she was expecting Gabe. Soon after his death, her mother had taken her younger brother and sister and gone back to Ireland to be near her extended family.

'What a mess it all was,' she says, as if to herself.

'But look at you now,' I say. 'You have a lovely home, a car, your own business...' I stop short at mentioning having a healthy son. It doesn't seem right to mention Gabe in light of what happened to Tyler.

'Count your blessings. Is that what you're trying to tell me?'

Her tone has been reflective and matter-of-fact; now she has reverted to prickly sarcasm.

'No, not at all,' I say. 'I was just thinking how tough it must have been for you, and how well you've done to recover from such a difficult start in life.'

'Ah well, we all do what we can to survive.' A smirk plays around the corners of her mouth.

The room has become hot, and Mel unfolds her legs and reaches across to lower the temperature on the fire. She resumes her position on the sofa, and I wait for her to continue. The dry heat is making me thirsty, and I would love a drink, but I'm reluctant to interrupt before she finishes her story.

'It was great to be back in Birmingham, even with no family around, and for the first few years, things went really well. Joel set up a drop-shipping business, buying handmade woollen goods from Scottish suppliers. Missing so much school meant I wasn't great at reading and writing, but I was good at figures. We worked together, and the business was successful. We bought a big house, had expensive holidays, clothes, cars, ate in expensive restaurants...' Her voice tails off, and I sit, holding myself still, not wanting to break the spell.

'Then, as they say, all good things must come to an end.' She sighs, and her eyelids droop with tiredness.

'What happened? Did the business fold?' I say.

She laughs bitterly. 'Nothing could be further from the truth. Joel turned out to be an astute businessman. He's still doing well, especially with sales in the States and Canada. Unfortunately for me and the boys, Joel was not the marrying type. He got bored with family life. There was always some young, fresh face available who could be bought with nice clothes and jewellery.'

'So you and the boys were just cast aside?' I say. 'That's a bit brutal, considering you helped him to build up the business.'

'It was gutting at the time. And, what was worse, everything was in his name. I'm not stupid, though. I got myself a good lawyer, and the settlement gave me enough to buy this house and have a bit left over. I knew a couple of people in Derby, and I wanted to get away from Birmingham by then, so I moved here with my boys. The rest, as they say, is history.'

I have a question for her. The problem is, I'm worried about what her reaction will be. She's over-

wrought and unpredictable. My asking it may well
undo any trust that has built up between us. Still, it's
been bugging me. Buzzing at the edge of my awareness
like an irritating insect. Hovering on the tip of my
tongue, requiring an appropriate pause or space. Now,
with a gap in the conversation, the opportunity presents
itself. I decide to take the risk, even if doing so demol-
ishes my plan.

'Do you have any idea why Tyler was killed, Mel?'

She raises her head and turns toward me, fixing me
with eyes that glitter like blue ice.

'Tyler was a sacrifice,' she says.

27

F or the first time in a while, it feels good to be back home. I make a very welcome pot of tea and a round of toast. Apart from a cup of coffee at the funeral home, I haven't had anything to eat or drink since breakfast. I feel shaky and a bit sick. It could be that my sugar levels are low, or it might be a reaction to what has been an emotionally charged few hours.

I watch Buddy, nose to the ground, sniffing and scrabbling amongst the latest batch of leaves accumulating on the lawn, and go over the events of this morning in my head. If I had hoped to have a better understanding of Mel and her motivations, then I have succeeded in some areas and failed in others. She talked a lot about her life, never once asking me about mine, which suited me fine.

Despite this, she persists as an enigma, and I remain conflicted. Is Mel victim or perpetrator, and what does she know about Tyler's death and who was responsible?

Her response to my question about why she thought Tyler was killed was disturbing and delivered without a hint of emotion. Attempts at getting her to elaborate were unsuccessful; she refused to be drawn further. What on earth did she mean by *Tyler was a sacrifice*?

I wrap up warmly and head into an icy wind with Buddy at my side. I'm hoping a walk will help unravel the jumbled thoughts circling in my head like agitated birds. It doesn't, and I return home more confused than when I ventured out. It would be so good to go over all this with Laurie, who is a great problem solver and more objective than I, but I've already decided that it's out of the question. I try to work out who else would be able to help me gain some perspective, and I decide on Sal. She might question my approach, but I feel sure she will understand what I'm trying to achieve. I will contact her, but not just yet. She dislikes talking on the phone. It will be better to arrange to meet up. Sal is shrewd and upfront, even though she is hostile towards Mel. She's likely to be a useful sounding board for what I've managed to glean so far. What Mel has told me is interesting, but not that enlightening. It's only what she wants me to know, and I can't rule out the possibility that I'm being manipulated.

FRIDAY COMES AROUND. It's my birthday, and I am fifty-two years old. Laurie was away overnight, and my phone pings when I switch it on. It's a text message.

Happy birthday, love of my life. Top drawer of my dresser for your pressie. Will ring later. Enjoy your trip to Birmingham.

Nestling amongst his socks are two envelopes. In one, there is a card. It's a beach scene. Blue sky and a glittering sea. There are two sets of footprints, side by side on icing-sugar sand. Inside he has written: *Perhaps we will get around to having our dream holiday before you reach fifty-three?* It's a standing joke between us. We never seem to be able to find the time to get away now. Not unless you count the odd couple of weekend breaks in Wales or Scotland. The other envelope contains theatre tickets for tomorrow night. I'm being spoiled. A pre-theatre meal followed by a production of one of my favourite plays, *The Tempest*, at the RSC in Stratford on Avon.

Late morning, I drive into the city centre and leave my car at the station car park. It's a short train journey into Birmingham, a little over half an hour. I arrive, and soon I am making my way through the milling crowds at New Street Station. I have time to kill before I meet Alice, and I wander up to Central Arcade to do some window-shopping. It's raining when I exit the building, and I'm glad of my waterproof jacket and fold-up umbrella.

Alice has sent the directions to my phone. I use the sweeping curves of the titanium-clad John Lewis store to orientate before I set off in what I hope is the right direction. I will never hear the end of it from her if I manage to get lost.

The bistro is down a narrow, brick-lined street and is located in a converted warehouse. From the outside it looks austere, with its red-brick facade and large windows clad in iron grilles. Inside, the decor is industrial chic with an unconventional layout. Instead of tables there are long reclaimed wood trestles lit from overhead by metal pendant lights. They cast soft, glowing pools of light over the assembled diners. There's a low hum of conversation, but I'm feeling too self-conscious to sit at one of the tables by myself. Ordering a drink, I sink instead into a low leather sofa and wait for Alice.

Arriving with a flourish, she stamps her feet on a

mat inside the door and runs her fingers through her damp hair. She waves at me and takes off her coat, gives it a shake and hangs it up on a wooden stand in the corner of the room. I hand her my wet coat, which has been draped over the back of the sofa, and she places it next to hers.

She gives me a peck on the cheek and goes off in search of menus. Returning a few minutes later, she has a young waiter in tow. He is carrying a small chalkboard and easel on which the dishes of the day are written. The two are flirting outrageously, and it reminds me of just how little I know about my daughter's private life.

We are taken through an archway into a book-lined room with half a dozen or so tables. Each has its own candle set in a wrought-iron holder.

'Can I get you lovely ladies some drinks?'

'A lime soda for me, and Mum will have a glass of wine. It's her birthday. Oh, and could we have a jug of iced water with the meal, please?'

The waiter winks at me, and a flush rises in my cheeks. He wishes me a happy birthday, then bows theatrically before departing.

'This is great, Alice. I was trying to get my head around sitting at that refectory table like a student, but this is perfect.'

'It's got a really nice atmosphere. Jess and I sometimes come at the weekend for breakfast. They do the best poached eggs with spinach and avocado.'

'Looks to me as if it's worth coming here just for that waiter,' I say.

'Oh, Mum.' Alice rolls her eyes in exasperation. 'He's gay, for goodness' sake. Can't you tell?'

'Ah well, never mind,' I say. 'He is good-looking, though.'

We order a sharing platter, and as we wait for it to

arrive, Alice takes a card and a package from the bottom of her bag.

'This is from me and Flynn. I hope you like it.'

They have both signed the card. Alice's writing is small and compact; Flynn's messy and flowing. *No graphologist required to assess their individual personalities,* I think to myself.

The package contains a silk scarf with a watercolour design of pink peony flowers on a blue background.

'It's gorgeous, Alice. My favourite colour, and my favourite flowers too. I love it,' I say, knotting the soft, shiny fabric around my neck.

The waiter arrives with our food, and we spend a companionable hour staying firmly on neutral ground and avoiding any subject that might spark friction. Alice has been selected for team management training at work and seems happier in herself. I want to ask if she is seeing anyone, but avoid the question, conscious that her private life is generally off limits.

'What about you, Mum?' she says. 'I know you have had a rotten time recently, but keeping busy will help. Are you doing lots of things that you enjoy? It must be great, in some ways, to have so much free time on your hands.'

It's a typical tactless remark from Alice. Before I get the chance to respond, the waiter arrives to clear our plates. I am saved, first from making a snippy comment, which could put a dampener on things, and second from having to muddle through a fabricated explanation of my recent activities.

The waiter returns, balancing a plate with two slices of cheesecake, one of which has a lighted sparkler at its centre.

'For the birthday girl,' he says with a puckish grin. 'On the house.'

. . .

ALICE LOOKS AT HER WATCH. 'I've managed to blag an extra half hour, but I will have to go soon. It's been really nice, Mum. We'll have to do this more often.'

After consuming the cheesecakes and a quick cup of coffee each, we collect our coats and step out onto the rain-slicked pavement. We say our goodbyes, and Alice hurries off back to work while I take a leisurely stroll to the train station. Although it has stopped raining, banks of heavy, grey cloud hang low in the sky, promising further showers before long.

Reaching the station, I'm glad to get back inside where it is warm and dry. The departure board is showing delays due to the weather. There's flooding on the line back to Derby. With more than an hour to wait, I find a coffee shop and text Alice to thank her for lunch. Flynn has sent a birthday GIF of a bunch of flowers from his phone, and I send him a return message, thanking him for his contribution to my birthday present. Laurie has also left a message to say the weather is causing traffic backlogs, and he expects to be delayed getting home this evening.

The coffee is strong and hot, just how I like it. From my seat in the window of the café, I can people-watch to my heart's content. Laurie and the kids find it an odd pastime and rib me gently about my 'nosiness', but it reminds me of happy times shared with Mum. We both enjoyed speculating on the lives of others. As a child, I treated it as a game and loved the intrigue associated with building a complex web of characters and adding to their daily activities. Complete strangers were imbued with fanciful identities and magical powers, long before Harry Potter and his friends were committed to print.

'See that man, Fran? The one with the bald head and trench coat? He's a spy, and his superpowers are advanced lip-reading and hyper-hearing. Quick, lower your voice and turn away. We don't want him to know we are talking about him.'

'No, no,' I would protest. 'He's really from another planet, and he's wearing a human suit. He has a transceiver in his skull to communicate with his friends. We will have to be careful. There are aliens like him everywhere.'

Mum would laugh indulgently, knowing a combination of a creative imagination and too many episodes of *Dr Who* gave me the advantage in the fantasy stakes. As I got older, our joint musings gained a higher level of sophistication. Our speculations would revolve around who might be having an affair, or whether the homeless man raiding the bins was really a multimillionaire who retired to his mansion at the end of the day.

I find myself smiling at the memory and thinking just how much I miss Mum's company. Glancing out of the window, I catch a glimpse of a figure passing by. It's a teenager. A boy. He is wearing a dark tracksuit top with the hood pulled up and a rucksack slung over his shoulder. There's something in the way he's walking, head down and shoulders hunched, that looks familiar.

It takes a few seconds before it dawns on me.

The boy is Gabe Ingram.

28

I'm not sure just what it is that is propelling me out of my seat to set off in pursuit, but I grab my coat and bag and follow Gabe's retreating back. He doesn't seem to be in much of a hurry. Slowing my pace, I manage to keep far enough back to avoid catching him up. I follow him out of the concourse, taking a different exit to the one I used previously. Even though the streets are less crowded, there are enough people around to make my presence less conspicuous.

We pass the iconic Selfridges store, its aluminium discs glinting in the watery, afternoon sun, and head towards Digbeth, a short walk away. It's been a few years since I was here. Alice and Flynn were teenagers when I brought them to nearby Deritend to see a graffiti art exhibition at the Custard Factory during the school holidays. Then, the whole district was undergoing regeneration. Today, it is buzzing with trendy eateries and expensive warehouse conversions. The flats are out of Alice's price bracket, either to rent or buy, but she loves the vibe here, and her social life at weekends revolves around the vibrant nightlife.

Deep in thought, I almost lose sight of Gabe. He has turned down a long stretch of road lined with cafés and restaurants. His speed has increased, and I have to hurry to catch up. Reaching the main thoroughfare, he crosses the road, then turns down a shabby street with boarded-up shops. It's a dead end, blocked by concrete bollards to prevent vehicle access. I don't want to be seen and duck into a disused shop doorway. From my vantage point, I can see beyond the bollards into a small industrial estate.

I watch as Gabe saunters towards a one-story building, its frontage almost completely taken up by a wide roller shutter. To one side, there is a steel door spray-painted in graffiti. The whole location has a run-down feel, and many of the units appear to be unoccupied. Somewhere close by I can hear the insistent clang of a hammer hitting a metallic surface, and I feel a sense of relief that there is someone around.

Gabe leans with his back against the door as though waiting for someone. His head is down, and he is fiddling with his phone. I can just make out a pair of earbuds dangling from his ears. Engrossed in whatever he is listening to, he doesn't look up as, with a swish of tyres, a black SUV sweeps around the corner. When he does notice, he pulls out his headphones, jams his phone into his pocket, and begins to walk at speed back in the direction he came from.

I push myself further into the recess of the doorway and wait for him to pass me. He doesn't appear, but there are the sounds of a scuffle and raised voices. Peering around the corner, I see one of the men has got out of the vehicle and is holding Gabe by the arm. The rear car door is open, and he is trying to force him onto the back seat. It crosses my mind that they might be police, but something doesn't feel right. Gabe is pleading with the man and sounds close to tears. Even though the words are muffled, I can tell he's in distress. He's struggling to escape and is begging the man to leave him alone.

In those few seconds, the memory of Tyler and his mute beseeching causes a wave of anger to rise within me. Without thinking of the consequences, I run in the direction of the voices, shouting at the top of my lungs like a banshee. I swing my bag in the man's direction, and there is a satisfying *thud* as it engages with his shaved head. He stumbles forwards, and as he does so, he lets go of Gabe's arm. With his head bent, I can see a familiar inked outline on the back of the man's neck. The clock face without hands.

The man looks up, and my stomach lurches. Whatever tricks my memory might have played up to this point, there can be no denying its veracity now. Standing in front of me is one of the men responsible for Tyler's death.

I hear a click as the catch on the driver's door is released. I don't want to wait around to see if I recognise the other man. With Gabe in shock and rooted to the spot, I shake him with all the force I can muster, then pull him roughly by the arm.

'Run!' I bellow in his ear.

AFTER THE INITIAL burst of adrenaline has worn off, I curse the fact that I've allowed myself to become so unfit. My breath is coming in short, ragged gasps, and my lungs feel as though they are about to explode. Gabe is lagging behind, and I'm struggling to find the energy to pull him along too. Reaching the busy main road, it's a relief to find the pavement crowded with pedestrians.

It's drizzling again, and dodging open umbrellas and sprays of water from passing cars, I slow to a walking pace. The jarring sound of a car horn startles me, and my nerves jangle in response. I half expect the SUV to come screeching to a halt alongside, and arms to reach out and pull us both inside. Still dragging Gabe, I dart across the pelican crossing as the lights turn green, much to the annoyance of waiting drivers, who have to pause to let us cross.

We reach the railway station, and I push Gabe up the steps ahead of me. The earlier crush has cleared, and I'm hoping the trains are running on time again. To my relief and Gabe's obvious discomfort, there are a couple of Transport Police officers posted close to the ticket barriers. I keep them in my line of vision while I scan the faces of passing travellers.

The departures board is showing the earlier train to Willington is running almost an hour late, but that's worked out in our favour. It now means it will be leaving in five minutes.

'Have you got your ticket, Gabe? The train is leaving soon.'

Gabe's face is pale, and his eyes are downcast. He doesn't respond, and I pull him towards me by the sleeve of his tracksuit.

'We have to go now, or we will miss the train.'

'I can't. I have to go back.'

'What do you mean, go back?' I say sharply. 'You can't go back. We're getting the train. No arguments.'

We board with seconds to spare. The compartment is crowded and, with no chance of getting a seat, we stand, holding onto the backs of seats for support. Gabe is sulky and ignores my attempts at conversation. He puts in his earbuds and selects some music to stream through his phone. The journey home is punctuated by the tinny vibration coming through his phone speakers. Some of the other passengers find this irritating. I know this, because they look in my direction and tut their displeasure.

Occasionally, I glance over at Gabe. His face has lost its pallor, and his cheeks are pink from the heat of the compartment. Close up, his skin is unblemished with no signs of the pimples that plagued Flynn when he was around the same age. Mel is correct about her boys. His similarity to Tyler is evident, but there are differences. Tyler had thick dark hair and brown eyes. Gabe's hair is finer and a shade lighter, and although his eyes are also dark, they are an unusual shade of slate grey. It's possible that in a couple of years, Gabe will become stocky and muscular like his brother. For now, an adolescent growth spurt has turned him into a lanky beanpole with rangy, uncoordinated limbs. It's such an awkward age, and I'm struck by how vulnerable he looks despite the outward show of bravado. I wish it were in my power to give him back a blameless boyhood. Whatever is taking him up to Birmingham cannot be innocent, if this afternoon's incident is anything to go by.

The train judders to a halt at Willington station, and Gabe pushes through the throng of standing passengers to get to the doors. I follow, trying to keep pace with his retreating back. We go down the stairs, through the subway and emerge into the gloom of late afternoon. Gabe, still a few paces ahead of me, turns when he realises I am following him.

'I'm okay. You can go now,' he says, looking down and scuffing his trainers on the pavement. 'Oh, and thanks.'

The begrudging acknowledgement makes me smile. I don't want him to think I'm laughing at him, and I turn my head to prevent him reading my expression.

'No chance, Gabe,' I say, grabbing him by the shoulder before he walks off. 'I want to take you home and make sure you're safe. It's important I talk to your mum about what happened.'

He screws up his face, then shrugs his shoulders in resignation.

'She's going to fucking kill me,' he mutters under his breath.

29

G abe unlocks the front door with his key, removes his trainers and throws his bag down in the hall. He doesn't invite me in, and I hesitate on the threshold, conscious I am an unwanted guest. For a split second, it crosses my mind that if Mel's not at home, I don't have to have a conversation with her about what happened this afternoon. I can go home, pour myself a glass of Prosecco and unwind by watching some crap TV until Laurie returns. Looking at my watch, I see it is just after 5 p.m. It seems an age away from when I was sitting having lunch with Alice.

My back and feet ache from walking, and my calf muscles are throbbing, stretched from the short burst of running. I will have to ring Laurie and let him know I'm getting back later than I said, although weather conditions countrywide mean his journey is likely to take longer than normal. At least it will give me time to make some sort of sense of the episode with Gabe. And there is the knotty problem of how to get my car, which is still parked at Derby station.

From inside the house, I hear the low murmur of voices, then growls followed by loud barking.

'Kai, Dexter. Heel!'

Mel appears, holding the dogs on either side of her by their collars. They lunge towards me, still barking. She pulls them back, nodding for me to follow her into the lounge.

From where I'm sitting, I can hear the rattling of crockery and slamming of doors coming from the direction of the kitchen.

'Gabe, take these dogs for a walk while I talk to Fran.'

His head appears around the door. 'But I'm starving. Can't I have something to eat first?'

Mel fixes him with a look that shuts down any argument, and he shuffles off, calling for the dogs to follow.

'What's all this about?' Mel says. 'Gabe isn't making much sense. What were you doing in Birmingham, and what the hell were you doing following my son?'

Gone is the exposed and vulnerable Mel of my last visit. Her expression is masking a controlled anger, if the tightness around her mouth and the throbbing veins in her neck are anything to go by. Shifting in my seat to ease the discomfort in my back, I feel a sudden flash of annoyance.

'Do you know what, Mel? I have gone to a great deal of trouble in pursuit of saving your son's ass and getting him back here in one piece. After the afternoon I've had, the last thing I need is a grilling from you. I think the least you can do is offer me a drink.'

Without a word, she gets up and goes to the kitchen, returning a few minutes later with a large mug of tea, which she hands to me. I sip the contents, glad of the warming liquid even though it's too weak and milky for my taste.

Exhaustion is creeping up on me. Sitting back in the chair, fingers wrapped around the mug, I wish I could stretch out on Mel's sofa and rest for a while. One thing's for certain, I've decided I won't be leaving here until I get some sort of explanation from *her* as to exactly what is going on.

She sits impassively as I tell her why I was in Birmingham and give her my account of what happened from when I first saw Gabe at New Street. I conclude with a sarcastic *'Great way to spend my birthday'*, and she cracks a weak smile in response.

I decide to go for the blunt approach.

'The thing is, Mel, it doesn't take much of a leap of imagination to work out what Gabe was doing there. I'm not stupid. He was collecting drugs, wasn't he?'

She looks off into the distance, then shrugs her shoulders and nods in agreement. I'm grateful she hasn't decided to play games. She could have denied everything; then what would I have done?

'Correct me if I'm wrong. My guess would be that you are involved in dealing drugs. You are sending the kids to collect, based on the assumption that if they are caught, they will be treated more leniently. Yes?'

'It's not that simple, but by and large, yes.'

'What I don't understand is why Tyler was killed, and in such a horrible way? Surely it's possible to kill someone by less dramatic means and get rid of the body. Or am I missing something? Unless...'

I remember what Mel said about Tyler being a sacrifice.

'Was Tyler killed as a warning ? Has there been some sort of double-cross? I've read about people who use drugs having their homes taken over by dealers. Cuckooing, they call it. Are you being cuckooed?'

She doesn't look like a user, but appearances can be

deceptive. A drinker, yes, but a crack or heroin user? I just can't see it.

Mel sighs, as though exasperated by the volley of questions. She looks across at me, irritation etched across her face.

'Ooh, quite the little detective, aren't we? We *have* done our homework,' she says.

It's a sarcastic retort, and her displeasure with me is making her Birmingham accent more pronounced.

'As there's no point in denying it, I'm going to come clean with you, Fran. The truth is I run my own deal line, if you know what that is, but let's get this clear: I'm not a user, and I'm not being cuckooed. I'm the one in charge, and what I say goes. It's a way of making money. Quite a bit of money, actually. It's kept a roof over our heads for the last few years. It's not cheap bringing up two growing boys on your own, you know.'

'I know, Mel, but hard drugs? There are better ways of making money.'

'And what would you know about it?' She sneers. 'With your lovely life and your perfect husband and kids.'

Of course, nothing could be further from the truth, but I'm queasy about defending myself if it means sharing personal details with her.

I can see she is agitated, and I know I have to calm the situation if I'm to keep her on side.

'I'm sorry,' I say. 'I know it must be difficult after all you've been through. It was just so appalling and inhumane what they did to Tyler. Those men are wicked. And what about Gabe? Why are they after him? Jesus Christ, Mel, what if they do the same thing to Gabe?'

She studies her manicured fingernails. 'They won't,' she says. 'I've seen to it.'

'How? They are dangerous; they have proved that. I

have no idea what measures you have taken to sort it out, but why the hell would you trust them?'

She looks across at me and smiles. 'Honour among thieves?'

'Come on,' I say. 'That's beneath you. It's certainly no laughing matter.'

'No, you're right. It's too serious to joke about. Despite what you think of me, I have dealt with the situation to everyone's satisfaction.'

It's odd. She seems so unmoved and matter-of-fact. We could be having a conversation about something innocuous, like selling party plan. When we first met, she told me she sold make-up, and I do wonder if that's a convenient cover for her criminal activities.

'I'm curious,' I say. 'What are you going to do to protect Gabe?'

Mel doesn't reply immediately, leaving an uncomfortable silence stretching out between us. A few minutes pass, and she takes a deep breath, then lets it out slowly.

'I suppose you might as well hear the whole story,' she says, drawing the words out precisely as though she's reading from a script. 'Then you will understand.'

She gets herself comfortable in her chair, and I wonder how long it's going to take.

'So this is how it works,' she says. 'My shipments are brought into Birmingham by an acquaintance of mine. He's a lorry driver. He comes through Rotterdam on a regular basis. The lorries are sealed, and checks are random. Resources at the port are mostly directed at finding large consignments of drugs and illegal immigrants. I buy heroin and ready-prepared wraps of crack cocaine from my Dutch suppliers. The big boys, the gangs running lines out of the big cities, have larger consignments coming in, and also prepare their own crack in home-based factories. That way, there's more profit for them. My operation is small scale, so I'm not much competition. Until recently, they tended to leave me alone. Then, last year, members of a gang from London arrived on the scene. They had been sent by the man at the top. He wants to spread out and gain control of rural areas in the region. Once they reported back to him, he sent his own runners and started to muscle in on my customers, giving them free samples and under-cutting my prices.'

She pauses and looks up at the photograph over the fireplace before continuing.

'My boy Tyler was furious. I told him to keep away, but he wouldn't listen. He could be hot-headed and stubborn. There was a bit of argy-bargy, and one of their lads pulled a knife. Tyler got angry and ran off with the lad's rucksack. Apparently, there was over £2000 in cash and a stash of drugs inside. Tyler knew having the money and drugs in his possession would be bad news if the gang got hold of him. He tried to find the boy to return the bag, but he was picked up before he found him. The way he was killed was a warning to anyone who might think it's a good idea to rip them off.'

'So that's what you meant by saying he was a sacrifice,' I say. 'But what about today? Why did those men try to take Gabe?'

'They don't want Gabe, they want me. Or, to be precise, what I have to offer. My deal line is already well established with hundreds of customer numbers. Taking over my operation will give them a foothold in the area and allow them to expand. Spooking Gabe was a way of leaning on me to get what they want, and it's worked. I am handing over my line to them. After what happened to Tyler, I've had enough. I want out.'

I have nothing to say in response, useful or otherwise. There's just too much to take in. Mel seems unconcerned by my lack of reaction. We sit for a while in silence until the click of the back door and the tip-tap of claws on the kitchen floor indicate Gabe is back with the dogs.

'I really must go,' I say. 'Do you have a number for a taxi, Mel? I got the train from Derby this morning, and my car is at the station.'

'I'll drive you. It's the least I can do after you helped Gabe.'

Too tired to protest, I follow her to her car. I don't see Gabe as I'm leaving. I can't say I blame him. He's probably had enough of me for one day.

In the car, neither of us is up for talking, and there's an awkward atmosphere between us.

Mel puts the radio on, and we listen to Rock Classics until we arrive at the station. She pulls the car into a vacant bay opposite the entrance.

'Thanks for the lift,' I say. 'I'll see you at the funeral.'

She nods, then reaches for my arm as I'm starting to get out of the car.

'If you're thinking about going to the police, I wouldn't, Fran. What they have been doing up to now is nothing compared to what they are capable of.'

'I understand what you're saying,' I say. 'But I'm not going to withdraw my witness statement. They have to be put out of action and punished for what they have done.'

'Look,' she says forcefully, her nails digging into my arm. 'I can get them to back off, but you have to keep what I've told you today to yourself. You've seen how ruthless they can be. Do you really want a life spent in witness protection? Because that will be your only option if you mention any of this to the police. From now on, not another word. Understand?'

I nod, and she lets go, slamming the door behind me as I stumble out into the night air.

I stand on the pavement, shaking, and not from cold.

I watch as her car headlights recede into the darkness.

30

I need to stop myself from unravelling. I feel as though I'm disappearing down a rabbit hole. It's all become too complicated. I've been foolish and naive and placed myself in even greater danger, that's become obvious. Unless I comply and avoid talking to the police, it could be me swinging from a tree like Tyler, or something equally horrible. I'm in a double bind; damned if I do, damned if I don't. It's a frightening position to be in, and I have no one to blame but myself. What started as an interest in Mel and a genuine desire to get to the bottom of what happened to Tyler has become a tangled web of labyrinthine proportions.

Sal was right. Mel is running a County Line, and I find it hard to believe she is going to take up a legitimate career after getting used to the lifestyle she has acquired on the back of dealing. She wants to portray herself as some sort of low-level entrepreneur, acting in the best interest of her family, but she is a criminal, not a victim. Now I'm faced with two stark choices. Either I place my trust in what Mel has said and rely on her being able to get the dealers to back off, or I tell the police the whole story and risk whatever might be unleashed as a consequence.

When I was at work, I had a reputation for honesty and fairness. Seen as upright – on occasion, even uptight. Those who knew me well would be shocked, now, if they knew what I have got myself into. Ordinarily, I like to think of myself as someone who would do the right thing, but this situation is riddled with grey areas. And it's not just me I have to worry about. Laurie and the kids are also part of the equation. The thought of anything happening to them is too awful to contemplate. I have to find a way of disentangling myself from the predicament I have placed myself in. And soon. Before it gets out of hand.

Flynn rings to wish me a happy birthday. It's good to talk to him, especially as he sounds so upbeat and enthusiastic. He tells me about his date the previous evening with Eloise while I tell him about lunch with Alice.

'Come and visit soon,' I tell him. 'And bring Eloise.'

I'm bone-weary and flaked out on the sofa with Buddy by the time Laurie gets back. He is tired and grumpy after being stuck in traffic on the M1 for hours.

'Eventful day?' he says.

I'm momentarily thrown by his question until it clicks. He's talking about my trip to Birmingham to see Alice.

'It was,' I say. 'Alice is looking well, and she was on good form. She's enjoying her training course, and the extra responsibility at work seems to be suiting her. She and Flynn got me a lovely silk scarf for my birthday, though it will have been Alice who chose it. She has a good eye for colour, and it's a perfect match for my blue dress.'

I desperately want to be able to talk to Laurie about

more consequential matters. Ask his advice about whether or not I should go to the police. I'm almost sure I know what his response will be. That is, after I have scraped him off the ceiling when he realises the depths of my stupidity. The whole convoluted mess has left me in a state of confusion. I'm starting to feel even more scared and isolated.

I heat up some food and get a cold bottle of beer from the fridge and hand it to Laurie.

'You not having a drink?'

'Nah,' I say. 'It's been a long day. I'm knackered, and I've got a headache coming on. I think I'll turn in early and read for a while.'

'Not a great end to your birthday,' he says, taking the plates and glasses to the kitchen. 'Tomorrow will be better. You haven't forgotten we're going to the theatre, have you?'

A trip to Stratford on Avon is the last thing on my mind, even if it is meant to be a birthday treat, but I manage a weak smile.

'No, I haven't forgotten. I'm really looking forward to it.'

The events of today have pushed going to the theatre to the back of my mind. I'm not exactly fizzing with excitement at the thought of over an hour's drive each way. What I am hoping, however, is that the evening will be a distraction. A breathing space where I don't have to worry about the mess I find myself in.

Tucked up in bed, having done the nightly ritual of checking doors and windows, I attempt to get to grips with another book borrowed from Jenny. I've had it for months, and so far I've only read three chapters. I try to concentrate, attempting to override the intrusive thoughts that keep bubbling unbidden to the surface, forcing me to attend to them. The book is not especially

well written, and I keep finding irritating errors that
jump off the page. To be fair, the author is not a professional writer, and I try to be charitable given the subject
matter. It's an account written by a father left to bring
up his young daughter following the death of his wife
from cancer.

It's a harrowing read and not the best subject matter
under the circumstances. The description of the daughter's reaction to her mother's death causes a lump to
form in my throat and tears to prickle at the corners of
my eyes. The book conveys well the aftermath of a
death as a time of heightened emotions and ambiva-
lence. How is it possible the author writes, to feel relief
and a sense of lightness, as though a weight has been
lifted, when you have just lost the person you loved
most in the world?

I can only hazard a guess as to how I might cope if
anything happened to Laurie or the kids. Not well, if the
truth be known. I do, however, wonder what it would
be like for them if something awful happened to me. I'm
sure Laurie would be fine. After he got over the initial
shock and had dealt with my estate, he would be a free
agent.

After Mum died, we made our wills. Apart from
some personal gifts to the kids, everything goes to him
anyway. Once a decent period of mourning has elapsed,
I'm sure he will find someone else, maybe a younger
woman. One still able to have children. He has time for
a new relationship, a new life. Alice and Flynn will be
okay, too, once their initial sadness has passed. Having a
stepmum and possibly younger brothers and sisters will
take some getting used to, but they have their own lives.
It won't be long before they have homes and families of
their own. I suppress a sob at the thought of not being
here to see the events of their lives unfold without me.

Oh, just stop it, you silly woman, I chastise myself, hardly believing how mawkish and self-absorbed I'm being. It's not like me, but then who am I? I don't think I know anymore.

Pull yourself together. It's not the first time I've said these words to myself over the last few weeks, and I doubt it will be the last.

My sleep is disturbed. Dreams running like water, one into the other, full of longing and loss. Clearest is the one I awake from, shaking myself free from the snare of sleep. There had initially been fear, poised as I was at the edge of a precipice, struggling desperately to keep my footing. Arms encircle and support me, then lose their grip, leaving me to plummet earthwards. I don't crash to the rocks below. Instead, I sprout wings, as soft and white as swan's down, and float gently to the bottom.

I'm not superstitious. Assigning meaning to dreams is, in my opinion, as nonsensical as voodoo. It's odd, though. The dream has left me with a residual feeling of optimism and a sense of how glad I am to be alive. *I want to be the one who grows old with Laurie. I* want to be there for my children and grandchildren. I don't want some youthful facsimile taking my place in this imaginary future I have conjured up.

I resolve to do everything in my power to try to keep us all safe.

Whatever that may take.

31

I have misplaced my scarf. I'm wearing my peacock blue wool dress to go to the theatre. It's my favourite, and I've been looking forward to pairing it with the scarf from Alice and Flynn. The scarf, however, is nowhere to be found. My newfound faith in the future dissipates, replaced by exasperation. How the hell could I have been so careless? I've looked in every part of the house, searched the car and its surrounds, and there is no sign of it anywhere.

'You haven't seen the scarf the kids got for me, have you?'

Laurie looks at me and gives me a wry smile. 'Don't tell me you've lost it already? Honestly, Fran, you only had it five minutes. Alice will have a fit!'

'I know,' I say. 'I'll have to ring around the train stations to see if anyone has handed it into lost property. I'm bloody well annoyed with myself, but it was quite a day. It's hardly surprising I got somewhat careless.'

'Mmm. Swanning about and having lunch with your daughter. Very arduous...'

I bite my lip before I say something in anger that

gives me away, and stomp off upstairs to find an alternative. Of course, he has no idea what transpired after I left Alice. I know it's unreasonable to expect a different response from him. Still, the unfairness grates.

I have a drawerful of accessories and scarves of every size and colour, and I still can't find one that matches. Instead, I pull out a pendant made of sea glass that belonged to Mum. The stone is a deep cornflower blue, set in a silver filigree locket. Mum bought it on holiday in Northumberland during a week of unseasonably warm weather. The necklace always reminded her of the sea, which throughout her stay had been the deepest shade of blue.

Laurie, shouting from the bottom of the stairs, interrupts my musings, and I grab a white pashmina as protection against the evening chill.

'You need to get a wriggle on, Fran. We have to leave, or we'll be late.'

WE EAT at the rooftop restaurant with the River Avon flowing alongside, its surface illuminated by a high, bright moon. The reflections from the lights glitter in the darker water on the opposite bank. We have been seated next to a window, and I can feel the chilly night air through the glass. I'm glad of the pashmina I brought with me, and pull it around my shoulders to ward off the chill.

'Do you remember our cheesy beans?' Laurie says, feeding me a forkful of our shared dessert, a tower of mini profiteroles. .

I give him a wistful smile. 'How on earth can I forget? They were all we could afford when the money started to run out at the end of the week. I think the highlight was when you persuaded the woman on the deli counter to sell you a heel of parmesan for 5p. Baked beans with grated parmesan, served with a sprig of parsley, became your signature dish. You called it Posh Beans.'

'And look at us now,' he says. 'We've come a long way since then. We could have only dreamed of a meal in a smart restaurant followed by going to see a play in a building as beautiful as this. In those days, we were more than happy with a Chinese takeaway and a bottle of cheap plonk.'

He raises his glass in my direction. 'Happy birthday, Fran. Here's to many more to come.'

The alcohol is making me dewy-eyed, and I reach for his hand. 'Thank you,' I say. 'Not just for this, for everything. I want you to know I love you. I know I don't say it enough.'

Laurie gives me one of his 'aw shucks' looks, but I can tell he's pleased. 'And I love you, too. It's been a roller-coaster ride, and I'm not just talking about the last couple of weeks. We're a good team, you and I. When we pull together, we can overcome anything.'

Ay, there's the rub, to quote the Bard. Pulling together requires there to be a bond of trust between us, and trust is something that's in short supply on my part.

I'm saved from my musings by the first bell, which rings to summon us to our seats. Laurie has chosen well. We are in the stalls and have a good view of the stage without being too close. It's a mesmerising production, set in the present day on a tropical island. The sensation of being at the centre of a wild storm during the shipwreck scene is unsettling. The experience feels so real.

It doesn't escape my notice that some of the themes covered in the play are not too far removed from what is going on in my world. If I'm not mistaken, love, betrayal, forgiveness, and repentance all have their part to play in the drama that is my life.

'Ready to go and face the real world?' Laurie says as the lights come on following the final curtain call.

My heart performs a somersault in my chest. He doesn't know how loaded with connotation that question is.

'Yes,' I say. 'As ready as I'll ever be.'

32

The loss of my scarf is maddening. I have looked in every conceivable place, and it's nowhere to be found. Nothing fitting its description has been handed in at left luggage at either of the train stations. I can only conclude that someone has taken a shine to it, or I didn't leave it on the train. The train station staff I speak to suggest I ring again in a few days. One tells me it can take days or even weeks for lost items to show up. The more I think about it, the more sure I am I had it when I got to Mel's house. Is it possible I left it there? The other alternative is that it could have slid from around my neck when I was getting out of her car. Surely she would have let me know if either had been the case? Then again, the celebrant was visiting over the weekend to talk about the funeral. With all that going on, it could easily have slipped her mind.

Rather than ring her, I send a text message with a brief description of the scarf.

Just wondering if I left it at your house or in your car? It was a birthday present from my kids. They will never forgive me if I've lost it. I insert a smiley face. I'm hoping the tone conveys urgency without sounding too heavy-handed.

To my consternation, I don't hear anything from Mel as the week goes on, not even an acknowledgement of my text. Conscious the day of the funeral is fast approaching, I need a distraction, as I'm filled with dread at the prospect of attending. It's been months since the house had a good clean, and it's just the sort of task that dulls the thinking processes if you throw yourself into it. Systematically, I go from room to room, vacuuming, dusting, polishing and cleaning the inside of the windows until the house is gleaming in almost show-home condition. That is if you ignore the odd chip in the paintwork and a dangling cobweb, unreachable at the top of the stairwell.

The sense of satisfaction I feel at my efforts in creating order is short-lived. Still at a loose end, I try ringing Sal. The phone rings out, and I leave a message to say I will try again later. After a few minutes, my phone buzzes, and I pick up to hear Sal on the other end.

'Fran? Hello, it's Sal here. We were walking to the car when you rang, and I couldn't get into my bag quick enough to get my phone before it rang off. How are you?'

'I'm fine. Are you and Al keeping well?'

'We are. We've been out for lunch at the marina at Willington with friends.' Her voice fades, then disappears, before returning at full strength in my ear. 'Hello, hello, can you hear me? I seem to be losing the signal.'

To save my ears, I place the phone on the worktop in front of me and put it on speakerphone. I had thought about making arrangements to go and see them, but it occurs to me that they will be passing close by on their way home.

'Sal, do you think you could detour here? I have something to tell you, and I don't really want to do it over the phone.'

There is crackling in the background and the sound of muffled voices; then Sal comes back on the line. 'Send us your address and postcode for the satnav. We are on our way.'

I'm wearing one of Laurie's old shirts and a pair of jogging bottoms. There's not much point in running around trying to make myself look presentable for their arrival; there isn't time. Instead, I bundle away the cleaning products lined up by the sink, rinse my hands and face, and run a comb through my unwashed hair. Finding one of Alice's old scrunchies lurking at the back of one of the kitchen drawers, I scrape my untidy locks back into a tight ponytail. The kettle is just coming to the boil when, with a warning woof, Buddy runs to the door just as their car kicks up a section of loose gravel on the drive, heralding their arrival.

'You found us, then,' I say, gripping Buddy by his collar before he bowls them over in his enthusiasm at having visitors.

Al raises his eyebrows and frowns. 'Just about. I think Sal needs a visit to Specsavers. She transposed the letters in your postcode. It's a good job I noticed, or we would have ended up going round in circles.'

Sal grins and shrugs her shoulders. 'Ah well, we're here now. It's lovely to see you, Fran, and Buddy too. He looks a lot better than when we last saw him.' She bends down to scratch behind his ears and is rewarded with a lick to her face.

'You have a lovely home, and the garden is so secluded.'

We have come into the kitchen, and she is peering through the glass door leading out to the back garden.

'Does that gate lead into the woods? It must be so convenient for walks.'

I follow her gaze, looking out over our undulating stretch of lawn, still carpeted with leaf fall. I try to put myself in the shoes of someone unfamiliar with the broad swathe of woodland that now seems to me so menacing. Some of the trees are almost bare after the last high winds. Others, like the ancient oaks, still hold onto the last remnants of their foliage, like elderly men huddled into tweed jackets.

'I used to love the walks. It's just not the same since...!'

'Oh, of course not. Forgive me, I'd forgotten. Me and my big mouth.'

Sal looks downcast, and Al moves to change the subject, rescuing her from further embarrassment.

'I'll have a look at that area you were thinking of turning over to a wildflower meadow before we go. I think I spy a great spot from here.'

We sit in the lounge and have tea and stale digestive biscuits I found at the back of the cupboard. Buddy has taken a shine to Al and keeps dropping his ball at his feet in the hope of a game.

'I could take him for a walk if you two want a chat. I'm not very good at sitting for any length of time, and Sal can fill me in on what's gone on.'

'Really, Al,' Sal says with disdain. 'It wouldn't hurt you to stay and listen to what Fran has to say. She will think you have no manners.'

'Actually, if you don't mind walking him, you will be doing me a good turn. Saves me going out later in the dark,' I say. 'Sal can tell you everything, and if you don't mind a chat over the phone, I could ring you. It would be good to hear your opinion on what I have to report.'

Al seems pleased to be let off the hook, and he sets

off with Buddy, armed with a tennis ball and poo bags in the direction of the park.

'Honestly, that man. He can't relax. He's not happy unless he's busy. He's always been the same. Not going to alter now, is he? Not at his age.' Sal says this in mock annoyance although there's a glint in her eye.

'You adore him, Sal,' I say. 'You know you would be lost without him.'

'You're right, of course. We've been married a long time and gone through so much together. It would be like losing a limb if anything happened to him, and I know he feels the same about me. Anyway, enough about us. You said there was something you wanted to tell me. Is it about that nasty piece of work Mel Ingram?'

I take a breath in through my nose, releasing it slowly to steady my nerves before replying. 'You were spot on, you know. About Mel. She is involved in the drugs trade. She has a phone full of users' numbers, wanting to buy drugs in the area. It's called a County Line. Tyler was caught up in it, too, which is how he got himself murdered.'

I expect Sal to say *I told you so*, or words to that effect, but she doesn't. Instead, she drains the last dregs of her tea and places the cup on the table in front of her.

'Shall I make a fresh pot?'

She shakes her head. 'No,' she says quietly. 'You're worried, I can tell. Whatever has happened, you need to get it off your chest.'

She takes a cushion, plumps it and places it at her back. 'I'm all ears.'

Sal lets me talk without interruption. I tell her of the difficult early years Mel spent within the Traveller community, of her estrangement from that way of life and ultimately from her family. How she and Joel created a home and family of their own and built up a successful business before it all fell apart and she was left to bring up her children alone. I recount what happened with Gabe in Birmingham and Mel's admission of her and her boys' involvement in the drug trade.

'I've achieved what I set out to do; I've found out what happened to Tyler,' I say. 'But it's gone beyond that. I've got myself into a mess, because now I know too much, and this leaves me exposed. I have to believe Mel and take her at her word. If she hands over her line to the gang, it will mean she and Gabe will be safe, and if I don't go to the police with any further information, she has said they will leave me and my family alone too. It's just…'

'It's just that your conscience is telling you that you should inform the police so that these vile pedlars of misery can be taken off the streets. That's the crux of it. Am I right?'

I'm not sure what to say. She is right, of course. I think of all the victims of this trade that I know of, including Baby C. Despite the findings of the investigation, I will always feel in some way that I failed him. I suppress the white-hot anger rising within me. I promised myself I would make sure Mel didn't get off scot-free. I just can't see how I can make certain she pays the penalty for her actions without putting us all in danger. And if I do go to the police? They will no doubt want to know why I didn't come forward earlier with my suspicions. They may even accuse me of holding up the investigation into Tyler's death. In my defence, I can give them a sanitised version of events from my perspective. Present myself in a positive light. Play down the obsessive, and frankly weird, stalkerish aspects of my behaviour with regard to Mel. I can do naive.

Even if I can plead shock and distress from seeing

the murder to explain away many of my actions, then what? I get a reprimand or even a caution? It seems a small price to pay if it leads to an interruption in the supply chain. Mel will be punished, and as a consequence, Gabe will too, though Sal would say removing him from his mother's influence can only benefit him in the long run. For a brief moment, I experience a sense of clarity. That is, until I am reminded of Mel's words. *Do you really want a life in witness protection?*

'Fran?'

I hear Sal's voice. It sounds as though it's coming from the bottom of a well.

'Are you okay? You've gone as white as a sheet.'

I realise that Sal is standing over me, looking worried.

'I was asking what Laurie's thoughts on the matter are, but you stared right through me. You zoned out there for a minute.'

'Erm, yes, I'm good. Just tired. I've not been sleeping well. It seems to catch up with me around this time of day.'

'I know exactly what you mean. I often snooze in the afternoon, too.'

Sal is now back in her chair and is resting her elbows on the cushion. She is looking at me expectantly.

'Does Laurie think you should go to the police with what you have uncovered?'

'This is where it gets convoluted. You see, I haven't told him.'

I'm saved from having to explain further by the reappearance of Al and Buddy.

'He's had a good run around with his ball,' Al says. 'Now, if you let me out into the garden, I'd like to have a good look at this patch you are turning into a flower meadow before it gets dark.'

Sal follows me into the kitchen as I let Al out and put the kettle back on.

'It's too much of a burden to carry all by yourself,' she says, rinsing the teacups under the tap in the sink. 'You have to tell your husband. Whatever you decide is going to affect him and the rest of the family. It's not a game, Fran. It's gone beyond a bit of amateur sleuthing. There's a lot at stake, and I think you know what my advice would be. Mel is despicable and a failure as a mother. I can't fathom the hold she has over you, but ultimately the decision you make has to take account of your safety and that of your family. As far as I can see, the only way you can achieve that is if Laurie knows what is going on and can help you gain some perspective.'

Sal is looking in my direction, waiting for a response.

'After the funeral,' I say, trying to keep my voice steady. 'That's when I'll tell him. Then we can decide together on the best course of action.'

Peering through the glass in the patio doors, I see Al. In the fading afternoon light. He is pacing out the section we have identified as suitable to dig over and sow with wild flower seeds. A feeling of melancholy washes over me, and there's a catch in my throat.

I can't help but think I may never see the project come to fruition.

33

'Y ou don't have to go, you know,' Laurie says. 'It's not as though anyone will notice if you're not there.'

It's the day of the funeral. Laurie is Skyping me as he's having his lunch. He holds up the sandwich he is eating for me to see. The bread is brown; granary, if I'm not mistaken. Bits of greenery and slices of cucumber and tomato are escaping from its innards.

'Nice and healthy. Vegan cheese and organic salad. How worthy is that?'

'Yum, looks delicious,' I say. 'You should be very proud of yourself for trying.'

Laurie laughs at this and leans into the screen. 'Have you had anything? You've been off your food recently. Are you worrying about the funeral?'

'I suppose I am.' This is true, but on the scale of things, the funeral is not exactly top of the list of my concerns.

'I was asking about food,' Laurie says. 'You had better make sure you have something before you go. Fainting at funerals is never a good look.'

'True,' I say. 'But Jenny called earlier, bearing home-made chicken soup, so I'm sorted for lunch.'

We sign off, and I put Jenny's Denby pottery bowl in the microwave. While the soup is heating, it gives off a delicious aroma, and my stomach rumbles in anticipation. Jenny had called earlier this morning. She was in a hurry and had thrust the bowl into my hands along with a piece of wrapped sausage for Buddy.

'I'm not stopping. Off to a meeting. Just to let you know I will be thinking of you today.' Heading for her car, which she left out on the road with the engine running, she turned and waved.'And wrap up warmly. It's going to get cold enough for snow later. You don't want to catch a chill. It's very open at the crematorium.'

The soup tastes as good as it smells. I am glad of something hot and nourishing. I've been living off tea and toast and the odd biscuit, only cooking something more substantial on the days Laurie is home. Even then, my portions have grown smaller over the weeks. To Laurie's dismay, I tend to pick at my food, consuming only a few mouthfuls at a time.

I rarely look in the mirror nowadays. When I do catch a glimpse of myself, I'm shocked to see how gaunt my features are. The bathroom scales reveal I have lost over half a stone. I know I needed to lose a few pounds, but that's too much too quickly to be healthy. I can't help but think the hollow-cheeked face staring back at me looks like a ghost.

I seem to recall that Mel requested that bright colours should be worn for the ceremony, and I rifle through my wardrobe to try to find something suitable that still fits. Eventually, I decide on a silky pink blouse, which I tuck into a stretchy wool skirt. My duck-egg blue military coat, bought a few years ago for a work colleague's winter wedding, hangs loosely from my shoulders. I pull on ankle boots with a low heel over a pair of thick tights and survey the effect in the full-length mirror on the back of the wardrobe door.

The look is surprisingly cheerful, and I wonder if it's really appropriate for a funeral. I decide I haven't time to choose an alternative; it will have to do. Remembering Jenny's advice about the weather, I think about adding a scarf for warmth. I dismiss the idea, but not before once again cursing my stupidity at mislaying my birthday present. *Idiot*, I say, grimacing at the wan figure in the mirror. *You really do need to get your act together.*

THE CAR PARK at the crematorium is full when I arrive. I manage to squeeze my little car into a tricky space flanked by two enormous four-by-fours. I can just about get the door open, swearing under my breath as I twist myself into an awkward position in order to get out without injury.

A coach pulls up at the side of the road and unloads its passengers. A sign in the side window reads *Derby Education Centre*. They are mostly teenagers, a mixture of boys and girls. They look about Tyler's age, and I assume they are his college classmates. They are flighty and argumentative at first, the boys shoving each other, the girls checking their hair and make-up in the mirrored surfaces of their phones. A middle-aged man, balding with wisps of sandy hair, comes down the coach steps, and they gather around him in a flock, their voices hushed. They listen attentively as he runs through a few basic guidelines; then they turn off their phones as instructed.

'Sir,' one of the lads addresses the man, who is obviously their teacher, 'what if we need the toilet when we are – you know – inside?'

'Good thinking. A sensible question from you for a change, Dylan.'

The boy flushes and smirks. Some of the girls put their hands over their mouths in an attempt to suppress giggles.

'Right, you lot. Pay attention.' He waits, holding himself still as all teachers do, until he has their full focus. 'I've spoken to you already about behaviour. I know you won't let me down, so no need to go over that again. I'm going to show you where the toilets are. Make sure you go before the ceremony starts. Then we have to queue up outside before we go inside, so make sure you've got a coat or jacket. It's starting to freeze already.'

There's a murmur of assent, and in small groups they follow the teacher along the path that leads to the main entrance. I walk behind, and for the most part, the group is quiet and respectful. It must be daunting for many of them. If they have attended a funeral before, it's unlikely to be one for someone of their own age group.

I try not to think of Tyler. I don't want to be overcome by sadness and start snivelling before I even get inside the crematorium. Instead, I stay at the back of the group, keeping just enough distance to enable me to hear the odd scatological comment or snippet of conversation.

'He was pretty fit, was Tyler.'

A couple of the girls are lagging back from the rest of the group. They are deep in conversation. One has a curtain of ash-blonde hair. When she turns her head sideways, it swings across her face, concealing her features. Hearing Tyler's name gets my attention.

'Yeah,' the other girl says. 'He was hot in bed, too. That's what Lara said, anyway.' They snigger, their heads close together, oblivious to my presence.

I slow my pace and allow a young couple holding hands to pass me and move into the space I have created.

I'm taken aback hearing the girls talk about Tyler in that way. Having had teenagers myself, I'm not generally shocked by teen talk, but it feels wrong, disrespectful even, to speak about him in those terms today.

I resist the temptation to remonstrate with them. Instead I slow down to allow others on the path to go past me. On reflection, I realise how foolish it is to get indignant about what I overheard. Young people can be thoughtless and say silly and inappropriate things. It won't have been malicious. After all, Tyler was a young, red-blooded male. Chances are, he had been sexually active for a few years before his death. A memory surfaces of a girl at the shrine in the car park being hugged by Mel. Was that his girlfriend? If so, she must be the Lara they were referring to.

I knew it was going to be a big funeral. Young people's generally are. The line of mourners, many shivering with cold in their lightweight clothing, extends as far as the access road and beyond, halting the progress of cars and those coming out of a previous funeral held in the smaller chapel around the corner.

An attendant opens the double doors, and the crowd surges forward in an unseemly manner, eager to get inside where it's warm. I am one of the last to get a seat. Those coming in behind me are directed to line up along the sides. I notice DI Holmes and DS Georgiou are among those standing at the back.

The air soon becomes muggy, heavy with the scent of lilies. They are part of the floral arrangements positioned on metal stands close to the lectern. The sickly smell causes the familiar buzz at the base of my skull, which signals a headache. I close my eyes, squeezing the lids tightly together to ease the building pressure. A cluster of dots seems to move like a swarm of gnats. When I try to open my eyes, the dots fuse into a solid black mass. Then there's nothing.

34

I come to as I'm being hauled to my feet. Someone is at my side, holding onto my arm, and I can hear the sound of a voice. It's slowed down, like an old record, and seems to be coming from the far end of a tunnel.

'Fran. Hey, Fran. You fainted. Come with me and get some air.'

I am propelled out of the chapel, through the foyer and out of the main doors, where an icy blast hits my face, causing me to gasp out loud. Slowly it dawns on me. The person holding onto my arm is Tash.

'I was coming from toilet, and I see you slide to floor like dying swan. Very dramatic.'

Tash can't have got the message about the dress code, because she is wearing a long, grey, shapeless shift. Her concession to colour is a pair of cherry red, 10-Eye Doc Martens boots and a necklace comprising coloured discs that resemble giant Smarties.

She's such a character. I hope with all my heart she manages to carry this baby to full term. She and Alex will be devastated if she miscarries again.

'Oh no, how embarrassing, Tash,' I say. 'Laurie joked about this happening. I'm never going to live it down.' As my head clears, mortification begins to set in.

Just then, the automatic doors open with a swish, and the attendant appears. 'Are you feeling better?' he says. 'I can arrange for a first aider to come and see you if you are still unwell.'

'I'm fine. I just fainted. I feel so embarrassed. It's the lilies. For some reason, they always make me feel woozy.'

The attendant looks relieved, no doubt pleased he won't have to deal with a medical emergency.

'The cortège is about to arrive,' he says. 'But you can sit in the waiting room if you wish. There is a screen and audio, so you can follow the service from there if you don't want to go back into the chapel. There's even a spare order of service.'

He hands me a booklet. The picture on the front is of Tyler sitting astride his motorbike.

'That's really kind,' I say. 'But if it's all right with you, I'd prefer it if I can slip back in and stand by the door.'

Once I assure Tash I have recovered, she makes her way back to her seat next to Alex. There isn't a great deal of room to stand; people are jammed in like sardines. A woman in a tweed coat, clutching a set of rosary beads, moves sideways, allowing me to squeeze in next to her. My whispered *thank you* goes unacknowledged. Her head is down, lips moving in incantation.

Holy Mary, Mother of God, pray for us sinners, now and at the hour of our death. Amen.

The attendant comes to the door and asks that everyone stand. He presses a button on a small remote control device he is holding, and music reverberates through the speakers.

According to the booklet, the song is called 'Brother' and is by a band that I have never heard of. The words are sweet and appropriate, chosen, I assume, by Gabe.

Walking ahead of the coffin, the celebrant, a slim, dark-haired woman in her fifties wearing a bright shade of purple, makes her way to the lectern. There is a pause, and the sound of coughing and shuffling can be heard as the congregation waits expectantly for the family to appear. The song ends, and the pause lengthens. Something is not right.

What's not right is that an argument is developing in the foyer. From my vantage point by the chapel door, I can hear raised voices, including Mel's, which is shrill and tearful. Not wanting to draw attention to myself again, I do a sideways shimmy so that I can look out and see what is going on. My view of Mel is blocked by the figures of a man and woman with their backs to me. I can just make out Gabe at his mother's side. He is pulling at her arm. She shakes him off, and her voice rises to a shriek.

'Why did you have to bring that tart? Today of all days!'

The man she is addressing is attempting to be conciliatory. 'We've been over this, Mel,' he says. 'And Amber is my wife. She is here to support me.'

The woman, attached to his arm like a limpet, is aptly named. Her hair, long and glossy, is the colour of burnished copper.

'Leave it, Joel,' she says dismissively. 'It's not worth it.'

This comment seems to incense Mel further. She is prevented from lunging forward by Gabe and the funeral director, who grabs her other arm, dropping his top hat in the process.

It's verging on chaos and descending into farce. I can

feel my face start to burn with anger at their lack of respect. Although it's not my place to intervene, I can't help myself. Without stopping to weigh up the consequences of my actions, I take a step forward.

'Just stop this nonsense now, all of you,' I say, indignation lending power to my voice. 'This is neither the time nor the place to air your differences. Today is for Tyler, and the least you can do is be civil to each other. Now get yourselves together and go into that chapel. You need to do the right thing for that boy. You won't ever get the opportunity again.'

Joel and Amber spin around to face me. Fearing I have spoken out of turn, I'm half expecting to be told to mind my own business. To my surprise, they look relieved. Mel, too, has stopped struggling and has shaken off both the funeral director and Gabe. Her face, though pinched and tear-stained, is still immaculately made up. Her outfit, a cobalt-blue tailored trouser suit, makes her look like a fashion model. The effect is striking, but I have to suppress a gasp when I see what is elegantly draped around her neck. There is no mistaking the pattern and colour. She is wearing my scarf.

Recognising that it's me who has spoken, Mel walks towards me. Instinctively I take a step back, unsure of what she might do. I needn't have worried.

'Fran, this is so awful. I can't face going in there. Not looking like this.' She waves a manicured hand in the direction of her face. 'I must look a complete mess.'

'You don't,' I say, resisting the urge to snatch my precious scarf and run. 'That waterproof make-up is worth every penny.'

She manages a ghost of a smile, then reaches for my arm.

'Will you come in with me?'

I can hardly refuse, given the circumstances. Retrieving my scarf will have to wait.

The funeral director and chapel attendant, hovering anxiously throughout, spring into action when I nod in their direction. As the music starts up once again, Gabe and I steer Mel towards the front pew, Joel and Amber following close behind.

The celebrant looks impassive as we take our seats, though a faint tic at the side of her mouth betrays her nervousness. She presses a button on a console, and the song fades. There is a collective sigh of relief as those who have access to seating sink down onto the polished wooden surfaces beneath them.

We are seated directly in front of the coffin. It's been sprayed a bright metallic red and is covered in images of Tyler's motorbike. A simple floral tribute bearing his name rests on top. Despite Mel's grandiose declaration to Nancy about no expense being spared, the funeral turns out to be simple and low-key. A slide show of photos of Tyler runs on a screen in the background as we hear heartfelt, stumbling speeches from some of Tyler's college friends. There is a moving tribute from Lara, Tyler's girlfriend, who comes to the lectern with a woman I assume is her mum. His teacher has prepared a eulogy. Formal to begin with, he speaks of Tyler's ambition to be a mechanic. Of how hard he was working to achieve his goals. He then makes us all laugh with accounts of Tyler's mischievous side and his love of practical jokes.

The celebrant reads a poem on behalf of Mel. As I try to follow the words in the order of service, they dissolve before my eyes. I can feel Mel's shoulders heave as she sobs quietly into a balled-up tissue in her hand. Her pain is raw, and I squeeze her arm in an attempt to offer comfort. My own tears, I hold in check. It seems an indulgence to weep openly for a boy I did not know. Not when his parents, seated on either side of me, have had their hearts ripped out and shattered into a million fragments.

Closing my eyes helps me focus on my breathing. With each inhalation, my nostrils fill with the faint cat-pee scent of rotting lilies. I swallow hard against the rising nausea, longing for it all to be over.

At last, the closing music. Mel walks unsteadily to the coffin. Leaning in, she spreads her arms wide and buries her head in the flower arrangement bearing Tyler's name. On the seat beside me, she has left the scarf. My scarf. I pick it up and press it into the pocket of my coat. Before I do, I catch a faint trace of her perfume rising from its silky folds.

35

It's a relief to step outside and suck in draughts of fresh air. It's so cold I can see my breath, and my nose is starting to run. The weather forecast mentioned the possibility of light snow flurries – early for the time of year, but already the odd flake is falling. Mel is with Gabe on the flower terrace, where an orderly queue, which includes Tash and Alex, has formed to offer their sympathies. Mel has an arm around Lara, who is weeping into her shoulder. I notice Joel and Amber are standing on the periphery, like outsiders.

Feeling like a spare part myself, I make my way back up the steps and across the access road. Taking refuge from the biting wind, I sit on a low wall. I'm shielded by a brick pillar, and if I get myself in the right position, I can observe what is going on without being seen. I open the order of service at the page where the poem read during the service is printed. The words are simple, yet they are suffused with longing and loss. A brief note beneath the text says it was written by a mother following the death of her son.

Tell me of some fond memory
Of you and my child together.
I need all the good memories
Of him I can gather up now –
Even second-hand ones.
Tell me you will miss him –
That I'm not the only one.
Your words will make me cry,
But your silence hurts more.
Tell me.

I can't help but feel like an imposter. I'm here for what reason? I had no tangible connection to Tyler, and the only memories I have of him are associated with fear and pain and death. My link to him is tenuous, grounded in a sense of helplessness that I couldn't save him. The relationship formed with Mel, too, is insubstantial. It is built around deceit and fraught with difficulties based on what I know about her. I decide I will ignore the invitation to meet at a local pub for the wake. It's unlikely I will be missed if I slip away. It's been an emotional afternoon, and if I leave now, I can get back in time to have a hot bath and cook something for when Laurie returns later this evening. Then I will tell him the truth about the last few weeks. It will be a difficult conversation, but once everything is out in the open, we can decide together on what course of action we should take.

The light is fading, and small groups are starting to make their way back to the car park. I'm about to join them when I hear raised voices coming from the other side of the pillar.

'No, Joel. Nothing will induce me to stay any longer.' A woman with a soft lilt – Southern Irish, if I'm not mistaken – is speaking. 'I came today for my grandson,

God rest his soul, and now I'm leaving. Nothing good will come of me staying.'

'Don't go, Bridie.' Joel's voice is conciliatory. 'Gabe is your grandson, too. He will be pleased to see you, and Mel won't kick off again. Not after she's shown herself up by having a go at me. Amber and I will look out for you. Please come to the pub and at least raise a glass in Tyler's memory.'

If I shift my position on the wall and peer around the pillar, I can see a stockily built woman with greying hair. She is wearing sensible black shoes and a tweed coat. It doesn't take much imagination to work out who Joel and Amber, just out of my sight line, are talking to. It's the woman from the chapel with the rosary beads. Mel's mother.

'I can't, Joel. I have to go. Mel is my daughter, but I'll never forgive her for splitting up our family.' Her voice has sharpened to flint. 'She broke her dad's heart. He was never the same after she left, but then, you'll know all about that. 'Twas you who took her away from us in the first place.'

'Now, you know that's not true, Bridie. Mel had gone off the rails way before I even came on the scene.'

Bridie seems to crumple. 'I know what you're saying is true, Joel. She was always bad. The things she has done. The people she has hurt. She has no conscience. It's just... It's all been too much, and when I heard about poor Tyler...!'

Bridie pulls a white handkerchief from her coat pocket and dabs at her eyes. 'I've been staying with some of our people in Birmingham, and they showed me the cuttings from the newspapers. There are some awful things being said about how Tyler was mixed up in drugs, and that's how he got himself killed.'

She's sobbing now, and Joel puts an arm around her

convulsing shoulders. I want to retreat out of sight, but I'm not quick enough. Joel has seen me, and his eyes lock onto mine. He holds his stare over the top of Bridie's head. Embarrassment causes my cheeks to redden.

The heat in my face isn't just because I've been caught eavesdropping. Joel is still an attractive man despite his greying hair and a slight thickening to his neck. His eyes, a deep smokey-grey like Gabe's, have a languid sensuality. I can see why Mel was drawn to him, and how he has now attracted a trophy wife young enough to be his daughter.

Eventually, it's me who drops my gaze, and I move sideways so that once again I'm concealed from view.

My thick tights are no protection against the cold seeping up through the brick. I long to escape, but I'm still disconcerted at being seen by Joel. I don't relish the thought of coming face to face with him if he is still around. Retreating footsteps indicate they may have moved on, but I want to be sure. Aching in every joint, I wait until there are no voices to be heard. No sound of car doors slamming. The light has now gone, indicating I must have been sitting on the wall for at least an hour. As I prepare to leave, I think about what Bridie said about Mel. *She was always bad. The things she has done. The people she has hurt. She has no conscience.*

Slipping my hand into my pocket, I take out my scarf and place it around my neck. On the scale of things, the significance of this piece of fabric, gifted to me by my children, is of concern only to me. It will have meant nothing to Mel, who picked it up and then discarded it, just as she will do with me when I am of no further use to her. Of course, my part in all of this is not without reproach. *Well intentioned* is not a good defence for lying and subterfuge. There is something that's puzzling me, though. Why has Mel chosen to confide in me? Is it because she trusts the person she thinks I am, or is there a more sinister reason behind it?

Trying to make sense of it all is draining. I've decided I don't want to be a part of this any longer. The whole saga has become wearisome and grubby, and I'm getting too far out of my comfort zone.

Telling Laurie will be a start. What's important is that we remain safe.

If I'm lucky, we can put all this behind us.

36

When I at last venture out, it's eerily quiet, and my anxiety levels climb. It was stupid of me to wait so long. It's freezing, and I plunge my hands into the pockets of my coat for warmth, checking at the same time that my keys and phone are still there, along with my bank card. Having decided against carrying a handbag, I had put the card in my pocket at the last minute in case of emergency.

My watch tells me it's after five. Low-wattage pillar lighting snakes along one side of the access road. The light being emitted is inadequate, the lamps partially obscured by foliage. I can't really blame the Council for failing to fork out on additional lighting with all the cuts they have had to make. It's not as though the place needs to be well lit at night. There can't be that many solitary individuals who hang around crematoria after dark, not live ones anyway.

I suppress a giggle, thinking of what Mum used to say when I developed a fear of walking through grave-yards. *Remember, Francesca, the dead can't hurt you. It's the living you have to fear.* If she was trying to allay the concerns of a highly imaginative child, she didn't succeed. I took what she said literally, and it was a long time before I could be coaxed out of viewing everyone I encountered with a degree of suspicion.

The footpath leading to the car park, bounded on either side by slender trees and dense bushes, is in darkness. I catch an occasional glimpse of a high, intensely bright moon. For the most part it's hidden, enveloped in a bank of cloud. In the distance, a downstairs light is on in the building where the office is located. I could go there and see if there's someone willing to walk me to the car park. Immediately, I dismiss the idea as ridiculous. What if there is only one member of staff and she is female, too? Or perhaps even elderly? I might scare her half to death banging on the door to get her attention. And anyway, I can be at the car park in half the time it would take to walk to the office.

Grabbing my phone from my pocket, I fiddle with it until I find the right button to turn on the flashlight. It casts a triangular beam on the path ahead, which is now glistening with frost. Below the surface, it's possible to make out faint imprints from earlier walkers. I'm glad of my boots with their grip soles, as I can see the frost is lying on top of a thin layer of treacherous ice. Now would not be a good time to fall and break something. Keeping close to the centre of the path, I avoid the hollows at the edges where water has pooled and formed into black ice.

My progress is slow, interrupted only by the rustle of dry leaves in the undergrowth. Suddenly, a sound to chill the blood fills the air. A reedy, high-pitched scream, freezing me in my tracks. For a heart-stopping moment, it sounds like the cry of a child. My senses go into overdrive. With a thumping heart, I swing the torch from side to side, trying to locate where it's coming from.

Then the soft, slow beat of wings overhead. My heart rate decelerates.

What is the matter with you? It's only a bloody bird.

The moon appears briefly, and there is my frightener, perfectly silhouetted against the night sky, its distinctive squat body settling into the forked branch of a large tree – a barn owl.

If Laurie were here, he would laugh at my foolishness.

'It gets you every time. You should recognise that shriek by now. We've lived in close proximity to their habitat for long enough.'

He's said this to me on more than one occasion. Now, the memory of those words conjures up an image of the two of us sitting in the garden at the end of summer. Wrapped in blankets to ward off the chill, we search the night sky for shooting stars and watch as the owls return to roost after a spell of nocturnal hunting.

When I at last reach the opening to the car park, I breathe a sigh of relief. A quick scan with my torch reveals it's emptied of cars from earlier; everyone's obviously headed to the pub for the wake. I head in the direction of where I left my car and reach for the keys in my pocket. I can't wait to get in and start the engine. It will soon heat up, and I can be on my way. Except, my car is not there. I'm confused. Surely I haven't made a mistake? Is it possible I left it somewhere else? Perhaps a different corner of the car park?

I've done that before. Mislaid my vehicle. Supermarkets and multistoreys are the worst. Everywhere looks exactly the same. You end up walking around for ages trying to locate the spot, or worse, have to summon the car park attendant, which is both stressful and embarrassing.

Standing with my back to the main entrance, I

remember driving in and feeling pleased at finding somewhere that could accommodate my little Fiat. It was definitely that weird, wedge-shaped space in the far corner. Pointing the flashlight at the ground confirms I'm not going doolally. The damp outline of where my car was is still visible. The area has not yet had the chance to freeze over.

There's only one conclusion I can come to. My car has been stolen, and not that long ago, either.

Bloody brilliant. Now what am I going to do? Ring Laurie? It's pointless worrying him. He's probably still in a meeting. And anyway, he's too far away to do anything constructive. Ring the police? I could, but I don't fancy waiting here in the cold and dark for them to arrive. My best option is to make my way back to the office. If I go out through the entrance gate, I can approach from the main road. There's no path, but I will be able to see any headlights approaching, giving me time to flatten myself against the hedge if a vehicle passes. From the office, I can ring the police and wait inside where it's warm. I just hope there's someone still on duty, or I will have to come up with a plan B.

Everything shrivels into irrelevance in the next few seconds. From out of the shadows, two figures materialise with such stealth they must have come from the lane that runs alongside the car park. I catch a fleeting glimpse, and from their burly shapes, I would say they are both men. They are wearing identical dark-coloured Puffa jackets, their faces obscured by balaclavas.

One reaches for my arms and twists them behind my back. My phone and keys fall to the ground with a clatter. There's a stretching and ripping sound, and I feel my hands being bound with tape. My attempts at screaming are silenced by a gloved hand over my mouth. I can smell the leather and the musky odour of nicotine. Another strip is torn off and pressed tight against my mouth. Weak from cold and fear, I can only stand, knees shaking, heart yammering as the figure in front of me removes his gloves and starts to unbutton my coat. He's close enough for me to raise my knee in the direction of his groin, but there's no strength in my leg, and it drops back weakly. I feel his hands run over and up and down my body. I'm petrified, racking my brains to try to find a way to escape. If I could speak, I would plead with them to release me before this goes any further. After all, I haven't seen their faces. I'd say that although I have no money on me, they can take my phone and bank card. I can even give them the pin number. There's close to a thousand in the account.

I want to appeal to their better nature. Let them know I have a husband, children and a dog waiting for me at home. Once they know all this, they may reconsider and let me go.

I close my eyes and feel my body slump forward. Resigned, I'm waiting for the worst to happen. I'm going to be raped, possibly even murdered. Tomorrow someone will find me and have forever preserved in their memory, the image of a frozen corpse in a crematorium car park.

A hush has descended, and for a single, suspended moment, it's as though I've stepped outside my body. Peering skywards, I see a subtle change in the quality of the light coming through the clouds. There is a softness to the air and a barely perceptible rise in temperature. I feel as though I'm floating, borne aloft on clouds of cotton wool. Perhaps this is what precipitates a deathbed conversion for those who have no religion.

The metallic clang of a car door slamming jolts me back to reality. I must have passed out, as I'm no longer outside. I'm lying in the foetal position on the rear seat of a vehicle, covered by a blanket. Lifting my head, I can just about make out the outline of a darkened car window.

It must have started snowing in earnest. There's no sound except the slap of wet snowflakes hitting the glass. They linger for an instant, holding their shape, then melt and slide down the window like winter tears.

37

I t can't have been that long since my hands were taped, but my shoulders are aching, and I've got pins and needles shooting down my arms. Every time I try to open my mouth, a strip of skin separates from my lip, and I wince in pain. I seem to recall reading somewhere that it's a fallacy, perpetuated in Hollywood kidnapping films, that duct tape can prevent you from opening your mouth. Well, let me tell you, it's no myth.

There's a low murmur of voices coming from outside, then a stamping of feet. The front doors of the car open, and I catch a whiff of cigarette smoke before both doors are slammed shut. The engine fires, and there's a low hum as it ticks over. The car is a four-by-four. Top of the range, if the padded leather seats are anything to go by. Newish model, too; it has that brand-new-car smell.

There is no conversation between the driver and passenger. All I can hear is the soft swish of the windscreen wipers. The blast of warm air coming from the heater, combined with our heat and breath, is causing the windows to fog. We seem to be racing along country lanes at high speed, the driver braking heavily into bends. It's not a smooth ride, and I am starting to feel car sick. Whirling snowflakes flash past the window, and I can make out the odd outline of a tree in the darkness.

There's a sudden screech of brakes, and the car comes to a halt, throwing me against the back of the seats. I have to push myself away using my knees, and I've now ended up lying on my back. This is putting extra strain on my arms, and I shuffle around until I'm once again on my side.

The pause is momentary. The passenger window is opened, letting in a gust of clear air. I can feel the seat in front of me rock as something is launched out into the night. The chink of metal against plastic follows, and I know my phone and keys have been flung into the undergrowth. I doubt I will ever see them again.

The realisation I haven't been assaulted or killed brought with it faint hope. Now even that is dissipating.

What the hell is going on here? Is it random, or was I targeted? And if so, who are these men, and what do they want with me?

Everything is jumbled in my head; it's difficult to think straight. I'm left with one explanation for what is happening. It has to be related to Tyler's murder. Mel must have had less influence on the incoming gang than she thought? Is getting rid of me their way of clearing the decks before taking over the line from her?

Now the fear is back, the fight-or-flight instinct flooding my system with hormones. Except I am unable to do either, trussed up like a chicken in the back of this car.

It's difficult to gauge how long we have been travelling, but the road is now straighter and lit by the orange glow of sodium lights. This suggests we are coming into a built-up area. The car slows and stops. Raising my head, I can see traffic lights reflected in a plate-glass window alongside. They are on red.

The tiniest flicker of hope struggles into life. If we are somewhere urban, there could be people around. I've probably only got seconds before the lights change, but I have to take a chance. I shuffle so that I'm closer to the side panel and kick as hard as I can against the rigid plastic, once, twice, three times. I try to scream, but the tape is wrapped too firmly around my mouth. All I can manage is a sound deep within my throat, hoarse and guttural. Too muffled to be heard from outside the car.

The lights change, and the car accelerates away, tyres spinning on the wet road.

I HAVE no concept of how much time has elapsed. Is it an hour, two hours since I last looked at my watch? I remember it was after five when I started walking to the car park, and it could easily be around seven now. Laurie will have tried to ring to let me know that he is on his way. He won't be concerned when it goes to voicemail. He'll think I've gone to the wake and switched off my phone. Even if I'm not there when he gets back in, he will see to Buddy, grab a beer and something to eat from the freezer, and stretch out in front of the TV. He might even fall asleep. It will be later, when he's tried my phone a few times and I'm still not answering, that he'll start to worry. Will it be too late for me by then?

All the fight has gone out of me; I feel drained. I want to be with Laurie and Buddy, curled up on the sofa with a glass of wine, watching something silly on the telly. The thought of home and everything associated with it brings tears to my eyes. The roller coaster of emotional highs and lows has depleted my physical and emotional resources, and I'm starting to feel a sense of hopelessness. With no ability to control what happens, I might as well resign myself to whatever lies in store for me.

Once again we are moving at speed through the darkness. The wind is whistling through the trees and whipping the snow into wraithlike flurries. I can't ever remember a time when we had weather like this in late October. No doubt Alice, who is taking an interest in Green politics and blaming us baby boomers for all the ills in the world, would say it's down to climate change.

Suddenly, the car skids to a halt. The driver jumps out and starts to open my door when there's a shout from the passenger side.

'Cover your face, you idiot.'

The man pauses to roll down his balaclava, but not before I catch the briefest glimpse of his face. It's only a microsecond, but it's long enough. Over the last couple of hours or so, it's become obvious my situation is perilous. What I didn't factor in was that someone known to me, whom I've always liked and trusted, could be implicated in all this. The man driving is Alex, and knowing that, it feels like the ultimate betrayal.

I don't have much time to think. I'm hauled to the edge of the seat by my legs and placed in a sitting position, facing outwards. Within touching distance is a hawthorn hedge. Through a gap, I can just make out a flat grey surface before the blanket is thrown over my head. Water. A narrow strip. I can just about make out the shape of trees on the opposite side. It must be the canal. I'm pulled to my feet and steered forwards. In a futile show of defiance, I shrug off the arm on my shoulder. In response, the grip tightens, and I'm pushed forward unceremoniously, the snow crunching beneath my feet.

A gate creaks, and a door is opened. Warm air, the aroma of freshly brewed coffee and something cooking. The aromatic fragrance is a mix of cloves and allspice. I've not had anything to eat since Jenny's soup at lunchtime, and this smell, both fragrant and meaty, is mouth-watering.

After they've manhandled me up the steep stairs, I'm pushed down onto a soft, yielding surface. My head is up against one end, and my feet are jammed against the other of what feels like a bed or sofa. Through the open weave of the blanket, I can see the soft glow of a lamp in a far corner of the room. There's a resinous odour of newly sawn wood and the smell of freshly washed clothes. I recognise the scent. It's one of the fabric softeners I've used myself, apple blossom and almond.

Laurie always takes the piss out of me for having such finely tuned senses and an ability to recall even the most insignificant details.

I can't help it. It's just the way my brain works. You wait. It will stand me in good stead one day. How fitting those words seem. I wish I could say them to him now and watch his face break into a smile.

I must have slept for a while, because I wake with a jolt. There's someone in the room. I can see their outline through the blanket and hear the sound of their breathing. My heart begins its familiar rhythmic pounding, and I try to get into a sitting position, my arms burning from the effort.

'Sssh, ssh, ssh.'

It's a man's voice, deep and resonant. Familiar.

The blanket is pulled aside, and I can see he is still wearing the balaclava. It's a pointless attempt at disguise. Alex can't have realised that I recognised him. He steps forward and pulls the strips of tape from around my mouth. I lick my lips. They feel raw and exposed, and I can taste blood. He reaches behind my back and snips the binding from around my hands with scissors. My arms flop weakly at my sides, but I can feel the warmth returning to my fingers. I massage my arms, then try to loosen my overstretched muscles and tendons.

'Eat,' he says, stepping back.

It's only now I see the tray with the plate and mug of coffee on the floor in front of me.

There's no knife or fork, just a plastic spoon. The food looks delicious. Sliced sausage and boiled potatoes in gravy. Polish food.

'Thanks, Alex,' I say, my voice barely a croak.

I want a response from him. An acknowledgement that I matter. That I am worth saving, but he leaves the room without a backward glance. He pulls the door behind him, and there's a metallic click as he turns the key in the lock.

38

The food has not only given me back some energy, it has had the effect of kicking my brain back into gear. This is Tash and Alex's house. I know because I've been here before. When they first moved in, it was in a bad state of repair, having been owned by an elderly man. He had lived alone in the house for over fifty years and had made few alterations during that time. Tash kept me up to date with the renovations during my hairdressing appointments. Laurie and I were looking forward to making arrangements to come over for a meal once the work was completed.

The room I'm in is the nursery. It has flamboyant touches, no doubt down to Tash. A woodland mural with matching curtains and a colourful rug on the wooden floor. Taking pride of place is a beautifully carved rocking cradle, which has got to be Alex's handiwork.

Is Tash here? I find it hard to imagine her allowing her home to be used in this way, especially if she knows I'm here and being held against my will.

With the bindings gone from my wrists, I'm now

able to look at my watch. It's showing 8:50 p.m. Laurie must be at home by now. Has he tried my phone? Is he starting to get concerned?

The front door opens and closes. There's a stamping of feet and the murmur of voices from downstairs. I desperately need the toilet. Unsure how to attract attention, I stand at the door and try rattling the doorknob.

'Hello, can you hear me?' My throat is hoarse, and my voice cracks when I try to shout.

There's no response, so I stomp down hard on the floor. It takes a number of tries before I hear someone coming up the stairs. The door is opened by Alex; this time his face is not covered.

How am I to interpret this? That there's no point in disguise if my fate is already sealed?

'What you want?'

'I need the toilet,' I say.

The Alex I know is a big bear of a man with a booming laugh. Always genial whenever I encounter him, he adores Tash and loves the life they have created for themselves in this country. It seems at odds to be presented with a different side to the man I knew and liked. He is troubled, I can see that. Torment is etched across his usually amiable features.

Holding me by the elbow, he steers me across the hall to the bathroom.

'Please tell me what's going on, Alex. Are you in trouble? Does Tash know I'm here? Laurie will be worried. Alex, please don't do this. Think of the new baby. You don't want to end up in prison just when Tash needs you the most.' My words are having no effect.

'No talking,' is all he says.

The bathroom is unfinished. There's a new white suite and highly polished chrome taps, but the walls are bare plaster, and the floor is rough chipboard.

There's a hook in the shape of a duck on the back of the door, and I take off my coat and hang it from its beak.

Filling the sink with hot water, I wash my hands and face, thankful that apart from a shaving mirror, there is nowhere for me to see my reflection.

The window above the bath is small and wooden with an old-fashioned casement handle. It's nowhere near big enough for me to crawl through, although the thought does cross my mind. Lined up along the ledge are numerous bottles and pots of creams alongside a shaving kit and bottle of aftershave. A tube of tooth-paste and a toothbrush holder sit on a small wooden shelf. The holder contains two toothbrushes.

Mel is in the room when I return. The name of the perfume she wears has eluded me since we first met. Now for some reason, it floats into my memory, *La vie est Belle*. The irony doesn't escape me. *Life is beautiful*. How appropriate that seems given the circumstances I find myself in.

She is sitting at one end of the sofa, looking relaxed. She's still wearing the outfit she had on for the funeral.

'Ah, I see you found your scarf,' she says.

I haven't given it a second thought since I looped it around my neck as protection against the cold. Now I reach up and touch it like a talisman.

'You must be wondering what's going on,' she says, patting the space next to her.

Are you talking about the last four hours, which have left me confused, terrified and in fear for my life? I think to myself.

I don't give her the satisfaction of a reply and stub-bornly stand my ground, ignoring her cue for me to sit down.

'Come on, Fran, sit here. I can't have a proper

conversation with you if you're looming over me like that.'

Her demeanour is normal, her tone friendly, as though we are meeting up for a drink. What the fuck is the matter with her? It was only this afternoon that her son was cremated, and here I am, having been kidnapped, probably at her behest, yet she is acting as though nothing has happened. Were her dramatic public manifestations of grief just an act? Can she turn it on and off like a tap when the situation demands? Was the visit to the funeral director's a prime example of her showboating?

Alex gives me a nudge in the direction of the sofa, and I relent, positioning myself as far away from her as I can. Somehow,I don't anticipate she has anything to say that will make me feel any better.

'Perhaps Alex will get us some tea?' She waves a hand in his direction.

I want to punch her in the face I'm so angry. I turn towards her and fix her with what I hope is a withering look. She ignores me and dismisses Alex with a nod.

'I know you're frightened, Fran. I'm afraid the London boys can be a bit heavy-handed. They are used to handling far more unsavoury characters than you. You have to trust me; everything is going to be fine.'

'Trust you. Now why would I do that? You've done nothing to suggest to me you are in any way trustworthy. And in answer to your first question, yes, I do want to know what's going on.'

I can hear the clatter of cups from downstairs.

Mel picks at a loose thread on the arm of the sofa, then scrapes at a chipped nail. The delay is aggravating. I want to hear what she has to say. To know what possible justification she can have for keeping me here.

And, more importantly, what the hell is going to happen to me.

'You know, you're a very nice person, Fran. All the support you've given me over the last few weeks is appreciated. I want you to know that.'

'Well, that's very big of you,' I say, trying to inject as much sarcasm as I can into my voice. 'But I want to know why I have been kidnapped, and why I'm being kept a prisoner? You told me that once you handed over your deal line, that would be the end of it. You said you would talk to the gang leader, and as long as I didn't go to the police, I would be safe. Well, I haven't spoken to the police, so why the hell am I here?'

'Ah yes,' she says, stretching her legs out in front of her. 'That was true – then. There's been a change of plan. Let's just say they made me an offer I couldn't refuse.' She laughs at her own joke, and I feel the blood drain from my face.

'You surely can't mean you're working for them?' I say, incredulous. 'After what they did to Tyler and how they treated Gabe? You said you'd had enough and wanted out. How can you even contemplate being a part of that operation? Is money really more important than living within the law and having peace of mind?'

'Oh, Fran.' She cocks her head to one side and gives me a look of faux sympathy. 'You have no concept of how much money we are talking about.'

Her eyes glitter in the lamplight. With what? Excitement? No, I decide it's more than that. It's greed. Pure unadulterated greed.

'And what about me? How do I fit in to all this?'

'I owe you a lot, Fran. Trying to save Tyler like you did, looking out for Gabe, taking care of me in the aftermath of Tyler's death. I haven't really got anyone to confide in, and you were, I should say are, a good listener. Very compassionate, but practical, too.'

'I'm not here for a job interview, Mel. Can you get to the point?'

'The point is, I let down my guard. I never do that, not with anyone. I let you in, and that was a mistake. I told you too much. About me, about the deal line. I shouldn't have exposed myself in that way.'

Mel is inspecting an expensive-looking charm bracelet around her wrist. She shakes it, and the charms tinkle like ice cubes in a glass.

'Then I got to thinking,' she says, her tone languid. 'What was your part in all this, Fran? What were you getting out of poking your nose into my business? I even considered the possibility that you were collecting information to give to the police.'

That explains why I was searched so thoroughly at the crematorium car park. They were checking for a recording device.

'I think you must be a bit paranoid,' I say. 'None of my family knows about any of this, not even my husband, Laurie.'

She raises an eyebrow, and I realise my mistake. Jesus, what a prat I am. I could kick myself for giving her that bit of information. I try not to let her see I'm rattled.

'It was all about Tyler to start with,' I say, trying to deflect her attention away from what I've just said. 'I felt guilty that I couldn't help him. Then I saw you at the shrine in the woods and on TV and social media. I identified with you as a mother. I felt sorry for you and wanted to help; that was my motivation. That and feeling as though I owed it to Tyler to find out who was responsible for his death.'

This is a slimmed down version of the truth, leaving out Sal and Al's contribution.

'Did you know your mother came to the funeral?' I say.

'Yes, I did. She came to the wake afterwards with Joel and that skank Amber. Didn't speak to me, though. Told everyone she was only there for her grandson.'

'It's fair to say she doesn't have a very high opinion of you, then?'

'Did you speak to her?'

Even though I want to hurt her, I still can't bring myself to be that cruel. I hold back from telling her how I'd overheard her mother's character assassination of her to Joel and Amber.

'No, I didn't. She was standing next me, praying for Tyler's soul at the crem,' I say. 'If I'd thought about it, I could have asked her to put in a good word for me.'

The ghost of a smile plays around Mel's lips.

'It's getting late, Mel. Laurie will be getting worried.'

Her smile twists into a smirk. 'Not yet he won't. We sent him a little message from your phone. He won't be calling out a search party just yet. *You* told him you were going to be back late.'

39

Mel has gone. She left with Alex soon after he had come up with a pot of tea and three chunky cups.

'We need to go. Now,' she said to him. A barked order, not a request.

They left abruptly, locking the door behind them.

They have some business to attend to, that's what she told me before she left. When they return, I am going to be picked up and taken to a 'safe' house for a while, no time scale specified.

'Honestly, Fran, this is for your own good. I can't risk you jeopardising the setting up of this deal. There's too much at stake. I promise no harm will come to you.'

She's lying. What's more, she knows I know she's lying. The gang she is now working with comprises of ruthless and brutal killers. It's in everyone's interest that I'm out of the way. There would be no point in releasing me. I know too much. The truth is, I am a dead woman walking.

I feel numb. Left alone, it's difficult to rein in my thoughts, to stop myself thinking about what's going to happen to me. The more I try to push it all aside, the more intrusive the thoughts become. It will be quick, I imagine, unlike poor Tyler. A bullet to the back of the head, then a burial deep inside a forest hundreds of miles from here. Amongst the dense pines, where no one ever goes. It might be that my body is never found.

Sipping the now-lukewarm tea, I listen hard for any sound or movement that would tell me that someone is still in the house. All is quiet apart from the gurgle of water moving through the central heating pipes. Going to the window, I pull back the curtain. If anyone is passing, I can try to attract their attention.

Outside, there's very little light and no sign of life. It's still snowing, and the imprint of tyre tracks in the road have already been covered in a light dusting. It's now 9:30 p.m. by my watch. There's nothing else for me to do but wait.

Resting my head on the arm of the sofa, I'm drifting into a fitful sleep when I hear a noise coming from somewhere in the house. It's barely audible and animal-like. I don't remember Tash and Alex having any pets. Tash doesn't like cats, and she would have told me if they had acquired a dog. Sitting upright, I wait. Minutes pass, and I'm about to dismiss it as a waking dream when I hear it again. It's coming from downstairs.

It's an old house, and this room has floorboards. There are bound to be gaps between the boards. Moving the rug aside, I find what I'm looking for. One of the boards has a missing corner. Lying down, I press my ear to the floor. There it is: a cry of despair, and it's definitely not an animal. The sound is faint, but unmistakable. A woman is sobbing quietly, and I'm pretty sure I know who it is.

'Hello, hello.'

Knocking with my knuckles against the wood

produces a dull thud that echoes in the void between floor and ceiling. There's no response. I need something more substantial if I am to attract attention. Scanning the room, there's nothing that looks suitable. Then my eyes alight on an object lying under the cradle. I scoot across the floor on my backside to have a look. Leaning in, I slide out a small hand plane, left there I would guess, by Alex when he was working on the cradle. Picking it up, I can feel it has some weight to it, ideal for making enough noise to be heard in the room below.

Returning to my spot, I bring the edge of the plane into contact with the wood. It makes a satisfying ringing sound. After a few more goes, I pause and listen. The noise from downstairs has stopped. I bring the plane down a few more times in quick succession and wait. This time a door opens, and there is the sound of footsteps on the stairs. I hold my breath as the key is turned in the lock. The light from the hallway is blocked by a figure.

'Tash,' I say, 'I thought it was you.'

I'm pleased to see her, but wary. She must have known I was up here, yet she didn't come to check and see if I was all right. So much for our long friendship.

I get up and walk towards her. She puts a hand up like a cop halting traffic.

'No. You stay there.'

She is trying to appear tough despite the waver in her voice. She looks rumpled, as though she has been sleeping in her clothes. Her hair is sticking up on one side and flattened on the other, and her face is blotchy from crying. I stand, holding myself still, conscious she might bolt if I say or do anything out of turn.

She points to the sofa.

'Sit,' she says. 'They will be back for you soon.'

'Oh, Tash. How on earth have you got yourself

mixed up in this? I thought you disliked Mel. You certainly seemed to disapprove of what she stood for. Yet here you are, holding a kidnap victim hostage in your home. That's major criminal activity, Tash. I thought we were friends.'

Her face crumples for a split second, then becomes defiant. 'No, not kidnap.'

'Then what else would you call it? They took me by force, and I am being held here against my will. It's very serious, Tash. You and Alex will go to prison for this. And if I'm killed, you will be an accessory to murder. What will happen to your baby then? They will put you away for a long time.'

All her bravado dissipates, and Tash sinks to the floor in an untidy heap. Clutching her knees, she rocks back and forth, tears streaming down her face. '*Matko Boska, Matko Boska.*' She repeats the phrase over and over again. I can only assume she is appealing to a deity that has not featured in her life for some time. I sit down on the floor next to her.

'Tash,' I say, keeping my voice low and even, 'can you tell me what is going on? How have you and Alex got yourselves involved with Mel and those crooks?'

Tash reaches into a pocket in her dress and pulls out a soggy, crumpled tissue. She blows her nose vigorously.

'I so angry and upset with Alex,' she says, tears coursing down her cheeks. 'He get us into this mess, stupid man. He never do anything like this before; then he go work for Mel.'

'Something to do with drugs?' I say.

'No, not at first. He start by doing odd jop.'

'Odd jobs?'

'Yes, things about house. Build big kennel for dogs in garden. Stuff like that. She pay him good money. Cash.'

'Then what?'

'Then he do driving. Deliveries. She pay money and give him bags.'

'Of what? Crack cocaine?'

'Yes, that gówno stuff. She is *dziwika*.' Tash spits the last word out whilst wiping her eyes with the disintegrating tissue. 'Now he have habit, bloody fool. We have debt for first time ever. He work for Mel, only way to pay it off.'

It's pointless trying to suggest that there are other ways of getting off drugs and clearing your debts. She isn't going to listen, and anyway, there isn't time.

'Tash, they will be back at any minute. They are going to take me somewhere and kill me. You have to help me!'

'No, no, not kill. Take you away for few days, then let you go. Alex tell me that.'

'C'mon, Tash. Don't be a fool. I witnessed Tyler's murder and saw the men who did it. I know too much about Mel and the new set-up. It's a huge drug operation. They aren't going to let me go.'

Tash shakes her head. 'No. You're wrong...'

I reach out and grab her arms, pull her to her feet and force her to stand and look me in the eye. 'The baby. The one who died from the overdose of methadone His name was Christopher. They called him Kit. Don't let there be another unnecessary death, Tash, I implore you. You have to help me before it's too late. You can tell them I tricked you into coming up here and that I locked you in.'

She is mute and withdrawn, so I shake her by the shoulders.

'Please, Tash. I don't have much time. I'm pleading with you for my life. Let me go. I will tell the police you helped me to escape. They will be lenient with you, especially as you are pregnant.'

Tash sits back down heavily on the sofa. She seems diminished. All the energy and sparkiness has gone, and she looks tired and resigned.

'Okay,' she says, shrugging her shoulders in resignation. 'Lock this door and go. But don't walk roads. They will find you in car.'

I shiver at the thought, and she looks at me in concern.

'You want sweater? Your top too thin. Is very cold.'

'I'll be fine,' I say. 'My coat is hanging on the back of the bathroom door. I'll get it on the way out.'

I go to the window first, open it, and look out at a picture-postcard scene. The snow is still coming down, and everything is blanketed in white. I listen for the sound of car tyres and search for headlights, but nothing is moving out there.

'Thanks, Tash. Look after yourself,' I say before closing the door and locking it behind me.

40

An Arctic blast hits me full in the face when I open the front door. I will have to keep moving to try to stay warm. There's no real plan, just a desire to get as far away as possible without being seen. The snow is two to three inches deep. Stepping down onto the path, I can see my boots are leaving indentations. Walking away from the house means I'm a sitting duck. I'm not going to be difficult to find if I leave a trail of footprints.

My luck is in for once. Propped up against the garden wall is a besom broom. I've seen Tash incorporate them into her Halloween window displays at the shop. She must be using this one for sweeping the path. I don't want to waste too much time. I experiment with walking backwards and brushing over the prints with the broom. The snow is powdery, and I take a couple of steps, stopping and brushing, until I am across the road and in front of the gap in the hedge. Looking back towards the house, I can see I've done a reasonable job of covering my tracks, and the falling snow is already filling in any gaps I've missed. Before I back my way in through the hedge, I spot a movement from the upstairs window. It's Tash. She's watching my departure.

Once I'm on the other side of the hedge, I heap the snow up into a mound and drop down the bank, still brushing behind me as I go. I've never walked here before, as it's lined with private boat moorings. I pass a couple of narrowboats. There is no sign of anyone on board, and they appear closed and shuttered for the winter.

I walk close to the boats along a narrow strip of concrete next to the canal. When this ends, the going starts to become more difficult. If I'm to stay off the road, I'm faced with a section of trees and dense under-growth, but I've got no choice.

Underfoot is hazardous. I'm glad of the broom, which I'm using as a stick to lean on to stop me from falling over. I try to increase my pace, but with no path to follow, my progress is glacial. It's a relief to come out into an area of well-tended allotments. I'm tempted to shelter from the wind in one of the greenhouses, but I know it's important to keep moving. Coming back into the open, the wind is now against me. Gusts are blowing snow straight into my face, soaking my hair and the front of my coat and dripping down into my boots. Pulling my scarf over my head, I plough on. It's not the best position to be in, but at least I'm giving myself a chance.

When I cross the railway line, the gravel at the side of the track shifts under me, and I skid down the bank, landing in an open field. In the distance, a beam of light appears momentarily, then disappears. A vehicle is approaching along the lane. I can hear the sound of tyres crunching on packed snow. I sprint and take cover behind the hedge, heart beating faster in anticipation. The car passes, flinging a pile of slush down on my head. Once the rear lights disappear from view, I skirt the edge of the field, staying close to the hedgerow. The snow is deeper here and harder to walk through, but I do have shelter from the bitter wind. I'm soaked to the skin, and my teeth are chattering. I know I need to find shelter and get warmed up soon, or I'm going to be in trouble.

The lights of the marina come into view. There's bound to be someone around who can help me. There's a restaurant on-site. I can call in there and ask to use their phone. My watch says 10:47 p.m. I've been walking for the best part of an hour.

I'm starting to feel light-headed, and I'm not paying attention to where I'm placing my feet. I've reached a line of tall tufted grass and immature trees, which my brain is telling me is the edge of the field. Suddenly, the ground beneath me slides away, and I'm falling backwards. Everything slows, and I land with a *humph* sound as the air is pushed out of my lungs. I've broken through a thin coating of ice, and my lower half is submerged in freezing water. The shock makes me gasp. I sit for a few moments, shivering uncontrollably, before hauling myself back up onto solid ground. What I thought was the boundary between two fields is a stretch of water where boats enter and leave the marina. On the coldest day of this unseasonable spell of weather, already wet and freezing cold, I've managed to slip into the canal.

To say I'm in deep trouble is a massive understatement. All along I've been concerned that Mel and her thugs are going to be responsible for my demise, when, in fact, it's my own carelessness that's going to be my downfall.

Stupid, stupid, stupid.

It's weird, because instead of concern about my

predicament, I'm starting to feel euphoric. It reminds me
of when I smoked cannabis a few times at uni. Floaty
and disassociated, I put my hand over my mouth to
suppress a giggle. The overall sensation is not unpleasant. If this is what it's like to die, then there is nothing to
be frightened of.

The path that leads into the marina is on the other
side of the water. I have to scramble up to the road, then
drop down to access it. It's uneven underfoot, and I
stumble a few times, but it's well lit, and there's a safety
rail to prevent people from falling into the water. A
slope brings me out onto the access road. It's stopped
snowing, and the wind has dropped. I'm warming up, I
can feel it; it's like being caressed by a warm breeze. My
clothes start to feel as though they are weighing me
down.

You're supposed to take them off when you fall into water,
aren't you?

Yes, but you are not in the water now, so how does that
work?

The voice in my head is reassuring and practical. I
want it to stay with me, to keep giving me advice, but
it's coming and going like a bad phone connection. I
unbutton my coat and discard it with a swing of the
wrist, like a Hollywood diva. Unwrapping my scarf
from around my head, I wind it around the nearest
lamppost. My saturated boots I kick into the bushes,
followed by my sopping wet tights. I feel as though I'm
walking on air.

There's a walkway leading down to the moored
boats. Suspended above are a row of fairy lights, their
haloes casting rainbows in the night air. It looks so
pretty I want to cry. The walkway has been swept of
snow to clear a path for owners to access their boats.
Stepping onto it, I can feel it rock gently beneath me.

There's a buzzing in my head, and my legs are starting to give way. I try to straighten up, wobble and lose my balance. This sends me crashing to the deck. Reaching out, I try to touch the diamonds I can see glittering in the piles of banked snow. I'm sleepy, so sleepy. I just need to rest my eyes for a while...

'Whoa. Be careful. You're going to end up falling in, you silly woman!'

A dog licks my face, and I force my eyes to open. A man is peering down at me, his voice a combination of anger and concern.

'Are you pissed?'

I reach my arms up towards him, conscious that I'm mumbling.

'Laurie, you and Buddy came to get me,' I say before everything dissolves and I disappear down a dark tunnel.

41

Pushing my way up through layers of sleep, it's a struggle to open my eyes. They feel as though they have been weighted down and glued shut.

I must have been dreaming. I remember the sensation of soaring high above the earth and looking down on a figure in a bed. I swoop downwards and see that it's me, lying pale and still. Then everything fades into darkness.

Now I'm conscious that I'm sinking into a downy nest, and I'm being bathed in currents of deliciously warm air. It's so peaceful I want to remain here forever. *Am I dead?* I imagine if I were, there would be nothing. That's patently not the case, but it's taking far too much effort to ponder such weighty issues. Sleep beckons, and with a deep sigh of contentment, I relinquish myself to its indolent charms.

The noises I awake to are muffled. The rattle of a trolley, the swish of a door and the irritating squeak of shoes on lino. A voice coming from far away, too indistinct to make out any words, is as irritating as a trapped wasp. There's a hiss, and the air fills with a pungent mix of floral antiseptic. I want to cough, but I haven't the energy to do so. Nor have I the strength to wave the person away, to tell them I just want to be left alone. To leave me to rest without interruption.

It feels like hours later that I wake from a deep and dreamless sleep, Someone is pulling at my arm. I snatch it away in annoyance and hear a woman's voice. Low and reassuring, it has a Caribbean inflection. 'Don't be frightened, Francesca. You're safe. I'm just changing your drip...'

I try to pay attention to what she's saying, but it's hard to focus, and my body feels leaden.

I'm aware of time passing. I have no idea how long ago it has been since the woman was here, although something around me has changed. Or is it me that is different? Noises are sharper, and there is a sensation of movement, as though the air is being disturbed. There are more voices. I try to force my eyes to open, but my lids are heavy.

'I think she's trying to open her eyes. Let's keep everything nice and calm. We don't want to startle her. She will be very disorientated.'

The person speaking is the one from earlier. I want to thank her for being so considerate. It would be nice to see who it is, too. Except my lashes are sticking together, and the light, when it hits my retina, is intense.

'Can someone pull down those blinds?' the woman says.

The room is a pale mushroom colour, and the bed I'm in is high, with starched white sheets. I have managed to force my eyes to open, but my head still feels fuzzy, and my vision is blurred. I try to speak, and what comes out is jumbled. 'Wheresamee. Where's me. I'm is where?'

I give up trying. I know what I want to say; it's just that what's coming out of my mouth is gibberish.

'Francesca, my name is Nancy, and I've been looking after you since you arrived. You're in hospital, recovering from hypothermia. The doctor will be along later, and he will explain everything to you. Let's try to sit you up so that you can see everyone.'

Nancy is not as I imagined. The authority in her voice made me think she was in her fifties and homely looking. Now I can see she's much younger than that, more like in her mid-thirties. She is lean and muscular and is wearing her hair swept up into a crown of tightly packed braids. Holding my arm, she leans me forward and plumps up my pillows, then presses a button to raise the head of the bed.

'How's that? Ready to face your audience?'

I nod in agreement, and she lowers the rails at the sides of the bed.

'One at a time now,' she says, addressing whoever is in the room. 'She's still confused. We don't want to overwhelm her.'

'Fran, it's Laurie.' He pulls a chair alongside and reaches for my hand. 'You gave us such a scare. Thank goodness you're okay. Alice and Flynn are here,' he says, gesturing to one side of the room.

Two figures materialise at the foot of the bed, their faces pinched and full of concern. I stretch out my arms, and they come to me. I hug each of them in turn. Flynn wipes away a tear while Alice weeps openly.

'We thought we'd lost you, Mum.' Flynn's voice is breaking with stress. He places an arm around his sister's quivering shoulders, and they lean into each other as though braced against a storm.

Laurie looks worn out, and I notice the shirt he is wearing hasn't been ironed.

'How long…?' I say.

'How long is it since you came in? Is that what you're asking?'

'Yes. What day is it?' My voice is still a dry rasp, and it's an effort to speak.

'It's Sunday. They brought you here in the early hours of Saturday. You were very sick, Fran. We didn't think you were going to make it.'

Alice gulps and begins to sob loudly.

'Can you remember any of what happened?' Laurie says. 'And what on earth were you doing at the marina? It was a miracle that the man found you when he did. His wife had been on a first-aid course at work and knew some of the basics of hypothermia. Mostly, what not to do. You weren't wearing any clothes, and she wrapped you up in a quilt and blankets from their boat while they waited for the ambulance. By the time they got there, you were unconscious.'

I can see that Alice and Flynn are becoming more distressed. I don't want them to hear anything else that will upset them further. Not yet, anyway.

'Y'know what me and your dad could do with?' I say. 'A nice cup of tea. Do you think you could find one for us?'

'There's a café by the main entrance,' Flynn says. 'We could have a walk down and see if they are open.'

He steers a reluctant Alice out through the door. I can hear their footsteps echoing down the corridor.

Laurie takes the opportunity to go into quiz mode.

'First of all, do you remember how you got to Willington? You had no keys or phone on you when you were admitted. And where the hell is your car? Fortunately, the couple at the marina gathered up your clothes and gave them to the ambulance crew. One of the nursing staff found your bank card in your coat pocket and did some detective work. They got hold of my name from LinkedIn, found my number and rang on the off-chance. I got here about an hour after you were brought in. I hadn't been too worried after you messaged me to say you were going to be late, although, when it got to after eleven, I knew something was wrong. I thought you might have skidded in the snow and were lying in a ditch somewhere. I was about to ring the police when I got the call from the hospital.'

My head is spinning from all the questions, and I'm conscious that Alice and Flynn will be back before I have the chance to say what I need to.

.'I have to tell you something important, Laurie. It will make the kids even more worried, so let's just keep it to ourselves for the moment.'

Laurie looks at me with a puzzled expression.

'It wasn't me,' I say.

'What wasn't you?'

'Whoever messaged you. It wasn't me.'

'Then who…?'

'I was kidnapped, Laurie. They were going to take me somewhere and kill me, but I escaped. They messaged you from my phone and then threw the phone away along with my keys. I don't know what they've done with my car. It was missing when I got to the car park at the crematorium.'

'You're not making any sense, Fran. Who would want to kidnap you? Are you sure you didn't have an accident? You could have banged your head. I'm going to see if I can find the doctor. I think you've got a delayed concussion.'

He gets up from his seat, and I reach across to grab his arm.

'No,' I say with as much force as I can summon. 'There's nothing wrong with my memory. I know it sounds as though I'm delusional, but it's all true, and I can prove it.'

'I'm not doubting you. I think you do *believe* that's what happened. Let me find a doctor to check you out, and then we can go from there.'

There's no arguing with Laurie once he has got an idea fixed in his head. Anyway, I feel too exhausted to continue protesting.

'Don't go too far,' I say to his retreating back. 'They will want to come and finish the job. I need to talk to DI…'

My words fall on deaf ears, as he is already out the door and walking down the corridor. The sound of his shoes squeaking on the polished surface makes me want to scream in frustration at his retreating form.

Lying back on the pillows, I realise how barking mad I must sound. An icy-cold rush of fear washes over me. What if I can't get anyone to believe me? What if they think I've lost my marbles, and end up sectioning me?

Laurie reappears with a man I assume is the doctor. Tall, dark and not much older than Flynn, he has a calf lick that causes his hair to fall over one eye in a rakish fashion. He is not wearing a white coat, but he does have a stethoscope around his neck.

'Nice to see you looking so well, Mrs Hughes. I'm Dr Shah. I was on duty when they brought you in. You were so cold you were barely with us. Your core body temperature was very low, and we had to get you warmed up nice and slowly.'

He squeezes the line on the drip attached to my arm. 'I can see that warmed saline has run through, so I'll take your drip out now. You've responded really well to treatment, and all your observations have been good. I just need to do a few checks to make sure you're in tip-top condition before we can consider letting you go home.'

Dr Shah takes my chart from the bottom of the bed and studies it carefully. He checks my pulse, listens to my heart and chest, looks down my throat, and then in my eyes. 'Any headaches, blurred vision?'

'I felt a bit groggy, and my vision was blurred when I first woke up. I still feel wobbly, but apart from that, I'm doing well, I think.'

'Let me be the judge of that,' Dr Shah says, winking at me. 'Now I'm going to ask you a few questions. Don't worry if you can't answer them all. It will take time to get back to normal after what you've been through.'

'Cognitive tests,' I say wearily. 'My husband thinks I'm going gaga.'

Apart from not knowing what time it is, I sail through the list of questions, and Dr Shah seems pleased with the results.

'You are doing great on all fronts, Mrs Hughes. I think the best course of action is to keep you in for a couple of days, just to be on the safe side. We can arrange your discharge once we are sure you are on the road to recovery.'

I look across at Laurie. Judging by his expression, he doesn't seem convinced by what he's heard.

'Is there any possibility she could have crashed her car and is suffering from concussion, Doctor?'

'Highly unlikely. There was no evidence of even minor injuries when she was brought in, just hypothermia. Of course, we can't rule out the possibility that her car broke down. If she tried to walk in the snow, she could easily have become disoriented.'

'Yes. I suppose you're right. Except she was nowhere near where she was supposed to be. Her explanation for how she got to where she was found seems so implausible. I just wanted to make sure she hasn't been hallucinating or suffering some sort of delusional episode.'

'It's unlikely, but you are right to be worried. We'll keep an eye on her over the next day or so. However, I don't think you have any need to be unduly concerned.'

Dr Shah's beeper sounds, and he dashes off to go and find his next patient. Laurie comes and sits on the chair next to my bed. He has deep furrows across his forehead. Linking his fingers with mine, he sighs deeply.

'You look tired. Why don't you go home and get some rest,' I say. 'And what about Buddy? You can't have left him on his own all day, surely?'

'No, I went back this morning to get a shower and change of clothes. I took him for a long run in the woods, and he was fine when I left him. I'm not happy about leaving you, but he will be due another walk soon. If I go now, I can be back in an hour or so.'

'Can you bring in some pyjamas and my toothbrush? This hospital gown is very unattractive.'

'Of course.' Laurie smiles, and some of the tension drops away from his face. 'You must be getting better if you're thinking about how you look.'

'And, Laurie,' I say, clutching his arm, 'you do believe me about the kidnap, don't you?'

'Kidnap, what kidnap?'

I'd forgotten about Flynn and Alice. They have arrived, balancing cardboard cups of drinks. Alice, standing in the doorway in front of Flynn, has a look of alarm on her face.

'Let me explain, Alice…' I reach for her hand with mine, but she shrugs it off.

'Don't even try to fob me off, Mum. I'm not a child. Are you saying you were kidnapped?'

_____

42

It's early evening, and they have moved me to a room closer to the nurses' station. It has a large glass viewing window and slatted blinds. They have been left open, and I can see the comings and goings as nurses, doctors and visitors congregate around the central hub. A police officer has been dispatched to guard my door. I can make out the top of his balding head through the porthole in the door and hear his booming laugh as he flirts with the female members of staff.

The light above my bed has been lowered and is casting a soft, warm glow. I want to sleep. All the activity this afternoon and the effort involved in talking has left me exhausted. Nancy has brought me a cup of tea and a stale ham sandwich. After taking a couple of bites of limp bread and sipping the lukewarm tea, I start to feel nauseous.

Earlier, after I had given Alice and Flynn a condensed version of what happened, Alice freaked out – and Laurie, for once, had been on the receiving end.

She instructed him to ring the police immediately. 'How could you not believe her, you idiot!' she screamed. 'She's at risk, Dad, and you're sitting on your arse as though nothing has happened.'

We are all used to Alice's outbursts, but this took us all by surprise. Laurie looked shocked at being the target for her anger for once.

I was too weak to remonstrate with her, and Flynn's attempts at trying to calm her were ineffective. I recognised the signs. Alice was winding herself up into a frenzy of rage. It reminded me of the terrible twos, which, in Alice's case, lasted until she started school. Like a summer storm, it tended to blow over. After a cuddle and milk and a biscuit, equilibrium would be restored, for a while anyway. If only it were still so easy.

The ruckus brought Nancy to the room. She looked at Alice, who was still railing at Laurie, Flynn holding her arms to prevent her from lashing out.

'What on earth is going on here? This is a hospital, not a playground, young lady. I will not have this on my ward. You need to calm down, or I will have to ask you to leave.'

Nancy's firm talking-to had the desired effect on Alice. She gulped a few times before taking a tissue from the box Nancy offered to her, then wiped her eyes and blew her nose. I nodded in Laurie's direction, and he got up andwent over to her.

'Come on, sweetie,' he said. It was a relief to see her collapse against his shoulder, her hostility towards him ebbing away.

'This is my fault,' he said to Nancy. 'My daughter has a right to be angry with me. I'm afraid I haven't taken my wife's account of how she ended up here seriously enough. The police are going to have to be informed. I'm sure the hospital will have procedures to follow in cases like this. Can you contact whoever needs to be involved, while I make the call to the police?'

Laurie left with a reluctant Flynn and Alice. He will return after dropping them at the station and seeing to Buddy. The whirlwind of activity in my room subsided with the arrival of DI Holmes and DS Georgiou. For some reason, I was expecting PCs to turn out on a Sunday evening. I apologised profusely to DI Holmes for taking her away from her family at a weekend.

She shrugged and said, 'Don't worry about that, Fran. It's the nature of the job. We're used to it.'

They brought chairs from the corner of the room and got out their notepads.

'We are aware you have been through a considerable trauma,' DI Holmes said, looking solemn. 'If we have your consent, we would like to interview you on the understanding that your medical needs take priority. The nursing staff have made that very clear. If you feel as though you want to take a break or it proves too much for you, you need to let us know. Is that okay with you?'

I nodded in agreement. 'I'm ready,' I said. 'It's just knowing where to start; there's so much. You're going to be furious with me when I tell you the full story. I've been a complete fool, and I've got myself into a mess. Even Laurie doesn't know the half of it.'

'Just give us as much information as you can,' said DS Georgiou. 'You can leave the rest up to us.'

I talked, with very little interruption from the two of them, trying hard to include even the most minor detail that might have significance. Some of it was jumbled and out of order, and I had to backtrack a couple of times, my head thumping from the effort.

'Is that everything, as far as you can recall?' said DI Holmes, flicking through the pages of notes she had written.

It had been over an hour, and fatigue was setting in. 'That's pretty much it,' I said. 'I'm so sorry, but I think I need to rest.' I lay back against the pillows and waited for my head to stop swimming.

'We have all the information we need for now, and your co-operation has been invaluable,' DI Holmes said. 'I don't have to tell you that you are in a vulnerable position, especially in such a public place. I'm going to have you moved, and an officer will be placed outside your room for your safety. No visitors are allowed apart from direct family. We will speak again about your ongoing security when it's time for you to leave the hospital.'

Not especially reassuring, but everything is now out in the open, with them at least. Telling Laurie the full extent of my foolishness will be a different proposition.

FROM MY NEW VANTAGE POINT, I see Laurie arrive. The ward has a buzzer-controlled door, and he walks in and strides past the desk where Nancy is sitting, tapping something into the computer. I wave, even though I know he won't be looking in my direction. He returns a few minutes later, looking frazzled, before Nancy points him in the direction of my room. I hear him exchange words with the police officer, who sticks his head around the door. 'This man says he's your husband. Can you confirm his identity?'

I want to laugh out loud at how ridiculous it all is, but Laurie doesn't look amused.

'Yes. That's my husband,' I say, feeling like an idiot.

Laurie looks around the room. 'Been upgraded to five star, I see. NHS patients don't usually get their own en suite.'

'Nothing but the best,' I say. 'Did the kids get off all right?'

'Yes, they did. And before you ask, Buddy is fine too. A bit put out that I was leaving him on his own again. He sat by the front door as I was going, looking very sorry for himself.'

Laurie unpacks the bag he has brought. It's one I use for yoga, and its bright blue and white spots stand out in contrast to the pastel tones in the room. I try not to turn up my nose at his choice of my nightwear and the plastic bag containing my toothbrush and toothpaste.

'Can you come and sit down? I need to talk to you.'

'Is it about Alice? She wasn't upset when I left her. We had a good chat in the car on the way to the station.'

'It's not about Alice.'

I wish by some alchemy I could rewind and go back to the time before that fateful day when Tyler was killed. Press the erase button on all the sordid events of the past few weeks. I feel tainted by it all. A clean slate is what I want, but I can't unsee what I've seen, or undo what I've done. And anyway, I'm kidding myself if I think everything was perfect before. It wasn't. I just happen to have made things complicated and dangerous for us, and I don't know how I'm going to make it right.

What I don't feel like doing is any more talking, but I have to. The thought of Laurie finding out how much I contributed towards my own downfall is causing my stomach to churn. I gave him such a hard time after the affair, it will be fair game if he switches to the moral high ground and turns the tables on me. I deserve it, after all.

HE'S QUIET, too quiet, after I tell him the full no-holds-barred version that led up to the kidnapping. I have to fill in so many of the gaps. Tell him about what I discovered about Mel and the full extent of her involvement in the supply chain. He flinches when I describe how I tried to defend Gabe during his run-in with the gang in Birmingham.

'Laurie...?' I say, waiting for some kind of reaction.

He shakes his head and runs his hands through his hair a few times, then rubs the rough stubble on his chin. He doesn't look at me for a long time. When he does, I see anger and disappointment in his eyes.

'What possessed you...? Were you bored? Unfulfilled? Was life really that lacking in excitement?' He's looking at the floor, still shaking his head.

His words are all too reminiscent of mine to him, not that long ago.

Yes, I want to shout. *All of those things and more. I did it for Tyler and for that baby and also for me, weak and pathetic individual that I am. I wasn't to know that Mel would turn out to be so toxic. I made an error of judgement, and now I'm paying the price.*

It doesn't feel like the right time for those words. I want to placate him, not create a space for an argument. 'I'm so sorry, Laurie,' I say. 'I've cocked up big time. I know that.'

He's pacing the room now, like a caged animal.

'Please come and sit down. I can't talk to you when you're like this.'

'Like this. Like this!' He's shouting, and I feel fear in the face of his fury. 'How on earth do you expect me to behave? This isn't just about you; it affects us all. It's going to have a major effect on the rest of our lives, and you expect me to suck it up. You're a fucking selfish cow.'

We have rowed before, but not like this. He's incandescent with rage, and his shoulders are heaving. I realise he's weeping, and I'm shocked. I've never seen Laurie like this in all the time we've been together.

There's a tentative knock, and Nancy's head appears around the door. The PC on duty has most likely heard raised voices and called upon her to come and investigate.

'Can I get you anything, Francesca?' she says.

I admire her diplomacy. She knows we are quarrelling and that her presence is likely to defuse the argument.

'Your evening meal will be here soon. Is there anything you would like, Mr Hughes? I can rustle up a cup of tea and a sandwich?'

Laurie shakes his head. I'm relieved to see he is starting to calm down. He goes to the bathroom, and I hear the tap running. When he returns, he picks up his coat and goes towards the door.

'Thank you, Nancy ' he says. 'I'm going for a walk to clear my head. I apologise for the shouting.'

'You mustn't overdo it, Fran,' Nancy says after he's gone. 'You have had a lot of visitors today, and your body is still recovering. You need rest, not aggravation. If there is any more nonsense, I will put a ban on all visitors.'

I feel pitifully grateful for her concern.

'Please don't be nice to me, Nancy,' I say, turning my head into my pillow to hide my tears.

I wait all evening for Laurie to come back.
He doesn't.

43

'They found your car and located your phone. No sign of your keys, though.'

It's morning, and Laurie is back, freshly showered and shaved and carrying his computer bag over his shoulder. He is wearing a clean shirt and chinos. I'm still feeling churned up inside after our argument and irritated to see he is acting as though nothing has happened. He doesn't mention his outburst from the night before.

After he'd gone, I had an awful night, my sleep interrupted by my usual anxiety dreams. It was close to midnight when Nancy came to do my observations. She offered me a sleeping pill, which I declined. I then tossed and turned for hours, conscious of the sweaty plastic under sheet and lumpy pillows. Eventually I slept, only to wake at 5 a.m. to the sound of the medicine trolley being wheeled up and down the corridor. After breakfast, Nancy had called a healthcare assistant to change the bed sheets and remain in the room while I had a shower.

It feels good to be out of bed at last. I'm sitting on a

chair in my clean pyjamas when Laurie puts in an appearance.

'Where was the car?' I say, trying to sound as normal as I can.

'Up a lane about a mile from the crematorium, at the entrance to a field. The farmer was going to check on his cows and called it in to the police. We can collect it once the police have finished with it. And they managed to track your phone to a ditch at the side of the road not far from Willington.'

The routine nature of the conversation is disconcerting. I want him to know how upset I am about him leaving and not coming back last night, but I can't face stirring it all up again.

'The doctor will be doing his rounds this morning,' I say. 'I'm hoping he will let me come home.'

'We'll have to see what the police have to say. They are coming back to talk to you this afternoon.'

'Oh, about what?'

'They didn't say. Just that they would be in later. About security, I would guess.'

We sit for a while in awkward silence until Laurie takes out his laptop and flips up the lid. 'You don't mind if I catch up on my emails, do you? Oh, and I almost forgot.' He draws out a slim box from the front pocket of the bag and hands it to me.

'It's a basic pay-as-you-go. It will tide you over until we find out whether we can have your phone back or need to get you a new one. I've put our shared family's and friends' numbers from my phone on there.'

'Thanks,' I say. 'I was beginning to feel a bit cut off from everything. I should have got you to bring in my laptop, too. Then we can sit and ignore each other and pretend everything's all right when we know it's not.'

There. The words are out in the open. I wait for the

eruption of anger, my eyes fixed on the porthole window in the door. The police officer from yesterday has been replaced. This one looks younger, if the back of his head is anything to go by. He has reddish blond hair slicked down with gel. A coiled wisp, having escaped his ministrations, curls around the back of his ear. If Laurie starts shouting again, what will his response be? Ignore us? Interrupt us? Call for a nurse or doctor to intervene?

I'm about to find out.

Laurie slams shut the lid of his laptop and turns to face me. I've known him for so long, yet his expression is difficult to read. Inscrutable. It's a word Mum and I liked to use when we were struggling to come up with a backstory for one of the characters we were observing. *In-scroo-tible.* My younger self would draw out the word, testing it on my tongue, and Mum would laugh at my efforts.

'What is it you want from me, Fran?' Laurie's voice is steely. 'An apology for the way I behaved? Because if you are, you're going to be waiting a long time. Under the circumstances I don't think I've been that unreasonable.'

I sigh wearily, knowing he's partly right.

'So where do we go from here?'

'What do you mean?'

'I've ruined everything. I know that,' I say. 'I was just thinking about how we might move on from this, if at all. Do you want us to separate?' My voice is tremulous. I swallow hard, trying to control my tears.

'What the hell are you talking about? Are you serious, or are you just being a drama queen? After all we've been through as a couple, are you seriously contemplating a separation?'

'No. It's not what I want,' I say miserably. 'But you

were so angry. I wouldn't blame you if you hate me and want to move on and start again somewhere else.'

The image of Laurie and his replacement family flashes briefly before my eyes.

'Really, Fran?' He shakes his head in disbelief. 'Have you really got so little faith in me? You think I am capable of swanning off into the sunset on my own when the going gets tough?'

'I don't know,' I say. 'Everything is so mixed up. I'm mixed up. Nothing is the same…'

Laurie gets up and comes to sit on the bed alongside me. He takes my hands in his and looks into my eyes. I can't bear it and turn away. I'm pathetic and angry with myself for feeling that way. I loathe being so weak, and I don't want him to stay with me out of duty – or worse, pity.

'Look at me, please. I have something important I want to say.' He shakes my hands from side to side to get my attention. 'First of all, and despite all that has happened over the last year, I love you, and I hope the feeling is mutual. Is it?'

'Yes.' I gulp, reaching for a tissue. I wipe away the tears coursing down my cheeks.

'Right. I'm glad that's clear. I know you are feeling unsafe after what has happened, and I've been doing some thinking about what we could do about that.' His voice is low and considered. 'What are your thoughts on us selling up and moving away from here?'

I sit up, and my mouth drops open in surprise.

'I will lose out by cashing in my pension early,' he continues. 'But I can still do the odd bit of freelancing from home. If we sold the house and your mum's flat, we could buy something smaller and cheaper. Maybe even move to Wales, near to my mum and dad. You get more for your money there, and we would be left with a sizeable nest egg for the future. You don't have to decide immediately. It's something you need to be one hundred percent in agreement with. Your mum left you her flat, and selling it will be an emotional wrench for you. In fact, if you wanted to, you could keep the flat on and continue renting it out if you can't bear to sell it.'

'No,' I say. 'I don't need to think about it. It's a great idea. Let's do it. And sooner rather than later.'

We toast to our future with water from the jug and plastic cups on the bedside table. When Dr Shah calls in on his rounds, I am still in good spirits and eager to get discharged.

'My, my, Mrs Hughes. You look like a different person to the one who was brought in. I'm satisfied that you have made an excellent recovery, and I'm happy to let you go home on condition that you rest and recuperate. I can arrange a follow-up appointment with your GP in a week or so. I will write up the paperwork, and Nancy will sort out your discharge.'

'Thanks so much to all of you for looking after me,' I say. 'Once the police have interviewed me, I will get out of your hair. I feel far too healthy to be taking up a hospital bed.'

Laurie leaves with a list of clothes I want him to bring from home. He's been down to the emergency room and critical care to see if he can locate what I was wearing when I was brought in, but there's no sign of any of it.

'They said your stuff was probably handed over to the police. They may have wanted it for forensics.'

THE DAY IS STARTING to drag, and I'm leafing through a pile of out-of-date magazines Nancy brought in from one of the waiting rooms, when DI Holmes and DS Georgiou arrive. They stop outside the door to have a word with the young PC before coming in.

'It's good to see you have recovered, Fran,' says Jo Holmes. 'Dr Shah says you are able to leave this afternoon.'

'I'm ready to go home, I can tell you. I'm raring to go. There's so much to organise. Laurie and I are selling up and moving away.'

I notice the familiar 'look' that passes between them, and the smile freezes on my face. I've seen this exchange before, and it usually means trouble.

'What is it? Is something wrong?' My heartbeat speeds up, and my breath catches in my throat.

'We can't let you go home, Fran. Not yet. We want you and Laurie to go into a safe house for a while. There have been some major developments, and we think you are still at risk.' DI Holmes is unusually curt, and her initial friendliness has evaporated.

'But I thought the security you mentioned would be at our house,' I say. 'We have the panic button and good home security. It was my understanding you would be just increasing police presence for a while.'

DI Holmes has on a heavy layer of make-up, which doesn't quite conceal the dark circles beneath her eyes. It's obvious she is tired; they both are. DS Georgiou looks dishevelled and in need of a shower. They both look as though they have been up all night working. DS Georgiou glances across at his boss for affirmation before speaking, and she nods her head in assent.

'I'm not at liberty to give out too much information on the case at this moment in time,' he says. 'But we have made significant arrests in operations involving other police forces. Unfortunately, Melanie Ingram, a major suspect implicated in your kidnap, has evaded arrest. We believe she may have connections to Europe, and it's possible she has left the country. But, whilst she is still at large, we are concerned your safety may be compromised. A safe house is the best option until she is apprehended.'

'What about her son Gabe?'

'He's being looked after. That's all I'm prepared to say.'

'Am I to conclude that by "significant arrests", you mean of the gang members? The ones Mel was about to go into partnership with?' I say.

'As DS Georgiou has explained, this is an ongoing operation, and until Melanie Ingram is arrested, we cannot guarantee your safety.'

There's no denying it. DI Holmes is weary, and it's making her tetchy. She skirted around answering my question, which is unusual for her.

'I'm so sorry,' I say. 'I do understand what you are saying, and I really appreciate all you have done, but I'm going home.'

'You do realise our resources are very stretched, don't you? If you do return home, the security cover we can offer will be limited.' Again, there's an edge to her voice.

'I am aware of that,' I say. 'But we are keen to pack up the house and put it up for sale. As soon as we are able to, we are going to move to a new location a long way from here. We aren't going to tell anyone where we are going, apart from close family.'

It strikes me that Laurie might be less than pleased with my unilateral decision not to go into the police version of hiding. I ring him as he's about to leave.

'Can you pick up some chocolates for the nurses?' I say. 'Oh, and they want us to go into a safe house until they catch Mel. She's on the run.'

'No way,' he says. 'If you are in agreement, I think it's best we sort the house out and get it on the market straight away. We can go to Mum and Dad's until it sells. I've spoken to them, and they would love to have us.'

I feel lighter, as though a huge weight has been lifted from my shoulders. We are both in agreement, and we have a shared goal for our future. We just need to put the plan into action, and we can be on our way.

'That's what I told the police,' I say. 'Now get your skates on and come and get me. I've got loads to do!'

44

W e have a police escort from the hospital, and then we are left to our own devices. A car will be sent to provide cover at the house, as and when resources allow. Other than that, we will have to remain alert and on our guard.

As we come through the front door, Buddy barks his stranger bark, then launches himself at Laurie. He keeps his distance from me, eyeing me warily.

'Buddy, come here. What's the matter?'

He circles around me a few times and takes a sniff at my outstretched hand.

'Bud, you silly boy. What is it? I thought you'd be pleased to see me.'

'You don't smell right,' Laurie says. 'I'm with him. You smell of the hospital. He'll be fine once that disappears.'

'I'll have a bath,' I say. 'The hospital shower was a weak trickle. It'll be nice to have a soak, and perhaps then I won't be so off-putting to the men in my life.'

Casting a glance around the room, I've never before

thought of our tastes in home decor as being especially vibrant. However, in contrast to the bland neutrality of the hospital, the navy blue feature wall and splashes of colour from the pictures, cushions and throws is a welcome assault on my senses. I feel a pang of sadness at the thought of leaving. The years we have spent here, turning it into a home, a safe place where we raised our kids, threw parties, enjoyed meals with family and friends, where we laughed and cried and planned for a trouble-free retirement, all that is over. There's no point in having regrets. We need to move on, to make new memories, create a home together and enjoy the rest of our lives. We can do that. It's only bricks and mortar, after all.

'You okay, Fran?'

'Of course. I'm feeling a bit sentimental, that's all,' I say, brushing away a stray tear. 'It's just memories, and we can take them with us.'

'Go and have a long soak. I'll do something quick for us to eat, and we can talk about our plans after dinner.'

The wood burner is blazing when I come downstairs wrapped up in my fleecy dressing gown. We eat Laurie's stir-fry, and I drink a little wine, my body adjusting to a diet richer than what was on offer in the hospital. Buddy sits between us, still unsure of me, though happy to have me stroke the silky backs of his ears.

'It's weird being back,' I say. 'It seems so long ago, yet it's only been a few days since the funeral.'

'I know. This is almost like old times, except so much has happened. I'm not saying at any level that's been a good thing, but in a way, being forced to evaluate our lives and make changes could be positive in the long run. We were coasting along, and that might have continued indefinitely. Horrible as it's been, this has given us the impetus to actually do what we've talked about for so long.'

We talk long into the night until we are both close to exhaustion. We agree that for safety reasons, we will do as much as we can online. Laurie will delegate his meetings and work from home for the next few days. The house will go on the market, and the tenants of Mum's flat will be given three months' notice before that too goes up for sale. Apart from a suitcase of clothes each, our personal belongings will go into storage, as will our furniture once the house has sold. Moving in with Verena and Bryn is only going to be a temporary arrangement. Staying too long with them is bound to result in frayed tempers. We will find a rental, and when everything is finalised here, we can then look for our new home.

'It's important that we put your safety first, Fran,' Laurie says. 'It seems to me your relationship with Mel was ambivalent, but you have enough information about her and the gang to put them all away for a very long time once this goes to trial. We can't take this lightly, and the police are right to want to take precautions against you being intimidated or coming to harm. But a safe house could have us ending up in some godawful backwater, and that's not what either of us wants. The sooner we get away from here, on our own terms, the better. Hopefully, they will capture her before long, and we can get on with our lives and stop looking over our shoulders.'

I CAN'T SLEEP. As Laurie snores quietly alongside me, I go over in my head the plans we are finalising and consider what the future might hold for us. Laurie is excited and eager to set the wheels in motion, whereas I suddenly feel anxious at the speed and scale of it all. The enormity of what we are about to do is starting to hit home. I know we can't remain in this house. Too much has happened, and I will never feel the same again about living here. Moving on has got to be the best option, surely?

The next morning, while Laurie takes a conference call in the office upstairs, I begin to tackle the list of seemingly endless tasks on my to-do list. It's something I'm usually good at. Today, however, I'm listless and unfocused. It all feels like a huge chore. Laurie comes down, and I'm glad to have a break from the computer. He sounds cheerful.

'Work has been surprisingly accommodating. I think it's because there's not much in the pipeline once these big contracts finish. I've told them I'm retiring, but that I'll be available in the future on an ad hoc basis for any work that doesn't take me away from home.'

He measures out the coffee into the cafetière, adds the water and presses the plunger. 'How are you getting on? You look a bit frazzled. Don't go overdoing it if you're not feeling up to it. You've only just got out of hospital.'

I give him what I hope is a reassuring smile.

'That must be it,' I say. 'I'm a bit dozy, and I haven't been especially productive this morning. I have spoken to the estate agent, though, and messaged the rental agency to give notice on Mum's flat. I've also looked at some storage places. It's only our personal stuff to start with, so it's not too pricey.'

We munch on home-made shortbread sent by Jenny at the weekend. Laurie has told her I crashed the car in the snow and that's why I was spending a few days in hospital.

'We will have to tell her the truth,' I say. 'You know how much I hate lying to people.'

The words are out before I realise their implication. He raises an eyebrow but doesn't say anything. 'Oh, shit, Laurie. I know what you're thinking. That I didn't extend the same courtesy to you when I got us tied up in this predicament. I promise you, nothing like this will ever happen again. Lies have consequences. It was all an aberration on my part, and I've learnt my lesson. From now on, everything has to be up front. I don't ever again want to be the sort of person who lies and deceives.'

I can hear the steady tick of the kitchen clock filling the silence. Laurie shifts in his seat. His face is creased with worry, and I realise he thinks I'm getting at him – which, if I'm honest, I probably am, at a level. The original wound is too deep to heal without the odd twinge of pain. He refills our coffee cups and takes a long swig before he replies.

'I know I've been an absolute bastard and hurt you deeply. I have no real defence except to say it was a bad time, and your grief and the stress you were under at work put an invisible barrier between us. That's not an excuse, and I'm not blaming you. I just felt left out and unable to help. The affair was a diversion, and I'm not proud of my behaviour. If there is anything positive to be gained from the whole sorry episode, it's that I've learned a lot about myself and what I want from life. I'm not suggesting we can pretend nothing has happened; that would be foolish. I just want to put it behind us and look to our future, and I hope you can do the same. What do you say?'

He has his coffee cup in his hand, and I pick up mine.

'I'll drink to that,' I say.

'Then we should go and ring the kids and tell them.'

We clink our cups together, and I feel my uncertainty start to dissipate.

Perhaps we can get back on an even keel after all.

I could do without any more drama, that's for sure.

45

November is always such a miserable month. The early snow from October has disappeared, to be replaced by a leaden sky. The rain beats down relentlessly, the staccato drumming on the windows adding to the pounding in my head. Being stuck in together is taking its toll, and we are niggling at each other. We can't even walk Buddy. He has to settle for a desultory amble around the garden twice a day.

We are making progress in boxing up our personal possessions, and tomorrow they will be collected by a local storage company. A charity shop has been to pick up bags of bric-a-brac, unwanted clothing and items of furniture we no longer have any use for. The house is beginning to look vacant and dejected.

Laurie is sorting out the shed, and I'm at a bit of a loose end. I ring Jenny and ask if she is free to come and have a coffee.

'That's perfect timing, Fran. I've made some banana bread this morning. I know how much Laurie enjoys it. I noticed his car as I was going out earlier.'

Buddy signals her arrival with a bout of excited

barking, and we sidestep boxes of stuff piled high in the hallway.

'My goodness. What's going on? Are you having a clear-out?'

'Come through,' I say. 'I'll explain everything.'

Jenny hands me a tin covered in a pattern of sweet peas and a small paper-wrapped item.

'For Buddy. I made a meat pie, and there was some leftover pastry.'

The bone-shaped biscuit with a cube of steak at its centre is carried by Buddy, like treasure, to a far corner of the room and demolished in a couple of bites.

'Oh my, I will have to make a few more of those. He seems quite partial to them.'

While I brew coffee, I can hear Jenny talking to Buddy in the front room. She's lonely, I realise that. It's going to be difficult telling her our news.

Laurie is outside, dressed in his waterproof coat, and I bang on the glass to get his attention.

'Coffee,' I mouth, mimicking drinking from a cup.

He nods and holds up both hands. 'Give me ten.'

'I'm sorry about the mess.' I can see Jenny looking around in puzzlement as I bring in the tray.

'It looks as though you are moving,' she says sadly, her hand balancing on Buddy's head.

'We are, Jenny. I know it seems a bit sudden, but we have had our hands somewhat forced.'

'When will you be going?'

'At the weekend. I'm afraid I can't say where. You see, we have to leave as soon as possible. It's not safe to remain here.'

I have almost finished filling in the background to our imminent departure when I hear Laurie stomp into the kitchen and wipe his feet on the mat. He appears, hair slicked down from the rain and water droplets running down his face.

'Hello, Jenny. Nice to see you. Filthy weather out there. I apologise for my appearance.'

I fetch a towel and a hot mug of coffee, which I give to him, along with a slice of Jenny's cake.

'Mmm, delicious,' he says. 'I will certainly miss your home baking. Fran has told you of our plans, I assume?'

'Yes, she has. I knew something was going on,' Jenny says. 'I recognised a police officer from one of our Neighbourhood Watch meetings sitting in a car outside. I completely understand why you have to leave. Fran has explained everything. That woman sounds unhinged. I will be very sorry to see you all go, though. People are a lot less sociable in the street nowadays, and it was nice to have you as neighbours. I'm just sorry your last memories of here are not pleasant ones.'

I might have known nothing would escape Jenny's notice. In anyone else – Avis for one – I would find her watchfulness and level of scrutiny irritating. Jenny, in contrast, is so gracious and thoughtful, I cannot imagine her revelling in gossip. I resist the temptation to say I will come back and visit. Drop in to say hello. Chat about old times. Deep down, I know it's not going to happen. There's no point in making promises I have no intention of keeping.

Laurie is keen to get back to clearing his shed and I have more packing to do. Jenny gets up from her place on the sofa and gives Buddy a quick stroke.

'I was thinking of how I might make myself useful,' she says. 'If you like, I can look after Buddy for a few hours tomorrow. It's probably best if he's not under your feet, especially when they come to collect the boxes.'

Later, as we are sitting in front of the TV, having the

last of the frozen pizzas from the freezer before I switch
it to defrost, a local news report catches our attention.

Police are appealing for help in tracing the whereabouts of
thirty-eight-year-old Melanie Ingram from Willington in
Derby. She is wanted on drug and kidnap charges. These form
part of an ongoing investigation involving East and West
Midlands Police forces. She fled the scene as police were
making arrests at a property in the village of Willington. She
has links to Derbyshire, Birmingham and Rotterdam in the
Netherlands. Ingram is of medium build and is approximately
five feet six with shoulder-length blonde hair and blue eyes.
Police urge you not to approach her, but instead to ring the
numbers at the bottom of the screen.

A photo of Mel appears on the screen with police
contact numbers underneath. I feel the hairs rise on the
backs of my arms.

'I wish they would hurry up and catch her,' I say.
'It's horrible having to be on our guard all the time. I
can't *imagine* her rocking up here, though. Her best bet,
surely, would be to get out of the country.'

Laurie reaches for the remote and turns off the TV.

'And our best bet is to get away as soon as we can. I
suggest we go before the weekend. There's no point in
hanging around any longer. By tomorrow, we will have
finished what we need to do here. We can leave on
Thursday and drop the keys off at the estate agent's on
the way.'

THE NIGHTMARES HAVE RETURNED with a vengeance. In
this one, I'm running through a forest of tall pines.
Someone is chasing me, and my feet are tripping over
boulders and tree roots. My breath is ragged, heart
bursting with the effort. Suddenly the ground gives way

beneath me. I scrabble, arms and legs flailing, desperately trying to keep my footing, but I tumble down, down, leaf litter and pine needles raining down on me until I'm covered in a dense blanket of decaying matter.

No psychologist needed to interpret this one.

It's still dark when I wake, gasping for breath and soaked in sweat. Not wanting to disturb Laurie, I ease myself out of bed and grab my dressing gown from behind the bathroom door. The air is cold, and my breath mists as I exhale. The security beam triggers, and a splinter of light glints through a gap in the window blind.

I draw the blind up a fraction and peer out, expecting to see a fox or some other nocturnal creature.

There's nothing moving out there. Just an eerie glow cast by the LED, illuminating an expanse of frozen lawn.

46

There are so many decisions you can make in life. So many turns in the road available to you, especially if you have access to resources. We are lucky. I know that others in society, for varying reasons, have not been dealt such a fortunate hand. Mum always believed in paying it back if you had an excess of good fortune. *It's not fair,* I would wail as she dragged (she would say encouraged) me to accompany her to yet another feed-the-homeless event, some community fundraiser or flag-waving march for an obscure, under-represented group she felt was deserving of her time and energy.

There's even a photo of the two of us at Greenham Common, joining in an anti-nuclear protest. I'm a bashful teen, head down, curly perm covering my face, whereas Mum is looking straight at the camera, eyes alight with fervour. Out of sight are the bolt cutters she would later use to cut a hole in the perimeter fence. The spark she lit in me to speak out against unfairness and injustice is there in Alice, too. *That's your legacy, Mum. That's how you go on. Your influence passing down through the generations and on into the future.*

'C'mon, Fran.' Laurie breaks into my thoughts, his voice impatient. 'We need to get a move on. The storage guys will be here soon.'

'Sorry. I was just thinking about Mum for some reason. About how fair she was and how much she hated inequality. I'm thinking that when we get ourselves settled, whenever or wherever that is, I'd like to give something back to the community. Maybe do some voluntary work? What do you think?'

Laurie doesn't reply. He is wrestling the fridge out of the very tight corner where it's positioned. A pool of water has gathered underneath from where it has defrosted. I get the mop and swirl it around. There's a metallic clink, and I bend down to untangle an object from the woolly fronds of the mop. It's a fridge magnet.

Mum brought it back from holiday one year. Knowing how much I hated anything cluttering up the face of the fridge, she declared I should make an exception in this case. Behind its resin face, a group of trees stands tall and straight, not unlike the copse of conifers you come to as you enter into the wood through our garden gate. The words written across the front are the first verse of a poem by Edward Thomas. It was a favourite of Mum's, and I read it at her funeral.

> *I have come to the borders of sleep,*
> *The unfathomable deep*
> *Forest where all must lose*
> *Their way, however straight,*
> *Or winding, soon or late;*
> *They cannot choose.*

The magnet is dusty and faded. It must have fallen

behind the fridge some time ago without me noticing. I hold it in the palm of my hand, then press it to my lips. 'Thanks, Mum,' I whisper. 'Thanks for everything.'

There's a knock at the door, and I go to answer it. It's Jenny. She's come to collect Buddy.

'Is three o'clock a suitable time to bring him back?' she says. 'I have a hair appointment soon after that. Now that Tash is unavailable, I'm going to try this woman in the village. She's meant to be very good, but I miss Tash. She always did such a good job on my hair.'

I'm unsure how much Jenny knows about Tash and Alex's connection to the drug gang. I haven't told her, and I don't feel like mentioning it now. I hand over Buddy, and when I have waved them off down the path, I search for a notepad and pen in a folder jammed full of correspondence and household bills. I feel I owe Sal and Al an explanation for our sudden departure, and with their mobile number on my lost phone, writing to them is the only way I can communicate what has happened.

The boxes have been collected and are en route to the storage facility. I have a plastic container with a few food essentials, including leftover slices of bread and a chunk of dry cheddar. We are both peckish after all the effort, including giving the house a final hoover and dust.

'Doesn't look very appetising,' I say. 'We should have picked something up for lunch.'

'I really fancy some fish and chips,' Laurie says, licking his lips in anticipation.

'Then go and get some. If we have something substantial for lunch, we can just have bread and cheese for supper.'

'No way. I'm not leaving you here by yourself.'

'Honestly, Laurie, I'll be fine. I'll get the kettle on.

You'll be back in no time. Post Sal and Al's letter while you're out, will you?'

'Okay. I won't be long.' He grabs his coat and puts the envelope into his pocket, then kisses me on the cheek. 'Put the chain on the door after me.'

I put some plates on to warm and fill the kettle. The radio is playing quietly in the background, and I hum along to a tune I recognise vaguely from childhood. I think it's called 'Bad Moon Rising'. Picking out the odd words I can remember takes me back to childhood and dancing in the kitchen with Mum.

I whirl around a few times, then freeze on the spot. Standing in the open doorway to the garden is a figure dressed in a baggy, grey tracksuit, a small rucksack strapped to their back. It's difficult to tell if they're male or female, as the hood of their top is up, partially obscuring their face. Escaping strands of straggly, dark hair are plastered to the sides of cheeks wet with rain.

'What the fuck…' The shock makes my voice waver, and I swallow hard. 'What are you doing in my house?'

They take a step forward. The trainers they are wearing are smeared in wet soil, and the bottom of their joggers are flecked with mud. There's a sense of familiarity. A flutter of recognition. I have a flashback to when I interrupted someone on the porch: Slight of build, androgynous, wearing a grey tracksuit. This is the same person I bumped into that day. I'd lay money on it.

'What do you want? I don't have any money. I suggest you piss off pretty quickly. My husband will be back at any moment.'

They stop a couple of feet away from me. I can feel a tremor at the base of my throat as my heart begins to pump faster. I back away. There's a smell in the air of sweat, damp clothes and outdoor air. Whoever this is, they've been outside in the rain for a while. Perhaps even living rough.

One hand is holding the end of a sleeve in their palm, and the other reaches up and pushes back the hood to reveal an unkempt bob of near black hair. A woman, then.

Her eyes are lowered, and when she raises them, I recognise immediately the shards of blue ice gleaming beneath wet lashes.

I suck in a breath, then exhale slowly. 'Mel?'

'Yeah, it's me. The one and only. Like the new hair-style?' she says, her voice hoarse.

She flicks a lock of hair, and her eyes scan the room. She seems agitated, and I take another step back to put some distance between us.

'How did you get in, and what do you want?'

'Weeeell, the first question is easy to answer. Your gate was unlocked, and the shed was open. I hid in that bush by the front door and sneaked into the shed after the removal men had finished loading. Going anywhere nice, by the way?' The question drips with sarcasm.

'*Shit.*' I curse under my breath. In all the commotion, neither of us had thought to lock the side gate.

'And the second…?'

'Ah, yes. What do I want?' Her voice has taken on a sing-song quality. She's either drunk, high or both.

She leans into the kitchen island and looks around.

'Very nice. Tasteful. Pretty much what I would have expected. You have it all, don't you, Fran. Perfect home, perfect husband, perfect kids. You're lucky. Very lucky.'

I'm racking my brains to try to find something to say to appease her.

'I know it seems like that, Mel…'

She's not listening. Her head is tilted back, and her

eyes are closed. 'I did almost have it all. The house, the car, my beautiful clothes, even the dogs.'

She pitches forward unsteadily, regains her balance, then wipes away a tear with a dirty sleeve. 'Now look at me. I've got nothing. Everything is gone. They've even taken my boy Gabe away from me. My life here is over.'

She's crying steadily now. Her hunched shoulders heaving. She's lost weight. I can make out the outline of her shoulder blades through the layer of fleece.

I almost feel sorry for her. 'Mel, I...'

She raises her head, and her face is contorted. 'Do you know what?' she sneers. 'People like you make me sick.'

'People like me? What do you mean?'

'*What do you mean?*' She mimics my voice, specks of spittle gathering at the corners of her mouth. 'I mean you and people like you with your cosy lives. You had it all handed to you on a plate. I had to do it all myself.' She is beating her fist against her chest, her voice rising. 'It's a pity you escaped. You deserve to be in that hole they dug for you. I can't believe that stupid bitch Tash let you go. And that idiot of a husband of hers, Alex. He went to try to find you before you froze to death.'

The car that passed me when I was in the field at Willington. It must have been Alex.

Her voice slows and becomes hard and edged with steel. 'Fuckwit went to the police and told them everything. Along with your evidence, they are going to send me down for a long time.'

My legs are starting to ache from standing, and I shift my position. Mel eyes me suspiciously.

'Laurie will be back soon,' I say. 'He's gone for fish and chips.'

'Ooh, luverly. Ah'm starving.' I don't know if it's

deliberate, but her Birmingham accent has become especially noticeable.

'Why don't we sit down while we're waiting? Then you can tell me what it is you want, Mel,' I say.

Ignoring me, she places her elbows flat on the countertop, then uncurls her fingers from the cuffs of her sleeve. They are white with cold. She reaches behind her and from the waistband of her joggers draws out what looks like a toy pistol. She slams it down onto the granite work surface in front of her with a muted clang. The silver body of the gun gleams dully in the afternoon light.

'Your help. That's what I want,' Mel croons. 'I need to get out of the country, and you're going to help me do it.'

47

W e survey each other across the expanse of black granite. I try not to look at the gun. I remember once reading about weapon focus. It's where victims become so fixated on the weapon, they forget other important details relating to the crime. This won't happen to me. Every tiny detail of this encounter is etched in my memory. There will be no forgetting if I do manage to get out of this unscathed.

'And how do you propose to do that? Get you out of the country, that is?' I say.

'It's easy,' Mel says. 'You are going to drive me to Hull. I have someone there waiting to pick me up. Fake ID, fake passport are all in place. Overnight ferry to Rotterdam, and I can start a new life there.' She pats the rucksack lying across the stool next to her. 'I've got plenty of cash. I might even move on from there and go to another country.'

My phone buzzes on the worktop, and I reach across to get it. Laurie's name is flashing up on the screen.

'Sit down. Don't answer it,' Mel hisses, picking up the gun and waving it in my direction.

I do as she says and wait for the knock on the door to tell me Laurie is back. He's been gone for ages. The minutes drag by, and my mind starts to wander, imagining any number of situations to explain why he has been so long. Perhaps he's had a flat tyre or an accident. What if he's written off the car, and the police were using his phone to contact me with the bad news?

I jump up when I hear an insistent knock on the front door. I move towards the hall, and in a flash, Mel is behind me. I can feel the snub nose of the gun pressing into my lower back.

My hands are shaking, and it takes a couple of attempts before I can slide the chain across and get the door open. Laurie has a carrier bag in his hand, and the aroma of freshly cooked food causes my stomach to growl with hunger.

'I know I've been a long time. The shop shut early for some reason. I had to drive to the next village. I tried to ring to let you know… Oh, who's this?'

Laurie has noticed Mel standing behind my shoulder.

Still holding the gun to my back, she increases the pressure, and I wince. Laurie looks at me in concern, but I give a slight shake of my head. 'This is Mel Ingram, Laurie. Just do as she says.'

Mel is ravenous. She is grabbing handfuls of chips and breaking off pieces of fish to ram down her throat before I even have time to share the food out onto the plates. She still has the gun in her other hand. Laurie and I pick at our shared portion. Before I can empty the remainder into the bin, Mel pulls the plate towards her. She stuffs the last remnants into her mouth.

'Cup of tea would be nice,' she says, her mouth full of chips.

I put the kettle on, and while I'm waiting for it to

boil, I watch as Laurie engages her in conversation. He appears relaxed and is chatting to her in the same way he would with my friends. He's jokey and flirtatious, leaning forward as though interested in every word she is saying. If you were looking in from the outside, you wouldn't know anything was out of place. It's surreal.

'So,' he says, 'you want Fran to drive you to Hull to catch the late ferry?'

He sits upright, steepling his fingers in front of him. 'Can I ask you, Mel, have you ever been to Hull?'

Mel laughs out loud and twirls her hair with her free hand. 'Nooo, I hear it's grim. But I won't be hanging around there for any length of time.'

I can't help but be impressed by Laurie. It's a while since I've seen him in full seduction mode, and Mel is lapping it up. I linger on the sidelines, not wishing to break the spell. If I didn't know him better, I might even be starting to feel a tad jealous. This is a game, though, and Laurie is good at it.

I pour the tea, and Mel demands sugar, which neither of us take. I bend down to search in our box of essentials, and she yells at me.

'Get the fuck where I can see you!'

I emerge with two sachets of white sugar, and she snatches them both from my hand. She tears at the paper and tips one into her tea, and the other she taps into her mouth and swallows. I look across at Laurie. His face is impassive, unreadable.

I have a proposition for you, Mel,' he says. 'How about *I* drive you to Hull?'

'No, Laurie...' I start to protest, but he waves his hand to silence me.

'It's fine, Fran. I can take Mel. It's less than two hours each way. I'll be back by early evening.'

Mel looks up, and there's a strange glint in her eye.

She slides off the stool and walks towards me, holding the gun at arm's length in front of her. Laurie starts to get off his seat, too, but she points it in his direction.

'No,' she says, her eyes narrowing. 'I know what you are playing at. Don't mistake me for a fool.'

Laurie raises his hands, palms outward. 'Okay, Mel. No worries. It's your call.'

Keeping a wary eye on Mel, I gather the plates and put them into the dishwasher. The clock on the wall is showing it's almost three. Jenny will be bringing Buddy back soon, and I feel a rising sense of panic at the thought of her becoming enmeshed in the situation. If I'm quick, I can intercept her.

'I have to go and collect Buddy, Mel. He's with a neighbour. She's elderly, and she doesn't need to be a part of all this. I'll come straight back, and then I'll drive you to Hull. I promise.'

Too late. I recognise Jenny's usual knock. Tap, tap, tap.

Mel follows me into the hall, holding the gun once again at my back. 'Not a word,' she hisses.

Her breath is hot, exuding a faint chemical smell I don't recognise. A drug, I would guess.

My mouth feels dry, and I swallow hard before turning the latch to open the door.

Jenny is balancing a greetings card and a plant in one hand and holding onto Buddy's lead in the other. Before I have time to say anything, he jerks on the lead, dragging Jenny into the hall. She crashes into me, dropping the plant and card as an overexcited Buddy jumps up at Mel, knocking the gun out of her hand. It spins across the floor in wide arcs, heading inexorably in my direction. Adrenaline has sharpened my senses, and I drop into a squat and snatch it away before Mel has time to retrieve it. It feels heavier than I expected. I hate guns, but fear is making me reckless, and I wave it in Mel's direction. From out of the corner of my eye, I see Jenny. She is pressed up against the wall, holding Buddy tight to her chest. I can hear her breathing in short, sharp gasps. There's no sign of Laurie, and I feel the panic rising. I wonder if he has gone to phone the police, leaving me to deal with Mel, who by now has staggered to her feet. She advances in my direction, holding out her hand.

'Give it back to me, Fran. It's fully loaded, and you have no idea what you're doing. We don't want anyone to get hurt now, do we?' Her voice is low, wheedling, as though she is talking to a child.

I stand firm despite the fact that my whole body is quivering. Hooking my index finger, I rest it on the trigger, sweat slicking my hands.

'No one is going to get hurt, Mel. We all just need to keep calm,' I say, my voice husky with anxiety.

The familiar smirk is back on her face, and I'm flustered. Why isn't she concerned? It's a loaded weapon. Does she really think I won't fire it?

She's less than two feet away, and I feel sick at the thought of what will happen if I'm forced to shoot her.

'I'll do it, Mel. Don't think I won't.'

Without warning, Mel kicks out at me, knocking me off balance. As I fall backwards, I instinctively tighten my grip on the gun. Mel is crouching over me, and I point it upwards.

'You can't do it, Fran. I know you. You're prissy and moral. You won't shoot me. Your stupid moral code won't allow it. A bleeding heart, that's what you are. You won't cross that line. I know you won't.'

In the infinitesimal unit of time that passes before I step over that invisible threshold, I realise beyond any doubt that Mel is beyond redemption. I close my eyes and squeeze the trigger.

There is no flash of light, no loud explosion. I look up in confusion, to see Mel grinning down at me. I try to get up, but she pushes me back. Reaching for the gun, she prises it from my trembling fingers. She steps away from me, then swings from side to side theatrically. Adopting the two-handed stance I've seen so often in crime films,she lowers her head, closing one eye as though lining me up in her sights.

In that split second, the only thoughts I have are that it's over and I will never see Laurie or my kids again. Buddy lets out a little yelp as a reminder he has been held too tightly for too long.

'Bang!' I hear Mel's wild, shrill laugh.

'See, Fran, the safety is on. I can't have anything happen to you. You're my ticket out of here.'

Over Mel's shoulder, Laurie appears, silhouetted against the light coming through from the kitchen. Mel senses his presence and goes to turn, but before she can, he grabs her arm, the one holding the gun, and twists it behind her back. She struggles and cries out in pain. He tightens his grip until she sighs deeply and relaxes against him as though in submission.

Laurie must have activated the panic alarm. Already I can hear the wail of sirens in the distance.

We wait for the police to arrive. A still and silent tableau in the darkening hallway.

EPILOGUE

TWO YEARS LATER

The views across the valley are breathtaking. Soon after we arrived, we bought a wooden bench and placed it by the back door of the cottage. It doesn't matter what time of day it is, there's always something interesting to see. Today a lone red kite performs leisurely sweeps of its territory, pausing only to momentarily beat its wings and utter a shrill, whistling cry before climbing in an elegant curve to soar high above on the thermals.

The cottage is a squat, single-level dwelling, dressed in local stone with a slate roof. A former dairy and milking shed, it's small in comparison to our last house, but perfectly adequate for the two of us. We spotted it on a walk to visit some Neolithic standing stones a short drive from Laurie's parents' house and immediately fell in love with its higgledy-piggledy quirkiness. It had been empty for a year, and it's taken us another year to restore it. It's located half a mile up an uneven farm track. I like that it's possible to see any approaching vehicle from every window.

The land at the rear slopes gently and ends in a

vegetable patch flanked by half a dozen or so apple trees. Al would be proud of us. Rather than cutting the grass, we have sown wild flower seed. Already corn-flowers, dog daisies, red campion and cowslips are flourishing beneath the trees. In summer, I can hear the low hum of honeybees from the open kitchen door.

'We can get the trees taken out if they spook you,' Laurie said soon after we moved in.

It was spring, and the pinky-white cloud of blossom filled the air with its heady scent.

'No, absolutely not.'

Laurie had smiled at that, knowing it was a sign that healing had begun.

Later in the year, we arranged for Alice and Flynn to visit. Together we dug a hole in the flower bed close to the house, into which we placed Buddy's ashes, along with his collar and favourite toy. He hadn't liked all the changes, and at first we thought he was homesick and missing what was familiar. As the months passed, he began to slow down and become listless. Eventually he stopped eating. After trying different medications without much success, we knew he was telling us it was time to let him go.

Rather than take him to the surgery, which he hated anyway, we arranged for the vet to come to the house. On a warm summer morning with the haze lifting from the valley floor, our devoted and faithful little terrier lay in my lap in a pool of sunlight and breathed his last.

I sent Jenny a copy of one of the last photos we took of him before he became ill. It's a jaunty pose, and I hope it makes her smile. He is standing on his short back legs with his paws resting on a drystone wall. His ears are flapping in the wind, and he's eyeing up the sheep in the adjoining field.

I don't spend much time thinking about what has

gone before. The trial was an ordeal. There was some satisfaction in knowing my evidence contributed to disrupting the chain of supply, as the police referred to the mass of arrests that were made following my evidence.

Mel had been about to go into business with one of the most violent gang bosses in the country. He was already running the majority of County Lines operations in the region, as well as having links to human trafficking and gunrunning. Mel was well placed to assist him in acquiring vulnerable young people to transport and deal drugs on the streets.

It turns out she had been under police surveillance even before Tyler's death. With local police intelligence focused on her, she inadvertently led them to the kingpin involved in controlling what was an extensive organised crime operation.

Mel got sixteen years. When I heard she had killed herself, I wasn't surprised. Those who exploit children, especially their own, don't get an easy ride in prison. I can't imagine anyone would mourn her passing, except maybe Gabe. As she said herself, everything that had meaning for her was gone. Although, if I remember rightly, her children were an afterthought, occupying a position well down on her list of losses.

There is no doubt she was deeply flawed, and no psychologist or psychiatrist will ever get to explain why that was. Ultimately, greed and resentment were her downfall, and if it hadn't been for Tash, she would have had me disposed of without compunction.

By now, Tash will have returned to Poland to live with her mother, leaving Alex to serve out his sentence. DI Holmes was able to tell me which open prison she had been sent to, and I applied for a visiting order. Tash had been handed down a short sentence for her participation and was about to be released on probation. I visited her in the prison's mother-and-baby unit soon after Zofia was born. Motherhood has mellowed and softened her edges. I almost didn't recognise her. With no make-up and her natural, light brown hair tied back in a plait, she looked young and vulnerable. As she nursed Zofia, there was a reminder of the Tash I knew in all her vivacity. From the sleeve of her sweater emerged the edges of a blood-red petal, its intensity contrasting with the creamy plumpness of Zofia's fingers.

For a long time, I felt I would never be free of fear. That anxiety would blight my life forever. It's true my heart still pumps faster when I see an unfamiliar figure in the distance, or I hear a vehicle rattling up the track to the house.

The bad dreams, though reduced in frequency, still manifest in times of stress or anxiety. Seeing a counsellor has helped me to recognise that recovering from a disturbing experience is a process that mustn't be hurried, and is one you can't necessarily tackle alone. When my sessions conclude, I hope to begin my own journey, training to be a trauma counsellor. It's my way of giving something back. A promise I made to myself on that fateful day when everything could have turned out so very differently.

Tomorrow we are going to pick up our new puppy, a female collie cross. We have named her Jenny, in honour of our dear friend and neighbour and Buddy's biggest champion. She's got a lot to live up to, in so many ways. As do we all.

WE HOPE YOU ENJOYED THIS BOOK

If you could spend a moment to write an honest review, no matter how short, we would be extremely grateful. They really do help readers discover new authors.

Leave a Review

ACKNOWLEDGMENTS

The germ of the idea for this book came as I was walking my dog in a small area of woodland at the back of my house. As the story took shape and evolved, it was heartening to have so much support along the way. I want to thank my family for believing in me. They are Matt, Adam, Persephone, and my daughter in law Daisy, who has been my biggest cheerleader.

I'd also like to thank Roz Watkins and Beccy Bagnall who provided the environment to nurture my writing skills when they started the original White Peak Writers group here in Derbyshire. Thanks to Pam for giving me constructive feedback on numerous pieces of writing. Her eagle eye has been invaluable. Also thanks to fellow writers Cheryl, Rachel, Isobel, Angela and Tom, all talented storytellers in their own right.

A huge thank you is owed to my ever patient and encouraging husband Lian, whose culinary skills have improved over the last couple of years by necessity. I mustn't forget to include my terrier Horace, who takes me on walks, even in the worst of weather and who was the inspiration for Buddy, the dog in the book.

I especially want to thank Brian and Garrett at Inkubator Books who took a punt on this debut author and eased me into the process of getting my book published with conviction and good humour.

The poem *Tell Me* is reproduced with kind permission from the author Alice Woodrome.

Published by Inkubator Books
www.inkubatorbooks.com

Printed in Great Britain
by Amazon

85251503R00185